Without a Trace

BRANTLEY WALKER: Off the Books, 2

DEAD HEAT RANCH
Boots Optional
Betting on Grace
Overnight Love

DEVIL'S BEND
Chasing Dreams
Vanishing Dreams

MISPLACED HALOS
Protected in Darkness
Salvation in Darkness
Bound in Darkness

OFFICE INTRIGUE
Office Intrigue
Intrigued Out of the Office
Their Rebellious Submissive
Their Famous Dominant
Their Ruthless Sadist
Their Naughty Student
Their Fairy Princess

PIER 70
Reckless
Fearless
Speechless
Harmless
Clueless

SNIPER 1 SECURITY
Wait for Morning
Never Say Never
Tomorrow's Too Late

SOUTHERN BOY MAFIA/DEVIL'S PLAYGROUND
Beautifully Brutal
Without Regret
Beautifully Loyal
Without Restraint

Without a Trace

BRANTLEY WALKER: OFF THE BOOKS, 2

NICOLE EDWARDS

Published by Nicole Edwards Limited
PO Box 1086, Pflugerville, Texas 78691

Without a Trace
Brantley Walker: Off the Books, 2
Nicole Edwards

This is a work of fiction. Names, characters, businesses, places, events and incidents either are the products of the author's imagination or used in a fictitious manner. Any resemblance to actual persons, living or dead, business establishments, events, or locals is entirely coincidental.

COVER DETAILS:

Image: © Andrei Bandarchyk (63466901) | 123rf.com
Design: © Nicole Edwards Limited

INTERIOR DETAILS:

Formatting: Nicole Edwards Limited
Editing: Blue Otter Editing | BlueOtterEditing.com

ISBN:
Ebook 9781644180297 | Paperback 9781644180303 | Audio 9781644180310

SUBJECTS:
BISAC: FICTION / Romance / Gay
BISAC: FICTION / Romance / General

Dedication

REESE TAVOULARIS

I always knew you would play a big role,
I just didn't realize it would be this big.

Chapter One

"SO HOW EXACTLY ARE WE S'POSED TO refer to you?" Trey asked, his words tipped with amusement. "Officer Walker? Special Agent Walker? Task Force Leader Walker?" He chuckled. "Naw. That last one's too much for the tongue."

Brantley Walker cocked an eyebrow, waiting for his brother to finish.

"How 'bout Governor's Pet?"

"You done?"

Trey tapped a finger on his stubbled chin as though considering it, then grinned wide. "Yeah. I'm done."

"Mama, you wanna know why I don't stop in more often?" Brantley turned to look at the woman flitting about the kitchen. "Him."

Iris smiled. "Your brother's harmless."

Brantley snorted. "Maybe. Doesn't mean he's not annoying."

Trey moved into the kitchen, smacking Brantley on the back of the head when he passed. "You say that like it's a bad thing. And you know I don't live here, right?"

Brantley cocked his head to the side. "Yet you're always here."

"Munchkin alert!" someone shouted from the living room.

Brantley turned on his barstool to see his nephew racing into the room. Without warning, the little boy donning his favorite cowboy boots and his daddy's trucker cap—which was several sizes too big for his head—launched himself in Brantley's direction.

Chuckling, he caught Eric, his sister Tori's boy, swung him up, and planted his butt on the bar. "What's up, kid?"

"Nothin'," Eric said, his grin revealing the fact he'd lost both his front teeth.

"Now why don't I believe that?"

"'Cause Mama said to play it cool," he whispered loudly.

"Play what cool?"

"She wants to know where Reese is."

That must've been the trigger word, because both his mother and Trey turned to look at him expectantly.

"Who's Reese?" Brantley asked his nephew, feigning ignorance.

The little boy shrugged, clearly just the messenger. "Maybe he's the chocolate and peanut butter guy."

Leave it to a six-year-old to think that.

"Like Reese's Pieces," Trey noted.

"Eww, no." Eric wrinkled his nose. "Not those, Uncle Trey. The peanut butter cups."

Great. Reese would forever be thought of as candy in this house.

"Why don't you go tell your mama to mind her own business," Brantley suggested, depositing the kid on the floor before turning his attention to his mother. "Anyone ever tell Tori she's nosy?"

"Mama! Uncle Brantley said to mind your own business!" The giggle that followed made Brantley smile.

Before Trey could launch his own questions, Brantley held up a hand. "Reese is off-limits."

Trey sulked. "For how long?"

"Until I say otherwise."

And he didn't intend that to be for a while. Right now, his relationship with Reese Tavoularis was new. The last thing he wanted to do was jinx himself by flapping his gums. While they weren't technically an item, they were exploring to see where this might lead. And Brantley was determined to enjoy the hell out of the journey.

"What I wanna know is why in heaven's name are you here on a Saturday night?" Frank inquired, joining them in the kitchen. "Shouldn't you be takin' that boy out or somethin'?"

Now his father was going to give him a hard time. Great.

Brantley shot a glare in Trey's direction. This was his doing.

He should've known his brother would run his damn mouth to the entire family. No one else knew about Reese. The only reason Trey did was because he'd swung by the house to check in after Brantley's last mission, when they had successfully located Kate Walker and delivered her back to her frantic parents. Brantley had suffered one of his migraines that night and Reese had apparently sent everyone on their way so he could take care of him. His brother had read into it how he chose to, then spread the word accordingly. Brantley wouldn't be surprised if his mother was gearing up to plan their wedding.

"Tell me this," Trey said, stepping up to the counter and passing over a beer.

Brantley waved him off. He wasn't staying.

Trey offered the beer to their dad, who accepted it easily.

"If you're seein' Reese," Trey asked casually, "does that mean Cyrus is fair game?"

Curious, Brantley studied his brother. "You interested in Cyrus?"

"Hey, it's just a question."

A question that had drawn the attention of everyone in the kitchen, taking the heat off Brantley. Thank God.

"What?" Trey glanced from one face to another. "Just a question. Damn."

Frank chuckled, evidently enjoying making his oldest son squirm.

"For the record," Brantley stated, "Cyrus has always been fair game. I've got no claim to him."

Trey glared his way. Probably pissed that Brantley hadn't simply said so in the first place.

Content he'd done his duty in putting his brother in the hot seat, Brantley got to his feet. "Well, I think I'll be headin' out now."

"No dessert?" Iris asked, her pale blue eyes shifting to him.

Patting his stomach, he grinned. "Watchin' my figure."

"Not gettin' enough exercise?" Trey quipped, the mischievous gleam in his eyes returning.

"Oh, I'm gettin' plenty," he mumbled, passing by his brother to give his mother a hug.

"You goin' to Curtis's house tomorrow night?" Frank asked when Brantley turned to him.

"Not this weekend, no. Got some stuff to deal with on the work front."

His father nodded. "Lorrie called, extended us an invite."

"You goin'?"

"Thought about it. Been a while since I've seen my brother's young'ns."

"There's a lot of 'em. Might bring your earplugs."

Frank chuckled. "All those little ones? That's the best part of goin' over there."

Yeah, Brantley happened to be quite fond of the kiddos himself. All twenty-plus of them.

Not that he wanted to spend every waking hour with them. He valued his sanity far too much for that.

Thirty minutes later, after saying his goodbyes to the rest of the clan, Brantley pulled into his driveway, parking beside JJ's SUV. He should've expected she would be there being that she'd spent a good majority of the past week in the barn, getting it in order, or so she claimed.

Rather than go inside the house, he made his way to the barn in the dark, briefly wondering if he should have a walkway put in. Would detract from the country vibe the property had, but might be better than trekking through the mud when it rained. For JJ, of course. Brantley couldn't give a shit less if he got mud on his boots, but she might.

Once he reached the big red barn, he slid the enormous door back, keyed in his code, then opened the steel security door he'd installed shortly after he acquired the property. Colt Ford's voice spilled out into the night, JJ's favorite country star singing about showing Vegas how the country folk party.

And because JJ'd gone to the efforts of installing it, Brantley instructed Alexa to turn the volume to three. The shift in decibel was instant, drawing JJ's attention from the computer screen.

"Hey. I like that song."

"I'm aware. Not sure the neighbors are fans though."

"Place is sound-proofed. Neighbors can't hear." JJ rolled her eyes. "Even if there were any."

Semantics.

"Whatcha workin' on?" he inquired, walking down the wide aisle created by the scattering of furniture JJ'd had delivered recently.

Using his credit card, JJ had outfitted the once empty space with desks, chairs, rugs, a couch, couple of small tables, and a foosball table. The state had coughed up the money for the electronics, save for what Brantley had prior to agreeing to put together a task force solely responsible for working missing person cases, both old and new, for the great state of Texas.

And while they'd brought in more computers, monitors, and a dedicated server, Brantley had agreed JJ could keep his original equipment, ensuring it wasn't connected to the government-owned stuff. While they had immunity and means when it came to solving their cases, JJ had convinced him there were perhaps a few things the government might not approve of; therefore it was important they kept the prying eyes of Uncle Sam out of their business. Who was he to argue with that?

"I've been goin' through the case files that were sent over," JJ explained, "tryin' to find one for us to work on."

"I thought we agreed we'd focus on Lauren Tyler." That was what they'd decided on shortly after he'd brought her on board. Their first official case would be that of a teenage girl who'd gone missing from Coyote Ridge nine years earlier. She'd been best friends with the governor's daughter, and since this task force had come together at the behest of the man himself, seemed fitting they would find some closure for Lauren as well as her family and friends.

JJ sat back in her chair, stared up at him.

She looked tired. And a bit out of sorts. Her dark hair was piled haphazardly on her head, face clean of makeup, her green eyes weary. The crease in her forehead gave away her worry and had him curious.

"We are," she said quickly. "Yes. We're definitely gonna prioritize that case. But…"

Brantley raised an eyebrow. "But what?"

She sighed, spinning around in her chair as she motioned toward a glass whiteboard she'd had him and Reese hang on the wall. The thing was roughly five feet by five feet, looking as large as it was because there were very few words scribbled across it.

"That's what I have on Lauren," she said, her tone clipped and anxious. "We know she vanished into thin air back in 2011."

"Okay."

JJ pivoted to face him. "That's the problem. That's all we know, Brantley."

"Which is why we've decided to take on the case."

Her green eyes were pleading as they stared up at him. "I don't know how to do this. I don't know how to unearth information on someone who's just gone." She gestured toward her desk. "That's why I was lookin' through some of the other files, hopin' to find something that has more for us to go on."

"Chances are, they wouldn't be cold if there'd been more to go on, JJ."

She huffed. "I know."

Brantley leaned his hip on the desk. "Unless we catch a current case, we're startin' with this one. Lauren Tyler's from here. From our hometown. We owe it to her and her family to find her. Bring her home."

"And if we can't?" She sounded desperate.

"We can," he stated firmly. "One way or another, we're gonna get closure for Lauren."

JJ sighed. "You're right. I know you are. I'm just… I guess I'm overwhelmed. I'm used to a definitive end goal."

"Finding her is a definitive end goal."

Another sigh, this one reflecting her frustration. "No. I mean … a structured path. Some sorta guideline. Hackin' a system, breakin' through firewalls, creatin' back doors. That's what I'm good at. Findin' clues … not so much."

"Good thing you're not doin' this by yourself then."

JJ rubbed her fingertips on her forehead.

"It's gettin' late," he told her. "You should go home, get some rest. We're not supposed to meet up until tomorrow night."

Another sigh, this one more resigned than anxious. "Fine. I'll go home." She marched to her desk, grabbed her car keys and cell phone. "Where's Reese?"

"He said he'd be over later."

JJ's eyebrows hopped. "Sounds kinky."

Shaking his head, Brantley planted his hand on her back, directing her toward the door. "Nothin' about that sounded kinky."

"Maybe not. But you should see the images I've got in my head right now."

"JJ."

She laughed, stepping out into the night. "Hey. Let me have my fantasies, Walker."

"Only because I can't stop you."

"No, you can't."

After locking the barn, Brantley walked JJ around the house to her SUV, opened her door, waited for her to get inside.

"Go home. Enjoy what's left of your time off. Because once we get started, you'll probably wish you had more of it."

She smiled. "I hope so."

Brantley huffed a laugh. "You would. Go home, JJ."

"I'm leavin'. Have a good night. And make sure you do everything I wouldn't do."

He closed her door, stepped back, then watched JJ do a quick K-turn to head toward the road. When her taillights disappeared into the darkness, Brantley went inside. Before making his way to the bathroom, he shot Reese a quick text, letting him know he was home.

Without waiting for a response, he headed for the shower.

WHEN THE TEXT CAME IN, REESE GLANCED at his phone, grinned like an idiot.

"Gettin' in the shower," he read aloud, thinking about Brantley naked and wet, waiting for him.

Sure, there was that anxious feeling he'd grown familiar with. The one that came on when he thought about the fact he had it bad for a man when he'd never even considered the idea of being with a man before Brantley. But he pushed that aside because it wasn't helpful, focused on the other feelings he got from the idea. Needless to say, there was an excitement that burned just beneath his skin, made him hot from the inside out when he so much as thought about Brantley.

Damn good thing he was pulling down the man's driveway, having just passed JJ's little SUV out on the main road. Reese knew from experience the front door would be unlocked, Brantley's way of encouraging him to come in and join him.

Truth was, it was what Reese had been looking forward to all damn day. Hell, all damn week. While Travis Walker had essentially fired him from Walker Demolition as a way of urging—which in Travis's book translated to shoving—him in the direction of the task force Brantley was heading up, Reese was sticking around until his replacement was fully up to speed. It hadn't been quite two weeks since the governor propositioned them with the idea, a week since Brantley told the governor he was all in. At that point, Reese had officially turned in his notice with Travis, offering two weeks to train his replacement. He figured by the end of the next week he would be available to Brantley.

He smiled. In more ways than one.

And because it required effort to transfer duties, Reese had been working a lot of overtime the past few days, including most of today—his day off—to get things in order. Not that he would let Brantley know he'd been counting down for this since he woke up this morning. Okay, that was a lie. He would most definitely be letting Brantley know.

After parking his truck, he grabbed the bag he'd packed for his sleepover, then made a beeline for the house. After dumping his things on the kitchen counter, he set out to find Brantley. As he headed down the hall, he yanked his T-shirt off, dropping it to the floor. One boot was discarded next, then the other. By the time he reached the bathroom, he was unbuttoning his jeans.

He pulled up short when he saw Brantley exactly as he'd imagined him. Gloriously naked, the water raining down on his delectable body. He paused for a moment to admire him, all six feet four inches of prime Navy SEAL. And while the man hadn't been active duty since the injury that ended his career roughly sixteen months earlier, one would not be able to tell from looking at him. He was long and lean, ripped, not bulky. And his stamina…

Yeah, Reese was fairly certain he'd just had a hot flash.

He continued to stare, curious as to what was on Brantley's mind. His palms were flat on the tile, his head hanging down as he leaned forward. The sight of him naked still tripped Reese up because just looking sent a bolt of lust through him. His gaze shifted to the long, jagged scar on his left leg, the leg that had been operated on numerous times in the hopes of fixing what had been broken during an op gone bad. From what he knew, the leg had healed, but it was the headaches—a direct result of the brain injury he'd sustained—that continued to plague Brantley, making it impossible for him to remain active duty.

His eyes trailed over him once more. Before Brantley, Reese had never felt any sort of sexual attraction to a man. And now, his body hardened simply from thinking about the guy. Looking at him… It made his blood pump hotter and faster.

Clearing his throat to get Brantley's attention, Reese waited until those stormy blue eyes lifted. As soon as they did, Reese stripped his jeans down his legs, enjoying the way Brantley's body went rigid. The man was certainly good for his ego. Didn't matter when or where, if they were talking or relaxing, Brantley's gaze always seemed to heat when he looked his way.

"Pretty sure this is the longest shower I've ever taken," Brantley said, that smooth, deep voice echoing off the tile. "Come here."

Without hesitation, Reese strolled across the bathroom, stepping into the glass enclosure and pulling the door closed. Seconds later, he was in Brantley's arms, their lips melding together, chest to chest. But he didn't stop, pushing Brantley all the way against the wall so he could eliminate every inch of space separating them.

The heat that churned between them rivaled that of the water, but more than that, Reese felt a comfort he hadn't expected to feel with anyone, least of all a man. This man.

Christ Almighty. This was the only place he wanted to be and it shocked him as much as it turned him on. Although he hadn't entertained the notion of being with a man, not in the first thirty years of his life, it had been recently that Brantley had pulled the rug right out from under him. And though he still battled bouts of anxiety, Reese was welcoming the familiarity that came with their connection.

"Missed you," Brantley murmured against his mouth, his calloused hands gliding over his back, gently, slowly.

Yeah, that was how Brantley operated. They might come together in a cataclysmic explosion, but it would only take a few minutes before the brakes were being pulled, their encounter slowing. Not by Reese's doing, either. Brantley had assured him they would take things slow and they were. Painstakingly slow at times.

Brantley's lips trailed along his jaw and Reese gave himself over to the exploration that was coming. The tides turned and Reese found himself against the wall, Brantley's fingers twined in his. Next thing he knew, his arms were extended over his head, pinned to the tile, while Brantley's mouth did wondrous things to his neck. Ensuring Brantley had better access, he tilted his head, inhaled sharply when Brantley nipped him.

This was what he thought about in the dark of night when he'd been sleeping alone this past week. Brantley. His touch, his taste, his smell. The man had overwhelmed his senses, made him ache.

That sensuous mouth moved to his once more, nibbled and licked before he pulled back. Their eyes met, held for long moments, and Reese could see the intent, knew what was coming next.

"I want you in my mouth," Brantley rasped as he relaxed against him.

Reese took his weight easily, keeping his hands up as Brantley's palms slid down his arms, over his shoulders, onto the muscles of his back, lower, pausing on his hips.

He knew Brantley was waiting for the go-ahead, wouldn't proceed until Reese was in agreement. It was the slow route Brantley was taking, easing Reese into this new experience.

"Put your mouth on me, Brantley."

Reese probably should've recognized the relief that had Brantley's shoulders relaxing, but he didn't. He was too focused on the way Brantley slid down to his knees, Brantley's thick chest never leaving Reese's skin as it brushed over the front of him. It felt so fucking good to be touched like this, by a man who knew what he wanted.

"Watch me," Brantley ordered, peering up at him as he palmed the backs of Reese's thighs.

With Brantley kneeling between his feet, there was no space between them, another way for Brantley to ensure Reese remained in the moment. Reese wasn't sure it was necessary. He was hyperaware of Brantley at all times. But in moments like this, he didn't mind the contact. It soothed the anxiety that still crept in. Why his nerves rioted when they were intimate, he wasn't sure. Probably had something to do with the fact he didn't want to disappoint this man. While Reese hadn't been with a man before him, the same could not be said for Brantley.

"Watch. Me."

Reese's eyes shot open, focusing on Brantley as his lips parted and wrapped Reese's cock in delectable warmth.

"Fuck." His arms slid down so he could cup Brantley's head, loving the bristle of his short hair against his palms.

As seconds turned to minutes, Reese endured the exquisite torture of being sucked and licked; all the while, he stared down at the sexy SEAL. He was in awe of the picture he painted. So fucking handsome, so damn cocky. Those were traits Reese was definitely attracted to, but it was Brantley's ability to own him that did him in.

Feeling emboldened by the eyes imploring him, the mouth working him to the point of distraction, Reese tightened his grip on Brantley's head, pulling him in as he pushed his hips forward.

The deep rumble that came from Brantley spurred him on.

"Let me fuck your face," Reese groaned. "Fuck … your mouth … feels so damn good."

More rumbles sent vibrations through his shaft. His balls drew up tight to his body. He was close, so damn close.

Brantley's hands fell from where they'd been clinging to his thighs and Reese was given free rein to drive his hips forward. He took what Brantley offered, fucking his mouth, taking all the pleasure the man was so willing to give him. He still didn't understand this overwhelming need he felt, but he wasn't questioning it, either.

"Brantley … goddamn … I'm gonna come."

The rumble that came next sounded a hell of a lot like encouragement. It was enough to send him over. Reese drove his cock into Brantley's mouth one final time, his body twitching and jerking as he came. His breaths slammed out of him, and by the time he was drained, he was boneless, the wall at his back and the man getting to his feet the only reasons he was still standing.

"Christ…" he said on a choppy exhale.

Brantley's eyes glittered and that devilish smirk sent another shudder through Reese.

But before Brantley could turn away, Reese did something he hadn't yet done. He reached for him, pulling him in and crushing his lips to Brantley's. As he expected, Brantley held back until Reese nipped his lower lip.

"Kiss me," he commanded. "Damn it, Brantley."

He wasn't sure if it was the demand in his tone or Brantley's desire to do so, but Brantley's mouth slammed over his, their tongues colliding. He could taste himself on Brantley's tongue, knew that was the reason the man had been holding back. Although he appreciated Brantley's efforts to be concerned for him, to worry that they were moving into territory he wasn't quite ready for, Reese was learning that there wasn't much—if anything—Brantley could do that would turn him off.

When their struggle slowed, their lips brushing rather than melding, Reese cupped Brantley's face, pulled back so he could look into the man's eyes. "I'm all in," Reese whispered, needing to remind him of the pledge he'd made before. "Don't hold back from me."

Brantley smirked, surprising Reese.

At least until those big hands cupped his ass, tugged his cheeks apart. "Not yet, you're not." Brantley released him. "But you will be. One day."

Yeah. One day. It was inevitable, even if he could admit he wasn't ready for it yet. Didn't mean he wasn't thinking about it, dreaming about Brantley sliding deep inside him, making love to him in a way no one had ever done before.

When Brantley turned away from him, Reese snagged the soap from the shelf. When his hands were slippery, he reached around Brantley, pulled him back against him, chest to back as he reached around Brantley's hip, his fingers circling his cock.

"I'm not done with you yet."

"Fuck, yes," Brantley moaned, relaxing against him as Reese began stroking his heavy cock. "Don't stop doin' that."

No, Reese hadn't experimented with all the ways he knew he could pleasure Brantley, but this was becoming second nature. He'd gotten familiar with Brantley's rigid cock gliding in his palm. Velvet over steel, thick and long. While he couldn't see his hand moving over Brantley, he didn't need to; the sensation was more than enough to guide him.

Brantley lifted his arm, reaching around and cupping the back of Reese's neck, holding on while his hips pumped. Reese groaned as Brantley fucked his hand. Every now and again, Reese would tease the head with his thumb, ragged moans escaping Brantley.

"I'm gonna come," Brantley warned.

Reese wrapped his free arm around him, holding him tightly as he jerked him faster, harder. The guttural groan that came out of the man was damn near enough to have Reese coming again.

Holding firm when Brantley's legs weakened, Reese chuckled. Only then did he realize the water had cooled significantly.

"Think I'm gonna have to invest in a bigger water heater," Brantley said, turning to face him.

Reese grinned, feeling complete for the first time in days. "Probably not a bad idea."

Not a bad idea at all.

Chapter Two

"TELL ME AGAIN WHY WE'RE MEETIN' ON a Sunday night? Is this when you plan to kick off our week?" JJ inquired as she took a seat on the black leather couch she'd bought for the barn, a paper plate with a slice of pizza and one breadstick in her hand. "Because I was under the impression the workweek starts on Monday."

"Until Reese is workin' with us full-time, it's the best time slot," Brantley explained, taking his own plate over to the desk she'd assigned to him. It wasn't anything fancy, but it did appear to be new. On the top sat a laptop computer, a single notepad, and a jar of pens. It was the mirror image of the desk set up for Reese, neither having been used for work up to this point, but it did make a damn fine dinner table.

"You get a replacement yet?" JJ asked Reese.

"Did. Yeah."

Brantley discreetly watched the ridiculously sexy man. At least he hoped he was being discreet. For whatever reason, when the guy was in the same room, Brantley wanted nothing more than to look at him. Okay, not necessarily true. He wanted to do a hell of a lot more than look, but he was keeping his lust under control. Mostly.

"Who?" JJ asked. "Do I know him?"

"Her," Reese clarified. "Autumn Jameson. One of Lorrie's nieces."

"She qualified?"

"More so than I am. Got her degree in business, was doing the corporate thing, decided she wanted to slow her pace."

"She live here?"

Brantley watched the exchange, chowed down on pepperoni, sausage, and green peppers.

"No. Closer to the city, but she's keepin' her eye out for real estate in the area. She's willin' to rent if it comes down to it."

"Not easy to come by." Brantley knew from experience. The house he'd purchased had been on the market for three hours before he managed to swoop in and snag it thanks to a rather aggressive Realtor referred to him by none other than his cousin Travis. Timing was everything when it came to buying in Coyote Ridge.

"Don't you have an apartment?"

Brantley frowned over at JJ, curious as to where she was going with this.

"What?" she asked around a mouthful of pizza.

"You want Reese livin' on the streets?"

JJ chuckled, wiping her mouth with a napkin. "Of course not."

Her eyes glittered with mischief, a sure sign she was about to venture down a path better left untraveled.

"Don't go there, JJ," he warned.

Another smile, but she nodded. "I won't. Promise. Any plans to bring on anyone else yet?"

"Let's get through our first case," he told her. "We won't know what we need until we've dug in deep, exhausted the resources we do have."

JJ set her plate aside, leaned forward, and grabbed her Pepsi from the table. "Where do we start?"

Finally getting down to the business at hand, Brantley gladly shared his thoughts. "I need you to get me a list of people the police talked to back when Lauren first went missing along with their current contact info. Family, friends, teachers. Whoever's still around. I want to get a clearer picture of what was going on at the time she went missing."

"This girl simply vanished," JJ replied.

"No one simply vanishes," Reese countered. "It might look that way from the outside, but Lauren went somewhere. Whether by choice or by force."

"And what if she did run away?" JJ's gaze bounced between them. "She was fifteen years old. We have no idea what was going through her mind at the time. Maybe she had a boyfriend. Older guy. He could've convinced her to run off with him."

Brantley had considered that angle, would definitely be digging deeper to rule it out. "Anything's possible."

"But you don't think so?"

"Right now, the only thing I think is that a young girl went missing nine years ago. That's all we've got to go on."

"Which is exactly the problem," she said on a sigh.

"No, the problem's the girl is missing." Reese stood with his empty plate, grabbing Brantley's and carrying both to the trash can in the kitchen before returning. "And it's up to us to trace her steps and figure out where she went."

Brantley could sense JJ's nerves, knew she was still trying to wrap her head around how this would work. Interesting considering how smart she was, but it seemed to him, she'd somehow created a box where she felt her skillset fit. It would take some work, but he knew JJ would find where she fit in. Her skills were unrivaled, and she would make a huge impact on whatever task they took on. It was just a matter of building her confidence.

"Out of curiosity, how will we learn about new cases?" JJ settled back against the cushions.

"The governor'll contact us initially, until he can get the word out to all departments and branches of law enforcement who deal with missing persons."

She flashed a smile. "Do we have a name? You know, like in Hawaii Five-O? They got a cool name. So much so, the five-o caught on and they started referring to all police that way."

"Aren't you a little young to remember that show?" Brantley questioned.

"They remade it. Alex O'Loughlin is smokin'."

Brantley cut his eyes to Reese, raised his eyebrows.

"Now that I think about it, he is kinda hot," Reese agreed with a grin. "And the governor's spiel reminded me of that show. Especially that whole immunity and means thing."

Brantley had no idea what they were talking about. Then again, he didn't spend a lot of time watching television. Unless it was the news. He kept up with current events, but even that had dwindled in the months since he returned home.

"Well, we're not the police," he told them both.

"No, we're not," Reese tacked on. "But we will need to work with them. Closely, at that. I doubt they'll take too kindly to us swooping in on their jurisdiction, either."

"We'll tackle that if and when we come across it. In the meantime," he told JJ, "I'd like to have that list started by tomorrow morning. We can start trackin' them down so I can pay them a visit. That way we can put together a timeline of events."

"A timeline." JJ's eyes widened. "That's a brilliant idea. I can do a timeline."

She could do a lot of things, Brantley thought. It would just take a little time for them to get her to see that.

"If you don't need me for anything else"—JJ got to her feet—"I think I'll head home. I want to get started on that list, and thanks to this trusty new laptop the governor footed the bill for, I don't have to be locked up in here all day to get things done."

"See you in the mornin'?"

She flashed a smile as she slipped the laptop into her bag. "You most certainly will."

"I'll walk you to your car," Reese offered.

"You don't have to do that."

"Have to, no. Want to...?" He smiled.

"Whatever. You guys are far too chivalrous for your own good."

When the two of them left, Brantley made his way up the ladder to what used to be the hayloft, glanced around at the space. While the main barn floor was roughly four thousand square feet, the loft was no more than twelve hundred. Which was a considerable amount of space that was currently unused. It was empty because getting furniture up here was damn near impossible without a set of stairs. Might make a good break area. Especially if they brought others on board. Wouldn't be too hard to build stairs, bring in some furniture. Relocate the foosball table that was currently down below. At the very least, it would offer some useable square footage for storage or whatever.

He turned and stared out over the lower level, taking it all in. It looked almost professional, in a very rustic sort of way. Then again, he didn't know much about professional. Brantley was familiar with war rooms and mobile command centers. Working in the field was more his forte. He hadn't really given much thought to what it would mean to put down roots. Now he had a house, what passed as an office, a task force to run, and last but not least, a man he was more than a little intrigued with.

Settling down, that was what he seemed to be doing.

The door opened and Reese strolled in, drawing his attention. Yep. Settling down.

In more ways than one.

REESE WOKE ON MONDAY MORNING, HIS NECK tight from sleeping on the damn couch in his apartment. Perhaps he should consider getting a bed. It was a studio apartment, but that didn't mean he had to be uncomfortable when he slept. Maybe just a couch with a pull-out bed. That would be a hell of a lot better than continuing to cram his six-foot-five-inch frame on this damn thing.

As for why he was thinking about it now, after years of living here, he didn't know. If he had to guess, he was getting spoiled thanks to those few nights he'd spent in Brantley's bed.

Forcing himself up, he went to the kitchen, flipped on the coffeepot, then made a detour to the bathroom. After a quick shower and shave, he dragged on his clothes, grabbed a travel mug, filled it with Folger's Best, and then headed out the door. He could've waited to get his coffee until he was in the office, but he found he worked better when he got his caffeine in earlier, even if it was only a three-minute drive.

When he pulled into the small lot behind the Walker Demolition office less than five minutes later, he noticed Autumn had already arrived, her truck parked in the spot Reese usually used. He pulled the Walker Demo dually in beside it, realized then that he was going to have to invest in a vehicle of his own. He hadn't bothered because Travis had allowed him to use the company vehicle as his own. Now that he would no longer be working for Travis, he would have to secure his own ride.

Mentally, he added it to the to-do list, knowing full well he would forget it and every other thing on it the next time he blinked.

The door to the office opened and Autumn appeared, a brilliant smile flashing at him. He offered one back because that was what you did in a small town. You smiled and/or waved at everyone.

Autumn Jameson was a beautiful woman, something he'd noticed the very first time he'd been introduced to her. Her hair couldn't be classified as either brown or blond, but rather somewhere in between. An interesting mix of color that hung to her shoulders in gentle waves. Her eyes were a deep brown, filled with curiosity, and always seemed to be smiling. Her mouth was a little wide, her nose a tad on the small side, but altogether her features created an intriguing mix.

"Mornin'," she greeted, stepping back and holding the door open for him.

"Mornin'. You're here early."

"I know. Excitement, I guess. I'm sure it'll wear off eventually, but right now, I'm riding that new job high." She closed the door behind them. "You're probably the opposite, huh? Eager to get out of here so you can move on to bigger and better things."

"I wouldn't say eager," he admitted. Excited, sure. He was venturing into something new on all fronts and there was a natural anticipation that came along with it. But he'd never been the sort to leap without knowing how deep the pond. Since he met Brantley, seemed he was taking the plunge over and over without knowing how shallow the water might be.

"Well, I hope you trust this place is in good hands," she said, her positivity and self-confidence coming out in spades.

That was one thing he liked about Autumn. She was confident without being cocky, smart without being overzealous. Reese knew she was a good fit for this job. She would be able to handle customers and employees with ease and grace.

"I was hopin' we'd get over to the mechanic shop today," she said when he headed for his desk. "Maybe after the first appointment, which is in an hour. We could swing through the diner first, grab some breakfast, and you can walk me through the current jobs. Two birds, one stone."

Yep, she was taking over as though she'd been born to do so.

Since there really wasn't much more for him to do other than get her up to speed on the jobs they had in the works, Reese couldn't find a reason to decline. And breakfast sounded damn good.

"All right, but I'm drivin'," he said with a smirk. She could run roughshod over him, but only to a certain degree.

Two hours later, after they'd chatted over fruit and oatmeal, Reese pulled the truck in front of the mechanic shop.

"I'm not sure how close you are with Ethan," he said before opening his door, "but I highly suggest you announce your presence before you go saunterin' in unexpected."

"Why's that?"

"Let's just say it's a family-owned business, and when Beau shows up, he and Ethan tend to think this place is an extension of their … bedroom."

Autumn laughed. "Ah. Understood."

Reese smacked the horn a couple of times before getting out. He met Autumn around at her side and the two of them wandered over to the open bay door.

"I hope to God y'all are decent in there," he shouted before motioning for her to go in first.

"Ain't no one naked off in here," Keegan said, making his way from the back of the building.

"You say that like it's not a usual thing." Reese motioned toward Autumn. "Autumn Jameson, meet Keegan Walker. Keegan, Autumn."

"Pleasure," she said, holding out her hand. "I've seen you and your brother around town. Never been formally introduced."

"Lorrie's niece," Keegan noted. "Bruce and Darlene's oldest."

"Very good."

Kaden appeared, wiping his hands on a rag. "Hey. Didn't realize we'd be havin' company."

"Not company," Reese clarified. "Your new boss."

"You must be Autumn." Kaden offered his hand. "Pleasure to meet you."

"Likewise." She stepped deeper into the building. "Nice setup you've got here. Holds more than I thought it would."

"More than it should's more like it," Keegan said. "Got a backhoe that's tryin' to claim it as a permanent address. Just had it overhauled two months ago and it's givin' us shit again."

"What's the problem with it?" she asked, heading over to the backhoe in question, Keegan hot on her heels.

Reese stayed back with Kaden while Keegan began rattling off details.

"So, what do you think?" Kaden asked. "She gonna fit in?"

"She's gonna be great. Hell of a lot better than I've been in the role."

Kaden's blue-gray gaze swung back to him. "You never do give yourself enough credit, Tavoularis. You've done a damn fine job."

He wasn't so sure about that, but he had enjoyed his time here.

"Now you're off to bigger and better things."

"So they tell me."

"You don't sound thrilled with the idea of detective work."

"Surprised me's all."

"Unexpected things'll do that to a man."

Reese's thoughts drifted to Brantley.

"Well, if it's any consolation, we're headin' into the slow season. She'll have some extra time to get her hands dirty and you won't have to put your boots up on the desk."

Reese grinned. He rarely did that, but he understood what Kaden was getting at. The guy was a natural at building people up.

"We will miss you, though."

"I'll still be around."

"You better be. Gotten used to seein' your ugly mug on beer nights."

Reese watched as Autumn grabbed a wrench from a nearby toolbox.

"Looks like you might have an extra pair of hands around here if you need 'em," Reese noted.

Kaden chuckled. "Looks like."

The rest of the day passed smoothly, ending with Reese taking Autumn back to the office to go over the Excel spreadsheet that tracked their production and cycle times. She was leaning over his shoulder while he walked her through a couple of the calculations when his cell phone buzzed, the screen lighting up with a text from Brantley.

Thought maybe you'd let me buy you dinner tonight.

His hand shot out to cover the phone, instantly darkening the screen, but he knew Autumn had seen the message.

"Got a hot date with Brantley tonight?" she asked casually.

"Date? No. Of course not. He's just a friend." Feeling both awkward and anxious, he flipped the phone over, grateful when she stepped away.

"Well, don't let me keep you," she said. "I've got you for the rest of the week. Plenty of time for you to transition all that knowledge over to me."

"You headin' home?" he inquired, desperate to shift the topic.

"Not yet. Figured I'd swing by Moonshiners, grab a glass of wine, relax a little. Drivin' back now'll take me an extra half hour with the traffic."

"Why don't you let me buy you a drink?" he offered.

Autumn's gaze slid to his phone briefly. "You sure? Don't wanna mess up your plans."

"No plans. Just a friend. He owes me a dinner. That's all."

As for why he continued to ramble on unnecessarily, and rather defensively, Reese wasn't sure. Probably had something to do with the strange tightness in his chest. He couldn't explain it, damn sure didn't want to think about it. The urge to be so self-justifying surprised him. This was the first time anyone had made an accusation that tied him to Brantley, and he wasn't sure what to do about it, wasn't sure how he felt about it.

"In that case, I'll take you up on the offer. Gives me a little more time to pick your brain." Autumn pulled out the bottom drawer of her desk, dragged out her purse.

"I'll meet you there." He motioned to the computer. "Just need to finish up a couple of things."

"Sure thing."

It wasn't until Autumn stepped out the door that he exhaled his relief, glancing back at his phone. He knew the right thing to do was to send Brantley a text and politely decline, but that choking sensation was still gripping him by the throat.

His gaze strayed to the door Autumn had exited through. What would happen when others started questioning his relationship with Brantley? How was he going to answer their questions? Denial? Just thinking about everyone inquiring as to the nature of their relationship bothered him. Wasn't like he could shrug it off and say it wasn't anything serious. That would imply there was something that might be serious at some point.

It wasn't prejudice that had him concerned, because Reese was the last person who would judge others. He respected every race, ethnicity, sexual preference. However, he'd never had to justify his own before. Especially when he didn't understand it himself.

His heart was beating a rapid tattoo against his ribs and he didn't like the feeling. He didn't like that he was inclined to deny that he even knew Brantley, much less that they were sleeping together.

Christ Almighty. This was too damn hard.

He glanced down at his phone. No, he couldn't respond to Brantley right now. He'd grab a beer, relax for a few minutes. Then he'd let Brantley know something came up. They'd get together tomorrow. It would give him some time to think about this irrational reaction and what the hell he was going to do about it.

Yes. That was what he would do.

And maybe by then, some of the weird tension would ease.

Chapter Three

AFTER SPENDING THE BETTER PART OF THE day helping JJ track down addresses for the list of people who knew Lauren Tyler back when she had disappeared, Brantley was looking forward to spending some time with Reese. Casual time, away from the house, away from the barn. Dinner and a couple of beers. He'd yet to take Reese out on a real date and had gotten himself worked up with the idea.

It wasn't that he was really the dating type, but he wanted to prove to Reese that this wasn't just about sex for him. He was genuinely interested in getting to know the man, doing things they both enjoyed. Outside of the bedroom.

Only his offer went unanswered.

Brantley waited an hour, figuring Reese was in the middle of something at work, before he shot another text, checking in.

Still no response.

A little concerned, he dialed Reese's number only to be kicked to voicemail.

Guy had a life, didn't he? Wasn't unusual for someone to be too busy to respond to a text or answer the phone. Happened to Brantley all the damn time.

Rather than jump to conclusions or worry, Brantley decided he would head into town. He'd already set his mind on eating out and he wasn't opposed to eating alone. He could stop by the diner, grab a burger. Reese would get back to him eventually, of that he had no doubt. They could meet up then. Maybe dessert and coffee.

He was heading toward the diner when he saw the Walker Demo truck parked in front of Moonshiners. Before he could think about what he was doing, he made a hard right, pulled into the parking lot. A couple of minutes later, he was strolling into the familiar bar, not surprised to see it was relatively empty so early in the evening.

What did surprise him was finding Reese sitting in a booth across from an attractive woman, the two of them leaning in, chatting. They looked rather comfortable, both smiling.

The strange knot that formed in his throat wasn't the least bit comfortable, but Brantley choked it down, then headed for the bar.

"Hey," Mack greeted. "What can I getcha?"

"Beer."

"Comin' right up."

Purposely taking a stool that wouldn't allow him to see Reese and his companion, Brantley accepted the beer Mack passed over. He didn't down it in one pull, but he didn't waste time, either. At the moment, he preferred to be anywhere but here, only his pride wouldn't allow him to storm out of the building. If Reese wanted to pull a stunt like this…

Brantley refused to care. There was no other option.

He could've pulled the whole caveman routine, stormed the table, confronted Reese. Where would that get him though? Into an argument in the middle of town? Last thing he wanted was to draw attention to something Reese clearly didn't want attention drawn to.

So, maybe this really was only sex, just without all the intercourse. Hand jobs and blow jobs galore, but that was about it.

Sex on the down low. He could do that, right?

Brantley nodded, answering his own question, and took a long pull on his beer. He could deal with that. Hell, he'd been doing that for most of his adult life. Relationships were for other people. Not him. He didn't need someone invading his space to be happy.

He would treat Reese the same way he'd treated Cyrus. Call him up when the urge hit, invite him over. Waste a few hours horizontal. Easy-peasy.

Only Brantley didn't want that with Reese, and the worst of it, he didn't know why that was. Here he'd been thinking they might have something. Which was saying a lot considering Brantley had never felt that way toward anyone. He'd never entertained the idea of more. His life had always been about the job, the mission. Being a SEAL wasn't simply a job, it had been his entire world. He had never needed more than that.

Not that he did now.

Nope.

No fucking way.

Brantley was not about to have a fucking pity party for himself. So what? He was no longer in the Teams. He was now living a different life. Didn't mean he couldn't be happy doing it.

Half an hour later, after attempting to settle his tab only to be told it was on the house for what he'd done to help out Travis, Brantley sauntered out. His appetite was now shot to shit, and the pit in his stomach wouldn't hold food well anyway, so he headed back to the house. After grabbing a couple of beers from the fridge, he started over to the barn only to make a U-turn, ending up right back in the house. He shoved the bottles back in the refrigerator, slammed the door, and went to change.

It wasn't until his feet were pounding dirt that he felt a modicum of calm even though he couldn't help but berate himself as he ran the five-mile route he'd gotten familiar with. Dusk had settled and it would be dark soon, but he wasn't too worried about it. He'd learned this path well enough, he could likely do it with his eyes closed.

The first five minutes he spent adjusting his gait, getting his muscles to work in tandem, forcing as much from his mind as possible. Running was always the best way for him to get out of his head. Oddly enough, it wasn't working for him today. No matter how hard he tried, he couldn't get the image of Reese sitting with that woman out of his mind. They'd looked so damn cozy. Too fucking cozy.

Was he honestly surprised that Reese had gone out with a woman?

Eh. Yes and no.

Sure, he'd suspected Reese was still on the fence as to whether he was comfortable with Brantley, but he'd gotten used to Reese's blatant honesty. He'd thought for sure when the day came Reese realized he didn't want this, he would've at least had the decency to say so to his face.

He was a fucking idiot. That was all there was to it.

What the hell made him think he could turn a straight man gay, he didn't know. That wasn't the way it worked. Everyone knew it, including him, but somewhere over the course of the past couple of months, he'd gotten his hopes up. What pissed him off was that Reese had led him to believe there was something more between them. Giving him that all in bullshit. Their definitions of what that meant clearly didn't align.

Better to find out now, he figured. Before he went and did something incredibly stupid, like fall for the guy.

Air was racing in and out of his lungs as he worked his body harder, pushed his legs to go faster.

Brantley didn't have time for this shit anyway. He had a job to do. One that had meaning, that would require a fuck of a lot of time. He had none left to spare for Reese and his waffling ideas of what he wanted. The guy could date all the women he could wrap his big fucking arms around. Brantley didn't give two fucks about it.

Keep tellin' yourself that.

Stopping to drag air into his lungs, Brantley planted his hands on his thighs, bent at the waist. He refused to think the tightness in his chest was from anything other than exertion. He hadn't developed feelings for Reese. Not in the short time he'd known him. It was sex. Not even phenomenal sex. Would've been, sure, if Reese would've fully opened up to the idea. However, the man continued to hold back, would continue to hold back because, despite what he said, he wasn't committed to whatever this was.

Fuck it.

With hands on his hips, Brantley started back toward his house. He decided to walk, needed a few extra minutes to clear his mind. He would grab a protein bar and a shower. Hopefully the combination would ward off the headache he could feel coming on. Then he would sleep, and tomorrow, he would get up and do it all again.

JUST AS THE CASE HAD BEEN FOR the past couple of years, JJ was hesitant to meet Dante for a date. Unfortunately, she'd put him off long enough and it had come time to put up or shut up. Stringing this along wasn't doing any good for either of them, which meant she now had to make a choice. Officially date him or don't. The man was becoming persistent, asking that they take things to the next level. And while she was skeptical about his motives, she wasn't sure what was holding her back.

So, here she was, walking into the diner on her way to have dinner with Dante. It still surprised her that he'd offered to meet her in Coyote Ridge. Being that Dante had moved out of their small town a long time ago and often looked on it with disdain, the kind that curled the lip, it was a bit disconcerting that this was where he wanted to meet.

He'd said seven, but it was fifteen minutes shy of that and he was already here. She knew that because his car was in the parking lot. JJ offered the waitress a smile and motioned toward the back before heading that way.

The instant she saw him, she found herself smiling.

One thing that never changed about Dante Greenwood was his good looks. In fact, she would say he'd gotten better-looking over the years. Although a bit more on the preppy side than he had been growing up, he still managed to pull it off. With the teal-blue polo shirt and the dark slacks, he looked like he should be sitting behind a desk, not having dinner in a backwoods diner. Because he'd tooted his own horn a number of times, she knew the watch on his wrist was a Rolex, the shoes on his feet were Ferragamos, as was the belt he wore, and the price tag on his entire closet was likely more than her house was worth.

But hey, not everyone was perfect.

"You look beautiful," he greeted, getting to his feet and leaning in to kiss her on the cheek.

JJ knew he was lying. She looked like she'd spent the entire day buried in her laptop, cooped up in a barn that had been converted into an office. But she had brushed her hair, put on minimal makeup, and changed into a fresh pair of jeans and a lightweight sweater to show effort.

"Thanks."

When Dante motioned for her to take a seat, she did.

"I took the liberty of ordering for you," he said. "I hope the special's all right."

It would have to be, even though she wasn't sure what tonight's special was.

"It's fine, thanks." She took a sip of iced tea, noticed it was unsweet. She added sugar since he hadn't bothered to get the sweetened tea she preferred.

It was the little things, the important things that Dante never seemed to pick up on.

"How're things with the new job?" he asked.

"First official day," she noted. "Good as can be expected, I guess."

"Well, you know I've always got a position open for you when you grow tired of it."

When not if, she noted.

Confused by his assumption she would grow tired of it, JJ opted to ignore the statement, took a drink. "How about you? How're things with work?"

"As usual, good. We've got more business than we can handle and I doubt it'll slow anytime soon."

No, it probably wouldn't and Dante would make sure everyone who knew him knew that. That was one of his flaws, one of the reasons she'd been keeping her distance. Dante was arrogant. And that was a trait he'd always had. Back in high school, she had mistaken it for self-confidence, even admired him for it. Although he had lived in the small town, grown up in a relatively small house, in an older neighborhood, Dante's family came from money. Or his father did, at least. His mother, on the other hand, had come from Coyote Ridge, and perhaps that was the reason Gerard had entertained the idea of living here and raising his children. That or he thought it would make him more pleasing to public opinion when he ran for political office.

"I hired a new assistant today," Dante informed her.

"What happened to the last one?"

"Creative differences," he stated, although he didn't meet her gaze when he said it.

JJ knew Dante. She knew him better than anyone in this town, probably better than anyone in his life. Which meant she understood that he considered himself God's gift to women. However, she thought he was making the effort to change his ways. At least, that was what he'd promised her when he started pursuing her again.

"How long was she there?"

"Month and a half."

JJ nodded. "Did you sleep with her?"

His brown eyes locked on hers. "I thought we agreed you wouldn't ask those questions."

No, they hadn't agreed to any such thing. Dante had insisted she not ask questions about his past relationships.

"I take that as a yes." She attempted to sound amused by the situation. She wasn't. "And this new one? Is she a redhead?"

He had the decency to blush, which told her, yes, the woman he had hired was likely a lovely redhead with green eyes and big tits. She would have long legs, prefer short skirts, and giggle whenever he spoke.

"We had a brief relationship," he admitted. "But that was before you agreed we would be exclusive."

JJ canted her head to the side. "I've never agreed to that, Dante."

"But it happened nonetheless." His smile was blinding, transforming his handsome face to almost beautiful. "And I'm holding you to it. Going forward, there's no one else for either one of us."

Since JJ hadn't been doing much in the dating arena, she had no argument.

Dante leaned forward, put his hand over hers. "I do want to see more of you, JJ."

So he'd told her. Many times.

"Starting with tonight."

Her eyebrows rose. "Tonight?"

"No better time than the present. I'd like to spend the night with you."

JJ wasn't sure what he was getting at. While they hadn't been exclusive, they had been having sex for quite some time. Mostly impromptu interactions, instigated by her. She could admit she had certain needs and she was comfortable with Dante when it came to the bedroom. Plus, they were compatible in that regard.

However, spending the night together hadn't been their thing. Usually, JJ would invite him over, they would have sex, then he would be on his way. It had worked for both of them.

"I have to be at work early," she informed him, trying to sound noncommittal.

"As do I. So we'll make the most of the night."

"Sure."

Another blinding smile was sent her way. "God, I've missed you, JJ. I can't tell you how happy I am you've decided to give me another chance."

JJ tried a smile of her own, hoped it held.

Because honestly, she wasn't sure she was as on board with his plan as he seemed to think she was.

"BRANTLEY?"

A firm hand landed on his shoulder, dragging Brantley from a restless sleep. He didn't bother opening his eyes. He couldn't. The pain was blinding, raging in his skull, his stomach threatening to revolt.

"Did you take medicine?"

He didn't answer, instead rolled over onto his side, facing away from Reese, pulling the pillow over his head, and letting his arm rest over it to apply pressure to his temple.

Behind him, the mattress dipped. Reese had taken a seat.

"I need you to take the pill, Brantley."

"Go. Away."

"I can't do that."

Well, he was in no shape to argue, so there.

Sometime later, Brantley woke, the pain in his skull to the point of excruciating. He knew he was going to vomit; there was nothing he could do about it. It took effort, but he got to his feet, stumbled to the bathroom. His knees crashed to the floor seconds before the remains of his protein-bar dinner resurfaced. He hugged the toilet, tried to get comfortable, the pounding in his head more intense than anything he'd felt in quite some time.

He gave his stomach time to settle, giving in to dry heaves a few more times before he felt slightly more at ease.

When he got over to the sink, desperate for one of those fucking pills, he found Reese leaning against the doorjamb. The only light came from the hallway outside his bedroom. It was enough to have the nerves in his fucking eyeballs throbbing.

"You finished?"

Brantley ignored him, made it to the medicine cabinet.

"I've got a pill right here," Reese said, his voice soft. "And water."

Because he would give anything to get rid of the pain, he held out his hand, took the pill Reese passed over. He used as little water as possible to choke it down before stumbling toward the bed again.

When Reese reached for him, he jerked away.

"You can be stubborn and you can be pissed," Reese whispered, "but I'm not leavin'."

Brantley was in too much pain to argue. Reese could stay or go. It didn't fucking matter.

The next time he woke, the pain had subsided.

He managed to open his eyes, glance at the alarm clock on the nightstand.

Six.

Which meant he'd slept for a solid seven hours. Funny how he only managed to sleep when he suffered another of those damn migraines. According to his doctor, they would possibly get better one day. Based on what he'd endured as of late, Brantley wasn't holding his breath.

"Headache gone?"

Frustrated and, yes, still fucking hurt, Brantley swung his feet over the side of the bed. He needed to shower and head out to the barn. He had shit to do today, people he needed to talk to.

"Brantley, talk to me."

Other people to talk to. Not Reese.

"Nothin' to say." He went to stand, but Reese's hand curled around his arm, pulling him back.

In a rare moment of anger, Brantley spun around, took Reese down to the bed with his hand planted firmly in the center of his chest.

Leaning, so he hovered above Reese, he growled softly, "If you know what's best, you won't fucking touch me."

There was defiance in the brown eyes peering back at him before Reese bit out, "I'm. Sorry."

Brantley jerked back, sitting on his heels and staring at him, surprised by the vehemence in his tone.

"I know what I did last night, Brantley. I know exactly what I fucking did. And I know you came into Moonshiners. I know you saw me."

Sounded to Brantley like Reese knew a hell of a lot.

Not that it made a bit of difference.

Lifting his chin, he stared down at Reese, unable to speak.

"I fucked up." Reese sat up, holding his stare. "In my defense, I told you I would." There was frustration and anger in Reese's voice. "I'm so fucking confused, Brantley. I know it seems normal for you, but this is so far outside of normal for me. I don't know what happened. I panicked. You texted me about dinner and I was working with Autumn. She saw the message, jumped to the conclusion that we were dating…"

Brantley choked out a laugh that lacked any mirth whatsoever. He scrambled to get off the bed, then went right for the bathroom.

"That came out wrong!" Reese shouted from behind him.

Brantley spun around to face him. "No, it didn't. We aren't dating, Reese. We're fucking. Or rather, you're gettin' your dick sucked and tugged while I wait around for you to figure out what the fuck this is for you. I'm just grateful you had the decency to let me know early on."

"I'm sorry."

"And I don't give a shit," Brantley snapped. "If you don't mind, I've got shit to do. And you do, too."

With that, he slammed the door and pretended his chest heaved because of exertion and not because Reese Tavoularis had managed to do what no man had ever done before: hurt him.

"WELL, YOU LOOK LIKE SHIT," AUTUMN SAID when Reese stepped into the office a little after nine. "Didn't get much sleep last night?"

"No." He went to his desk, sat down, opened his laptop.

"Have somethin' to do with Brantley?"

Reese's eyes cut over to her. "What? No. Of course not." He exhaled heavily, shot to his feet. "Yes. Goddammit. It has to do with Brantley."

Autumn's eyes had widened, but she remained in her seat. "Want to talk about it?"

"No."

"Okay."

Reese took a deep breath, sat down once more. He pulled up his email, skimmed the couple of things that had come in. Nothing of any importance because the majority of his job functions had been transferred to Autumn already. No, scratch that. Everything had been transferred to Autumn. There was absolutely no reason for him to still be here. Reese knew the only reason he continued to come back was because he was hesitant to take the leap in the direction his life was headed. It was a stall tactic. The last one he could hold on to before he found himself right in the middle of what was starting to feel like an alternate reality.

He turned on the out of office in his email, which directed people to Autumn, then signed out of his account, looked up at Autumn. "You need me to go over that spreadsheet one more time?"

She paused her typing to look over. "Um. No. I spent some time on it this morning. I've got a knack for reading formulas, so it's easy to navigate."

"Anything else you have questions about?"

Her golden eyebrows lowered. "I don't think so. You've been a really good trainer."

Getting to his feet before he changed his mind, Reese walked over, held out his hand. "Then I'm officially passing the reins over to you."

Autumn stood slowly, gripped his hand. "And I'm officially accepting them."

"I will need to keep the truck for a couple of days," he explained. "I'll have somethin' by the weekend."

"No worries. I've got my truck. It'll get me where I need to go."

Because there was nothing more to say or do, Reese nodded. "Good luck, Autumn."

"Hope to see you around."

He offered another nod and headed out into the brilliant Texas sunshine.

Half an hour later, after swinging through the bakery on Main Street and grabbing a dozen donuts, Reese headed for Brantley's.

When he got there, he parked the Walker Demo truck behind JJ's SUV, grabbed the generic white box with the sugary crap inside, and made his way to the barn. After keying in his pass code—only briefly worried it wouldn't work—he unlocked the doors and stepped inside.

Both Brantley and JJ turned to look at him. While Brantley's eyes narrowed on his face, JJ's darted to the box of donuts in his hand.

"Are those what I think they are?"

Clearly she didn't need an answer, because she was directly in front of him, relieving him of the box before he could say a word.

"Reese Tavoularis, you are my new best friend," she declared, going to her toes and kissing him on the cheek. "Want some coffee?"

"Would love some," he told her, still not looking away from Brantley.

If eyes could shoot daggers, Brantley would've slayed Reese where he stood. There was so much anger flashing in that blue-gray gaze, Reese wondered if he might go up in flames.

"Here's your coffee. Can I—" JJ came to a stop, eyes bouncing between them. "You know what? I actually forgot to add sugar. In fact, we're out. None out here. No sugar. Need to go over to the house and grab some."

Reese didn't stop her. He doubted Brantley wanted to be alone with him, but he would take the opportunity presented.

The door opened and shut, sealing them alone inside.

"I know you're pissed," he began.

"Not pissed," Brantley countered.

"Okay, upset."

"Not upset, either."

"Brantley…"

Brantley's chin tilted up, his eyes going to the ceiling, fists landing on his hips. "Now is not the time for us to have this discussion."

"So when will be?" He suspected never.

"Why are you here?"

"I work here."

"Thought you weren't startin' until next week."

"Things changed."

"Tell me about it."

Reese felt not only the words but the emotion behind them like a physical blow.

Rather than slink back into a corner and let Brantley continue to get riled up over something Reese couldn't take back, he continued forward, not stopping until he was standing directly in front of the man.

"Look," he said softly.

Brantley didn't look at him, so Reese helped him along, reaching up and putting his hand on his cheek, guiding him so he would meet his gaze.

"I fucked up. I'm well aware of that."

"It's not a big deal."

"It's a damn big deal," he bit out hotly. "Look. I get it, I do. You want to send me on my way, pretend there's nothin' between us. And I'm almost terrified enough to let you."

Brantley's eyes flared, likely surprised by his admission.

Reese stepped closer, eliminating the space between them. He lowered his voice when he said, "But I'm not goin' anywhere, Brantley. I can't. Not when I know that whatever this is, no matter how fucking terrifying... I've never felt like this before. Not for anyone. I don't know what it means, don't know where it's going. And I shouldn't have panicked, but I did. I'll probably do it again. Maybe more than once."

Brantley exhaled heavily, shaking his head. "I'm sorry, Reese. I'm not willin' to share. You wanna date women, feel free. But leave me out if it, would you?"

"That wasn't a date. What you saw last night. That was me havin' a beer with Autumn. We talked about her old job, some of the pain-in-the-ass customers we've both dealt with. It never got personal. I swear to God, it wasn't a date, Brantley. Yes, I ignored your call because I panicked. But I wasn't with her in that way. I don't want her that way."

Brantley remained silent.

Reese reached for him then, sliding his hand behind Brantley's neck, pulling him closer. Despite the fact he'd never touched a man like this, in such an intimate, emotionally charged way, it felt right with Brantley. "I'm sorry. I just… I need you to help me here."

He hadn't meant for so much emotion to escape, but he couldn't help it. He didn't understand any of this. How he could've gone his entire life without wanting a man and now feeling like this. When Brantley had told him to leave last night, the words had pierced him. A stab right in the heart. The thought of not seeing Brantley again … it was more terrifying than the realization he was falling for a man.

"I can't make you want me, Reese."

"Trust me, I don't need help in that regard." Reese leaned in, let his lips hover near Brantley's. "I've got that covered. I want you more than my next fuckin' breath. I think about you day and night. When I'm not here, I want to be here. And when I'm here, I don't want to leave."

He pulled back, met Brantley's gaze. "I'm not askin' you for anything. That's not where I'm goin' with this. I just need you to be patient with me."

"I'm not sure how much more patient I can be, Reese."

Okay, he had him there. Reese couldn't deny the man seemed to have an endless supply where he was concerned.

Before Brantley pulled away, Reese grabbed for him. He brought his forehead to Brantley's, keeping him close. "Please. Give me another chance."

"Fine."

Reese forced himself to let Brantley go. He knew the man was merely agreeing because Reese needed to hear it. But it was a start. He'd said what he had to say. For now.

Chapter Four

WHEN REESE STEPPED BACK, STARING AT HIM as though he'd just shot his dog, it was more than Brantley could take.

"Goddammit, Reese," Brantley bit out, grabbing Reese's arm and yanking him closer.

Cupping both sides of his face, he drew him in, crushed their lips together. The kiss exploded when Reese's arms wrapped around him, holding him securely as though he didn't want Brantley to pull away.

He absolutely detested how he felt in that moment. So fucking helpless, completely out of sorts. All thanks to Reese.

Brantley was a man who valued his control, had honed it over the years. It was what made him a phenomenal leader. He had led his SEAL team into dangerous situations time and time again, always managing to stay calm and cool under pressure. Then this man came along and rattled the very foundation of his being.

All because he was scared of what was happening between them.

In a sense, Brantley understood where Reese was coming from. Despite what he'd told Reese earlier, this wasn't just sex between them. It would've been a hell of a lot easier if that were the case. For both of them.

No, they were both dealing with heightened emotions brought on by uncertainty. Brantley didn't know which direction Reese was headed, and he suspected Reese didn't know, either. Leaving them in this perpetual state of question.

"I'm sorry," Reese mumbled against his lips.

"Don't say it again." Brantley pulled back, still holding Reese's head. "It's done. We're movin' on."

"Are we?"

He came to a decision immediately. "Yes."

Some people wouldn't understand his need to move forward, to leave shit in the past, but Brantley knew it was more about self-preservation than skill. He was not the sort to bring old shit up, to throw it in anyone's face. He would give Reese the benefit of the doubt because he wanted to, because he knew that throwing this away would only lead to a whole lot of what-ifs, and Brantley was opposed to those, too.

The door lock disengaged and Brantley instantly released Reese, not wanting him to feel uncomfortable when JJ returned. To his surprise, Reese didn't move away. The opposite, actually. He stepped forward, drew Brantley's mouth back to his, and kissed him softly, letting his lips linger for a few seconds. The hand that gently squeezed the back of his neck had a strange warmth swirling in his chest cavity.

When Reese pulled back, their eyes met, held.

JJ cleared her throat. "Should I leave and come back later?"

"No," Reese replied. "We're good."

Brantley held his gaze while he stepped back, space opening up between them once more.

"I handed Walker Demo over to Autumn this morning," Reese explained. "I know it's a few days early, but if it's all the same to you, I'd like to start workin' today."

Brantley nodded, mentally saw the line they were crossing. Moving forward. Not back. Never back.

"We're glad you're here."

"I am because you brought donuts," JJ declared, coming around to her desk.

"Where's the sugar?" Reese asked, grabbing his coffee cup and turning toward her.

She waved a hand over her shoulder. "In the kitchen. But I put some in your cup before I left."

Brantley watched Reese's grin form. Nope, they weren't low on sugar. Brantley knew because he'd stocked it on Sunday.

Taking a full breath for what felt like the first time that day, Brantley turned back to the whiteboard they'd been marking up before Reese's arrival.

"I was able to talk to Lauren's mother, Ellen, yesterday. She moved to Round Rock shortly after she and Lauren's father divorced. I wouldn't go so far as to say she has moved on, but she isn't the sort who has been hounding the police about her missing daughter. She admitted to contacting them at least once a year, but she said it's difficult because the case keeps being passed from one detective to another every few years. It was obvious she's disappointed in the lack of answers."

"I can imagine," Reese said, staring at the whiteboard.

"Did you learn anything we don't already know?" JJ asked.

"Not much, but there's something that might help." He glanced at Reese, then at JJ. "Like Governor Greenwood said, the day Lauren disappeared, she walked home by herself because Corinne had stayed home sick. What the governor didn't mention was that Lauren had stayed after school to work on a project with a couple of her friends. Rather than leave the school at three thirty like normal, it was closer to five according to those who saw her exit the building. Her mother didn't know who she was with, but she did give us a list of names of the girls she was closest to."

"If you'll give me those, I can see if I can track them down," JJ offered.

"You can reach out to them, too. Not sure how much they'll remember, but anything's better than nothing. I also want to talk to the teachers again," he added. "There are notes from interviews back then, but if there's even a remote chance we'll learn somethin' new, I want to ensure we cover all bases. A couple of them have since moved out of the area, but if they're nearby, I want to find them."

"What about Lauren's father?" Reese asked. "You speak to him?"

"Not yet." Brantley glanced over. "I was hopin' to do that today. He moved to San Antonio shortly after the divorce, remarried, has a couple of kids. According to Ellen, Rob Tyler spent most of his time at the office. Rarely was he home back then. She said he wasn't close to Lauren, but I'd still like to talk to him."

Brantley had actually been a little bothered by the way Ellen tried to dismiss Rob's relationship with his daughter. As though the man hadn't cared that she had disappeared. Perhaps that was because Brantley had come from a big family who all pitched in to take care of one another when necessary. He couldn't imagine any scenario in which they wouldn't want to find one of their own. He had suspected she was projecting her own anger on her ex-husband.

"What about sex offenders?" Reese inquired. "Do we have a list of those who were in the area at the time? Or anyone nearby who did, or is currently, serving time for a similar crime? Rape, kidnapping?"

"Good idea." Brantley glanced at JJ. "If there were any sex offenders in Coyote Ridge specifically, the sheriff'll know offhand. But broaden the search to the surrounding cities. See if you can track them down."

"Will do."

He glanced over at Reese. "Whaddya say? Wanna go for a ride to San Antonio?"

"Where you go, I go."

For the first thirty minutes of the hour-and-forty-five-minute drive to San Antonio, they rode mostly in silence. The radio played, set on a country station. Brantley didn't engage conversation, nor did Reese. The quiet wasn't wrought with tension, but it wasn't the comfortable kind. It just was.

And then it wasn't.

As the minutes passed and the silence became heavier, Brantley kicked off with the one thing that had been on his mind for the past few days. "I want to take you on a date."

There was no surprise in Reese's voice when he answered. "A date? Like dinner?"

"For starters, yes. You make it sound like a foreign concept."

"It's just…"

"What?" He glanced over. "You think gay guys don't like to go out?"

Reese chuckled, but it sounded strained. "I guess I haven't given it much thought."

"And you find it awkward?"

Reese turned his full attention over to him. "Yes, but not the way you probably think."

"And what do I think?"

"It's not the date part. Two guys goin' out, dinner, movies, whatever. The concept's not awkward for me."

"No?"

"No. I like doin' things with you."

"But?"

"But I'm not used to bein' on the receivin' end of the request."

Brantley hadn't considered that. Now that he thought about it, made a bit of sense. Reese was definitely an alpha male, liked control. It was something they had in common.

But Brantley was nothing if not flexible.

"Fine. You take me out." He shot Reese a grin. "I'm not opposed to you footin' the bill for dinner."

Reese laughed. "I don't imagine you are."

"But you'll need to be spontaneous."

"Is that right?"

"Yep. Can't be tonight. I'll already expect it."

"Fine. Then I'd like to take you out on Friday."

"Hmm." Brantley pretended to consider it. "I might have other plans."

"That so?"

"It's possible. I'll have to check my calendar."

"Well, you do that. And I'll be by to pick you up on Friday night. Seven o'clock."

Brantley cut his eyes over once more. "You'll pick me up? In the Walker Demo truck?"

"No. I'll have somethin' by then."

"You want help pickin' it out?"

Reese was silent long enough Brantley peered over at him again.

"What?"

"Yes. I'd like you to help me pick it out."

He laughed. "You just need a ride to the dealership. I've got your number, Tavoularis."

The chuckle that followed eased some of the tension and gave Brantley something he hadn't had in a long time.

Hope.

Brantley's first impression of Rob Tyler was that he was a man who loved his children beyond measure. And he wasn't only referring to the two he had now—Max, a boy of six, and Gabrielle, a cute little girl of four. Based on the nice two-story house situated in a quiet cul-de-sac, Rob and his wife, Reba, were proud parents who liked to show off their kids. Along with the pictures of Max and Gabrielle they had lining the stairs were numerous pictures of Lauren. Placed chronologically to depict her life from before she could walk right up to one that looked to have been taken at a high school dance.

"That's the last picture I have of her," Rob said softly.

Brantley looked at the picture of Lauren with a couple of other girls, all of them grinning widely, as though they were happier than they'd ever been.

"She disappeared shortly after that," Rob noted.

Brantley detected the pain in his voice. It was the same inflection he'd heard when he had spoken to Lauren's mother. Despite the apparent problems they'd had between them, both of Lauren's parents loved her very much and they were still suffering after all these years.

"I was a little surprised to get your call," Rob told them, motioning them into the family room. "It's been quite some time since I've managed to get anyone to give me information on her case."

"We just recently took it over," Brantley admitted, lowering himself to the sofa.

"Can I get you something to drink?" Reba offered.

"We're good, thanks." He turned his attention back to Rob. "Both Reese and I grew up in Coyote Ridge. We've recently been assigned to a task force created by Governor Greenwood. We're lookin' into missing persons cases. The governor mentioned this one specifically, so we decided it would be the first one we focused on."

Rob was staring back at him, and if Brantley wasn't mistaken, there was a glimmer of hope in his eyes.

"I haven't seen Gerard in years," Rob said, his voice low, as though it took effort to project it. "Not since shortly after Lauren's disappearance. He still calls from time to time to check in."

"If you don't mind, sir, maybe you could walk us through what happened the day Lauren went missing," Reese suggested.

Rob's eyes turned glassy. "Of course." He took a deep breath, exhaled slowly. "It was a normal day, I guess you could say. I woke up that morning, left for work while Lauren was having breakfast." He smiled at the memory. "Frosted Flakes. Her favorite. She had a bowl every morning."

Brantley listened intently as he continued to explain how he had gone to work and was on his way home when Ellen called him to let him know Lauren hadn't made it.

"She thought maybe I'd picked her up that day. I figured she had gone to a friend's house."

"Did she normally do that?" Reese inquired.

"Not unless she was at Corinne's. But she did have a lot of friends and she was starting to hang around more people. Part of high school, I figure. It's when kids blossom, establish the basis for who they will be."

Brantley nodded, encouraging him to continue.

"By the time I got home, Ellen was frantic. She'd called the police. They were checking in with the school, reaching out to her friends. Corinne had stayed home sick that day, so Lauren hadn't gone over there."

"Do you know if she had a boyfriend at the time? Or did she have a lot of interactions on social media?"

"She had the regular accounts, but we had the log-in information. We were relatively strict about her online interactions, what with the dangers and all. I looked through her accounts, didn't find anything out of the ordinary, but I gave all that information to the police at the time."

"What about boys at school? Did she like someone in particular?"

Rob's eyes narrowed. "No. Lauren wasn't interested in boys."

Brantley was curious as to the statement. Ellen had said something almost identical. And he got the feeling they didn't mean because she wasn't at that age yet. Something in their tone.

"She preferred her friends over everyone. And she was into her schoolwork. Most of her friends were focused on what college they would eventually get into. I think it was a game they played. Who could get the best grades."

Wow. If Brantley'd had friends like that, imagine where he might've been today.

"Were any of her friends boys?"

"No." Rob's gaze lowered. "Like I told you, she didn't date, didn't talk about boys. Probably had something to do with the fact Ellen forbid her to. Said she had no time for boys in her life and she could focus on that when she was finished with her schooling."

A little harsh, but it went along with the way Ellen had reacted to Brantley's question.

"We heard she stayed after school to work on a project," Reese said. "Do you happen to know which class the project was in?"

"No." Rob's eyes lowered. "I'll admit, I wasn't as involved in her school as I should've been. I didn't help her with her homework, didn't even check to make sure she'd done it. I left all that to Ellen. Figured Lauren didn't need us both micromanaging her."

When no one said anything more for nearly a minute, Brantley decided to conclude the conversation.

"Mr. Tyler, you've got my number," he said, getting to his feet. "If there's anything else you can think of that might help us in our investigation, please don't hesitate to call."

"And you'll keep me informed?" he asked hopefully.

"Of course. I'll make sure you receive frequent updates."

Half an hour later, Brantley was sitting at a table at Whataburger with Reese. As they waited for their food to be delivered to them, he went back to a couple of things the man had said.

"Rob was pretty adamant his daughter wasn't dating anyone at the time."

Reese leaned forward, drank from his straw, sat up. "I know. I caught that, too."

"Not that I remember a whole hell of a lot about bein' fifteen, but I'm pretty sure hormones played a big part for me that year. And many years to follow."

"All the way to present day," Reese quipped.

Brantley quirked a brow. "What about you? What were you doin' when you were fifteen?"

"Probably ridin' my Haro to Jenny Andrews's house."

"Jenny Andrews?"

"My girlfriend from sixth grade through tenth."

"Ah. So you were the settlin'-down type back then."

"No. It took me that long to round all the bases with her."

"Go, tiger."

Reese rolled his eyes. "It's not the fact Lauren's father said she didn't have a boyfriend. It was the way he said Ellen forbid it, therefore it couldn't have been true."

"Yeah. Almost like if he said it enough, it would be true."

"What're you thinkin'?" Reese prompted.

"I don't know. Maybe she had a bad relationship. Somethin' Mom and Dad didn't approve of."

"Like an abusive asshole? Maybe someone older? Or…"

"Or what?"

"A girl?" Reese suggested.

That was actually the first thing that had come to his mind. "It's possible."

"And maybe this is me bein' naive, but if she was gay, I don't see her girlfriend kidnapping her."

"No, wouldn't've been the girlfriend. Not if she was her age, anyway. And if Lauren was gay, I'd think Corinne would've known," Brantley explained. "They were best friends. Chicks share all that shit with each other."

"Not if they don't want word spreadin'."

Brantley watched Reese, wondering if he was talking about their current situation.

"You know Ethan, right?" Reese asked, pushing his drink to the side.

"Of course. He's my cousin."

"You went to school with him?"

"He was a few grades back."

"Did you know he was gay? I mean, back then. Were you aware?"

"Doubtful. Not somethin' that interested me."

"I don't think anyone knew," Reese explained. "Based on what I've heard from his brothers, Ethan was bullied brutally. His boyfriend took his own life and the kid's older brother terrorized Ethan for years." Reese exhaled. "What I'm sayin' is that not many people knew Ethan's story because he didn't want anyone to know. Could be Lauren kept it on the DL."

"If you twist it enough, yeah, it could fit. When I talked to Lauren's mother yesterday, she said the same thing. There was no way Lauren had a boyfriend. If she had, they would've known. I took it more to mean they kept a close eye on her."

"Oh, the misconceptions parents have," Reese teased. "I can tell you, my parents had no idea who I was datin'."

"Mine did," Brantley admitted. "But only because I've got three older sisters who could never seem to mind their own business. Still can't."

A young guy carrying a tray strolled up to the table, handed it over before swinging another around. This one held a variety of condiments.

Reese waved him off while Brantley snagged a couple of spicy ketchup tubs.

When the guy walked away, Reese leaned in. "I hope you know I'm not takin' you out for a burger on our date."

The comment had Brantley's eyes darting upward. He probably should've said something pithy, but the truth was, he was too stunned to say a damn thing.

THE LOOK ON BRANTLEY'S FACE LOOSENED SOMETHING inside Reese.

He wasn't sure why that was.

Nor was he sure why he'd spoken his thought aloud.

What he did know was that when he was around Brantley, the anxiety wasn't there. At least when they were hanging like this. Casual, comfortable. No pressure. When they were naked, yes, he was anxious, but he suspected it was different than the strange tension that had choked him when Autumn had seen that text.

It wasn't something he could explain because it wasn't something he understood. But he hoped with time, as he figured out how he fit in this new puzzle that was his life, it would all make sense.

"I'm lookin' forward to it," Brantley said, his eyes blazing with heat.

"Me, too."

By the time six o'clock rolled around, Reese was hungry.

After they'd eaten lunch, Brantley had driven them back to Coyote Ridge. They had met up with JJ in the barn, walked through what little they'd learned, and begun jotting down the millions of questions their conversations were producing. They were no closer to finding Lauren Tyler, but it did feel as though they were making inroads.

After deciding Brantley and Reese would reach out to Corinne Greenwood tomorrow and see if they could pick her brain, JJ had slipped out for a date with Dante, something she hadn't told Brantley but rather disclosed to Reese. For whatever reason, Brantley had a beef with Dante, even though, according to JJ, Brantley and Dante had talked over dinner one night about the past. She'd been under the impression they had cleared the air between them. Reese wasn't so sure.

Nor was he interested in discussing it with Brantley right now.

"What's on your mind?" Brantley asked from where he was sitting on the couch in the barn. He had his hands folded in his lap, head tilted back, as though the position might help bring him clarity on the case.

"Just thinkin' about what I'm gonna have for dinner."

Brantley's head tipped forward. The cocky grin that formed on his mouth said he could think of a few things. Brantley patted the cushion, so Reese made his way over, dropped down beside him.

When Brantley reached for his hand, Reese didn't flinch, didn't pull away, just watched the way their fingers twined, linking together comfortably. Reese was aware of the warmth of Brantley's skin, the roughness. Without thinking, he pulled Brantley's hand into his lap as he rubbed his thumb over the back of Brantley's hand. The next thing he knew, he'd untangled their fingers and was using both of his hands to explore Brantley's fingers, his palm.

"I like when you touch me," Reese muttered as he continued to hold Brantley's hand between his. "I like the feel of your skin on mine."

He wasn't sure if he spoke because he wanted Brantley to know what he was thinking or because he needed to hear himself say it aloud. To admit what he wanted, accepting it as he went along.

"But more than that," he whispered, "I like touchin' you, too."

Brantley remained silent beside him. Every now and then, Brantley's thumb would move, rubbing against Reese's wrist.

"That first time I touched you," he continued, "on the way to Mississippi, the plane… I'll never forget that moment. I was terrified, but not because of what we were doin'. Because of what I wanted to do. I've never thought of two men bein' together as taboo or wrong. My brother's gay and he's had plenty of boyfriends in his lifetime. For him, it's normal. For you, too. But for me, it's … different. I've never been turned on by a man before."

Reese glanced over, saw Brantley was watching him intently, listening.

"Then you came along and everything I thought I knew about myself went right out the window."

He brought Brantley's hand to his lips, pressed a kiss to his knuckles, then placed Brantley's palm against his cheek.

"When you touch me … it feels better than anything I've ever known before. But I can't say it feels natural. Just … better." He looked at Brantley again. "I'm sorry about last night. Truly sorry. I just…"

"You don't have to explain it," Brantley said, his voice deeper than usual.

"I do. I need you to understand."

Bringing Brantley's hand back to his lap, he turned it so his palm was up, began massaging it with his thumbs.

"From the first night I saw you at IHOP, I was fascinated. Not sure why, but I was. Then I saw you with JJ at the gun range. It was the same. For those couple of minutes we talked, I was more interested in hearing your voice than talking to the beautiful woman with you. I knew something was … off. Inside me. And when I saw you at the gun range alone the next time, I thought it was fate." He smiled shyly. "Sounds stupid, I know."

The hand in his lap squeezed his fingers gently. "It doesn't."

"I didn't want to go separate ways that night. After dinner. I wanted to talk to you, look at you. I tried to tell myself it was because you're an interesting man, that it was normal for me to be curious about you." He met Brantley's gaze again. "It was more than that. I wanted to know when I would see you again. I didn't want to walk away until I was certain I would."

He shifted his attention back to Brantley's hand.

"It's not that I haven't felt a pull toward a woman before. I have. Couple of times. But nothin' like what you make me feel. I didn't understand it. Still don't. It scares me shitless. Not just because you're a man, but because it's so powerful. This feelin'…" He locked eyes with Brantley, his voice dropping to a whisper. "It's so fuckin' powerful."

Brantley moved, shifting his upper body, angling toward Reese. The hand he'd been exploring moved to cup his cheek, pulling him closer.

"It's mutual, Reese. The feelin's mutual."

When Brantley's lips brushed his, Reese exhaled slowly, letting himself get swept away by the current.

His hands slid to Brantley's neck, curling around it, feeling the strain of the muscles in his shoulders, the rasp of his stubble against his thumb. He was aware of this man on every level and it didn't scare him. That wasn't the right word. It confused him, sure. But at the same time, it settled him.

"I want to touch you," he said softly, pulling back and meeting Brantley's stormy blue eyes. "Let me touch you, Brantley."

"Whenever, however you want," Brantley replied.

So Reese did.

Right there on the couch in what was their new office, Reese touched him. He maneuvered Brantley down to his back, settling beside him, curling one leg around Brantley's to keep from falling to the floor. They kissed, but it wasn't rushed. Brantley was giving him full control, something Reese had gotten used to. He knew the man was holding back so much for him, letting him explore.

Flattening his palm on Brantley's stomach, he dipped his fingers beneath his T-shirt, working the fabric up, revealing all the hard ridges of his torso.

"You don't have any tattoos." He lifted his gaze to Brantley's face. "Why not?"

"Too distinctive."

He nodded, understanding. Brantley had been a SEAL, which meant he knowingly put himself in dangerous situations. Situations that could've easily ended with him being taken by tangos. Made sense that he wouldn't want any identifying marks that might give the bad guys insight into who he was if they somehow were able to connect the dots.

Reese propped himself up so he could watch his hand as it glided over smooth golden skin. Brantley helped him along, tugging the T-shirt off, letting it fall to the floor. He admired the flex and pull of muscles, the delectable musky scent that was unique to this man. His head was spinning, his body hardening.

He continued to trail his fingers over Brantley's chest, across his nipples, watching the small discs harden from his touch. His mouth soon joined the exploration, gliding over warm, supple skin as he licked and tasted. All the while, Brantley remained where he was, watching, never rushing him, never guiding him elsewhere. He seemed content to let Reese do what was necessary for him.

It would've been easy to push this to the point of no return, but Reese didn't want that. Not yet. Not here. He wanted to be somewhere he could spread out, so he forced himself to stop, to pull back. He kissed Brantley again, shifting so he was over him, letting the man bear his full weight.

"Let's take this into the house," he whispered.

"Lead the way."

So he did.

NOT SINCE HE WAS A TEENAGER HAD making out been something Brantley had looked forward to. With Reese, it was a constant thought in his head.

It wasn't only the touching, the teasing. He enjoyed that part, of course, but it was watching Reese, the heated gleam in his eyes, the way he would lick his lower lip as though he wanted to taste but wasn't sure he should that enraptured him. And if this was all Reese wanted, Brantley was more than willing to lie there, to let him explore for as long as necessary.

Once they'd made it to Brantley's bedroom, he continued to let Reese lead. He had no desire to control this moment. No, he happened to enjoy being at this man's mercy. There would definitely come a time when the roles would reverse, when Brantley would take back the control he was loaning out. But for now, he didn't mind it.

When they were stretched out on his bed, they picked up where they'd left off in the barn. Reese's body covered his, but this time, Brantley did some touching of his own. He slipped his hands beneath Reese's T-shirt, drawing the cotton up, urging him to remove it. It was discarded easily, as were their boots, their bodies never separating, tongues continuing to mingle.

Seconds ticked by as Reese undressed them both. When they were finally naked, Reese returned to his position over him, their bodies pressed together from chest to knee, skin stroking skin, lips brushing lips.

Brantley had never made love to a man before. His sexual encounters had always had one main objective. Release. With Reese, it wasn't about the release, it was about the exploration. Brantley was content to touch and taste, not needing more because this was more. More than he'd known before. No man had ever driven him to madness the way Reese could. Perhaps it was the vulnerability he sensed, or maybe the uncertainty.

Reese's lips trailed down his jaw, brushing over his neck. He tilted his head and drew in a ragged breath when Reese sucked and licked. When their hips began a delicious grind, their cocks pressed intimately between them, Brantley cupped Reese's ass, holding him in place while the man continued to torment him with that exquisite mouth.

"Christ … Brantley…"

Reese's mouth returned to his, the kiss heating, their bodies continuing the easy glide against one another.

"You feel so fuckin' good," Reese moaned softly. "It's not enough."

It would be. Brantley would make sure of it.

He took Reese to the mattress, coming over him, rolling his hips while he took the kiss to the next level. They shared breath while they worked themselves into a frenzy.

"You're gonna make me come," Reese warned, his arms banding around him, holding tight.

"Come for me," Brantley urged, nipping Reese's lower lip. "Let go, Reese. I've got you."

Reese's head lifted, his mouth finding Brantley's again. They were both breathing hard, their moans and groans turning urgent as they chased the elusive release with nothing more than skin-to-skin contact.

Brantley slid his fingers into Reese's hair, tugged his head to the side, and fastened his mouth to Reese's neck. He sucked roughly, not caring that he might leave a mark on him. Hell, he wanted to.

"Oh, fuck. Brantley…"

Reese's hips punched upward as he came.

Brantley felt Reese's cock pulse, the warmth of his cum as it spilled between their bodies. It triggered his own release and he came on a strangled groan, relaxing on top of Reese when every ounce of his energy drained out of him.

"I don't know what to do about you," Reese whispered.

Brantley could think of a few things, but he didn't say anything, content just to be right where he was.

An hour later, they were sitting down to dinner. While Reese had showered, Brantley'd seasoned several chicken breasts, tossed them on the grill. And while Brantley showered, Reese had cooked them up, put together a couple of sides—poblano peppers and rice, with some ranch-style beans to go with it.

They ate at the bar, the tension from last night and that morning behind them.

Finally.

Chapter Five

THE NEXT COUPLE OF DAYS WERE SPENT going over the details of the case, adding notes, scheduling appointments, and essentially waiting for Corinne Greenwood to be free. The woman was a student at UT and currently under a lot of pressure for midterms, so Brantley had given her a reprieve, agreeing to meet on Monday of the next week, a full week and a half away, so they could chat. Although Brantley was the sort to prefer to get things out of the way faster, he figured pushing the issue was pointless. Lauren Tyler had been missing for nine years. He wasn't sure what a week was going to do now.

Because they weren't overwhelmed with work, Brantley had suggested they go on the search for some wheels for Reese, figuring it would be easy for the man to walk into a dealership and walk out with a vehicle.

Boy, was he ever wrong. He had sorely overestimated Reese's desire to get this done as fast as possible.

"This is the third dealership we've been to," Brantley said, though it was unnecessary.

"Third time's a charm."

"If you say so." Brantley exhaled, turning into the drive for what he hoped would be the last Chevy dealership they visited.

As it was, they'd spent the better part of the afternoon test-driving one truck after another for Reese to walk out of each dealership without making a decision. The only explanation Reese had for why he hadn't picked something out was that he hadn't found what he was looking for. According to the man, he would know it when he saw it.

"Ever think maybe you're not a Chevy guy? Maybe you should try on a Ford for size."

Reese peered over. "Not a chance."

Brantley grinned. "Good. Guys who drive Fords don't really do it for me."

"Cyrus drives a Ford."

"My point exactly."

And it was the smile that pulled at Reese's lips that he'd been going for. He knew Reese had his issues with Cyrus. For whatever reason, he was jealous. Quite frankly, there was absolutely nothing for him to be jealous about, but deep down, it pleased Brantley that he cared enough to admit it.

He pulled his truck up to the building, put it in park.

When they stepped inside a couple of minutes later, they were bum-rushed by an older man with thinning hair and a cheap suit. His cheeks were ruddy, his smile wide, his eyes wider, and he seemed hell-bent on doing whatever it took to make a sale today.

"And what brings you boys into our fine establishment?"

Reese strolled toward him. "I'm lookin' for a truck."

"Well, you're in luck. We've got the largest selection in Central Texas." The guy thrust his hand in Reese's direction. "Name's Billy. And you are?"

"Reese."

Before Billy could offer up his hand to Brantley, he opted to take a detour, moving around to check out the Corvette sitting in the middle of the showroom. A little too flashy for his taste, but then again, he'd never been the sort to seek his adrenaline fix behind the wheel of a car.

"You'd look mighty fine in that car."

Brantley glanced in the direction of the sultry voice, offering a grin when a leggy blond woman sauntered toward him.

"I'm a truck guy myself," he admitted.

"Leisure car then," she suggested, moving to stand a couple of inches from him. "Or maybe your wife'd be interested."

"No wife."

"Well now, that's a shame."

Brantley's gaze swung to Reese and he grinned. "Not really, no."

"I've got a couple more of these right outside. Perhaps a test drive? You never know, you might like it once you've tried it."

He fought the urge to laugh, knowing full well she was referring to the car and maybe hinting that she'd be interested, too. There was no ring on her finger, but that didn't mean a damn thing.

"I'm just gettin' familiar with what I've got," he told her, continuing with the riddles. "I prefer my rides … bigger."

The blonde giggled, her hand going to his arm in that casual, flirty way women did when they wanted a man to know they were into them.

Brantley glanced over at Reese once more, noticing the tall, handsome guy with the stern look on his face was now looking his way. Nope. Scratch that. Reese was now strolling his way.

"Speakin' of bigger…" Brantley mumbled, turning to face the sexy man whose eyes were taking in the situation.

The blonde turned toward him. She instantly stood a bit taller, her chest pushing out a tad more. Definitely liked what she saw.

Not that Brantley blamed her. He was quite fond of Reese himself.

"Any luck?" he asked when Reese approached.

"Got my eye on a red one out there." Reese held up his hands, dangled a key. "Let's go for a test drive."

"I'm right behind you," he said, wondering if the woman would understand that riddle.

With a nod and a wink to the woman, Brantley fell into step with Reese. He made sure he kept a safe distance between them, only to be surprised when Reese moved close enough their arms brushed as they reached the door.

When Reese turned to push it open with his back, their eyes met, held. Brantley could see a hint of jealousy flashing in that intriguing brown gaze. His response: a smirk.

"Please tell me this is the truck you've been waitin' your whole life for," he said as he hopped in the passenger seat while Reese got behind the wheel.

"Doubtful, but can't let Billy know that."

Frowning, Brantley glanced over. "You have an agenda."

"I do," Reese admitted, backing the truck out of the parking spot. "Plan to buy the charcoal-gray one we saw earlier."

"The one at the first dealership?"

"Yep."

Seriously? "So why the hell are we here?"

"Politics."

"Clue me in," Brantley urged.

"That first sales guy we talked to was too cocky," he said, steering the truck out onto the service road. "Acted like he'd be doin' me the favor of sellin' me a truck."

Yeah, Brantley hadn't been all that fond of the guy. A tad on the pretentious side.

"So?"

"Well, this dealership doesn't have a charcoal-gray one."

"Meaning?"

"Meaning I'll just have Billy call down there, see if they can do the swap. Because they're in direct competition, they won't. I'll get a call from the cocky jackass with a damn good deal for me. I'll tell him my problem with the service, he'll bump me to a supervisor because partial commission is better than none, right?"

Brantley sighed. "Fuckin' hell."

"Trust me, Navy boy. I know what I'm doin'."

Two hours later, Brantley realized Reese did, in fact, know what he was doing.

Now back at the dealership they'd started from, Brantley was sitting in the waiting area, knocking back a Dr. Pepper, while Reese took care of the paperwork on the first truck he had driven. Not only was he getting a good deal, he was now dealing directly with the man who owned the dealership on the truck he'd had his eye on originally. It wasn't much different than Brantley's, current year model, all the upgrades. That was one thing that people in Texas did, they took tremendous pride in their trucks.

He probably could've headed home, left Reese behind. Reese would have the keys before he walked out the door, but Brantley figured he had nothing better to do. Or rather, nothing else he wanted to do. Well, except maybe dinner. Lunch had been hours ago and he was starving. He wasn't sure what he had to cook back at his place and briefly wondered if Reese wanted to come over. He hated asking because they'd been spending a ridiculous amount of time together as it was. The last thing he wanted was to come off looking desperate. Then again, he didn't want to seem aloof, either.

Fucking dating.

This was why Brantley didn't date. There was too fucking much to worry about. It was a hell of a lot easier when it was simply sex. There was no worry about offending someone or making them feel less or more important. Brantley'd done a damn fine job of it over the years, balancing the scales of his sex life. Then Reese came along and suddenly he was worried he might be too fucking needy.

"Hey."

Reese's voice dragged him from his thoughts, had him glancing up over his shoulder.

"All done. You ready to head out? Or you wanna hang around and check out their reading material?"

Brantley tossed the magazine he hadn't bothered to open back onto the table, got to his feet. He pitched the empty Dr. Pepper can in the recycle bin on the way to the door.

"You headin' home?" Reese asked when they stepped outside.

"Yeah." Was he supposed to invite Reese over? Or shrug him off like it didn't matter if he came by or not?

Reese nodded. "All right then. I guess I'll see you in the mornin'?"

It was a question, he realized. "Works for me."

Another nod.

Not sure what to say, Brantley tilted his head toward Reese, then made his way to his truck. He climbed in, pretending not to watch Reese do the same. He pulled out of the parking lot, hit the turnaround to head back to Coyote Ridge. He was about to pull off the toll road when his cell phone rang.

Reese's name appeared on the screen, so he hit the button to take the call.

"What's up?"

"I'm comin' over."

"Are you now?" he shot back, pretending he wasn't grinning like a fucking idiot.

"Yep. I'll make dinner."

"I'm capable of makin' dinner," he countered.

"I want to."

"Yeah, sure," he said, aiming for casual. "See you in a few."

"Brantley?"

"Hmm?"

"There's a few things I think we should talk about."

"Yeah?"

"Yeah."

"Well then, I guess we'll talk while you cook my dinner."

The soft chuckle that came back was almost enough to loosen the knot that had formed in Brantley's gut.

Almost.

REESE COULD TELL SOMETHING WAS BOTHERING BRANTLEY. He'd seemed awkward when they were leaving the dealership, almost as though he wasn't sure what to say, if anything.

It was the very reason he'd decided he would go to Brantley's, hash this out before it could go sideways.

That was one thing Reese was good at. Talking. He'd always been brutally honest. Sometimes to his detriment. But when it came to Brantley, he figured it wasn't such a bad thing. The man wasn't exactly an open book when it came to his life. They'd shared no details about their time in the military, nor had either one broached the subject. Family was a different subject altogether. Brantley would talk about Mom and Dad, brothers and sisters, nieces and nephew until his tongue dried up. But that wasn't exactly the same as revealing his deepest, darkest secrets.

Not that Reese was looking to wrench his way into Brantley's psyche. But he did want them to continue on this path, and because they were working together now, it was important their spare time be spent on a personal level whenever possible.

At least, that was the direction Reese hoped they were heading. He was getting mixed signals from Brantley, so best to knock down those walls now before they got too high.

Kind of a complete three-sixty from when Reese had panicked, but hey, he wanted to believe he was evolving.

"I'm just curious, does your mom know I'm spendin' time over here?" Reese asked as he scanned the refrigerator for dinner ideas.

"Why?"

"Well, one, there's more selection in food. And second, it looks like she's shoppin' for two." He lifted a Styrofoam tray of salmon up to show him.

"Are you askin' if my parents know about you?" Brantley's tone held more than a little edge.

"I don't care if they know," he said quickly, setting the salmon on the counter. "You have maple syrup?"

"Pantry. I didn't tell 'em. Trey did."

Reese nodded. "The night I kicked him and Cyrus out."

Made sense. He'd taken a stand that night, and looking back, he wasn't ashamed that he had. He'd wanted to take care of Brantley then. The same as he did now.

"Got a bottle of Jack?"

"Cabinet over the stove."

Reese snagged the whiskey bottle, cracked open the lid for the first time. "Not a big whiskey drinker, huh?"

"Beer's more my thing."

This was good. Casual conversation. Brantley seemed to be relaxing a little.

"You mind heatin' up the grill for me?" he prompted as he started preparing the salmon.

Brantley went out, started the grill, returned, and grabbed two beers. After popping the tops, he passed one over. "You said we needed to talk."

Reese looked up, noticed the frown line marring Brantley's forehead.

"It's not doom and gloom, Navy boy," he said, hoping to lighten the mood.

The way Brantley stared back at him said he didn't believe him.

"Let me get the fish on first."

With a grunt, Brantley stepped back outside, checked the grill. Reese could see him through the glass doors, watched as Brantley turned to stare out into the yard. It didn't surprise him when he didn't return. It was that distance thing. Brantley was damn good at putting space between them. And it was instantaneous when he did. No argument, just immediate retreat.

Once Reese got the salmon seasoned to his liking, he took the plate and his beer and went outside. He got the fish laid out in foil, closed the lid, turned to face Brantley.

"When we were leavin' the dealership, I didn't know whether to assume I was comin' here or you were comin' to my place," he said, getting the words out before he changed his mind. "I didn't want to go home alone, but I didn't want to impose on you, either."

Brantley's gaze swung his way.

"I know we're takin' things slow because you think that's what I need, but … I guess what I'm tryin' to say is I don't want slow. Not as far as this goes." He gestured between them. "I want to spend time with you, Brantley. But I don't want to push, don't want to assume."

Brantley turned away from him.

"It's been a long time since I've really dated anyone," Reese continued. "A couple of one-nighters here and there but never anything serious."

Still nothing from Brantley.

Reese decided to come out with it. "Is this serious, Brantley? For you?"

That got him the attention he was hoping for. Brantley turned, took a long pull on his beer.

"It's not a one-nighter, if that's what you're askin'," Brantley said gruffly.

Reese nodded. Not exactly an answer. They both knew it wasn't a one-nighter already. Too much time spent together to qualify. Didn't do a damn thing to clarify what it was though.

He turned, took a drink, stared out at the barn as night continued to swallow up the earth.

"I haven't dated anyone," Brantley finally said. "Not since I got my trident. The Teams became my life. It was the only thing that mattered. One-nighters were all I could offer." He glanced over. "Cyrus was a consistent hookup but never serious."

Reese did his best not to flinch at the mention of Cyrus.

"So I don't really know how to do this. I wanna take you out because I want to spend time with you. Do things with you," Brantley said. "Not because I'm tryin' to seduce you. Although, I wanna do that, too."

Reese couldn't hold back the smile.

"And certainly not because I want to flaunt this in front of everyone. I know you're not ready for that."

No, Reese wasn't ready for that. One day. He hoped.

When Brantley didn't continue, Reese let all the spoken words settle between them before he made a decision for both of them.

"Then we'll agree this is more. That we want to spend time together. So unless one of us says otherwise, we won't try to put distance where it's not needed."

"I like that plan."

Content that they at least had one, Reese went back to cooking dinner.

Another hour and a half passed while they talked about growing up in Coyote Ridge, some of the things that had changed. Main Street and the numerous new businesses that had appeared, the constant festivals being put on by the new mayor. And the fact the Gas 'n Go had undergone new management. Mundane, boring. Comfortable.

Reese declined another beer when Brantley started cleaning up the kitchen. He wasn't interested in another drink when the only thing he wanted was standing right in front of him.

"I'm gonna shower," Brantley said when he finished loading the dishwasher. "Join me?"

Reese followed but stopped when they stepped into Brantley's bedroom.

"Not yet," he said, curling his fingers around Brantley's bicep and turning him so they were face-to-face. "Not yet."

Without preamble, he leaned in and found Brantley's lips with his own. The warmth that greeted him was a balm to his soul, giving him the distraction necessary to settle his nerves. This was his comfort zone. Didn't matter that everything around it was the red zone; once Reese had pushed past that, he was fine. More so now that he knew what to expect from Brantley. Or more specifically, what not to expect. He knew the man wouldn't push him for something he wasn't ready for and that had gone a long way to easing his anxiety.

"Reese…"

"Please," he whispered, sliding his hands up Brantley's chest, cupping his neck, his thumbs brushing over the stubble along his jaw. "I need you right now."

Brantley's blue-gray eyes swirled with a mixture of frustration and confusion, the same emotions that warred inside Reese.

"Let me have you," he rasped, stepping in close.

"You've got me," Brantley returned, reaching for him, those solid arms wrapping firmly around him.

Right here. This was where he wanted to be. In Brantley's arms. He wasn't worried about tomorrow or the next day. With Brantley, Reese found himself only concerned with that moment in time. Whenever he was with him … it was the only place he wanted to be.

There wasn't much grace when they crashed to the bed, nor was there any when Reese started tugging at Brantley's clothes. Their lips met and parted again and again as they worked to get the other naked. When they finally were, Reese spread out over Brantley, soaking up his warmth, his strength, his desire. It was familiar to him, not to mention something he'd never had with anyone else.

But right now wasn't necessarily about comfort. It was about need. A reminder that they were both here, together. That they had one another if no one else.

"Don't move," he whispered to Brantley, letting his lips trail down his jaw, his chin, working his way over Brantley's throat.

He didn't stop, getting lost in the exquisite taste of this man.

"Reese…"

Reese shook his head because he was not going to let Brantley talk him down. Not this time.

He skimmed his lips over Brantley's pecs, past his ribs, over his washboard abdomen, licking and laving the ridges he encountered, continuing his trek lower.

He paused, kneeling between Brantley's spread thighs, his mouth hovering over the hard ridge of his erection.

"We can take this slow," Brantley said.

A reminder? A request? Reese didn't know, but he needed neither. This was what he wanted, what he needed.

He let his breath fan the swollen head, keeping his eyes open because he wanted to watch as he took Brantley in his mouth for the first time. He wanted to memorize this moment because no doubt he would relive it a thousand times over later. It was important he remembered how eager he was, how anxious to pleasure Brantley in every way possible.

Brantley shifted, dragging a pillow beneath his head, propping himself up. The fact he wanted to watch, too, only spurred Reese on.

Leaning in, he let his lips brush the smooth head. A shudder scurried down his spine, lust blazing through his veins as he lapped at Brantley's cock. He moaned, the taste of him going right to his head.

"Fuck," Brantley rasped. "Reese…"

He brushed another kiss over the head, another lick. He stopped thinking about what he was doing and let the sensations take over, the desire to feel him in his mouth. He parted his lips, taking the engorged head between them, closing his mouth around him as he flattened his tongue and tasted more, explored more.

"Holy … fuck."

Oh, yeah. That was working for him, too. The way Brantley panted and moaned, as though this was the most intense thing he'd ever felt.

Reese got bolder, opening his mouth wider, drawing more of him in. He sucked as he retreated, letting Brantley's throaty groans drive him to do more. He was aware of every ridge along his tongue, the vein that ran up the underside. He had no firsthand experience with giving head but knew what pleased him, so he used that knowledge, giving back until he was sucking deeply, his head bobbing up and down as Brantley's cock fucked deep into his mouth.

"Careful, Reese," Brantley groaned. "You're gonna make me come. Not yet."

He slowed his ministrations, licking rather than sucking, venturing lower, letting his tongue glide over Brantley's heavy sac.

Another grunt, a deeper groan.

"Fuck me," Brantley pleaded.

Reese paused, lifting his head, not sure he'd heard him right.

"Fuck me, Reese. Get inside me."

He hated to stop but the temptation was more than he could handle.

Hoping he didn't appear too eager, he reached out, grabbed a condom and lube from the nightstand, shifted so he was kneeling beside Brantley as he leaned over, kissing him because he couldn't resist.

When he sat back to roll on the condom, then reached for the lube, Brantley rolled onto his stomach. Reese was behind him in an instant. There was no hesitance like the first time. He slicked his fingers, sliding them deep inside Brantley's ass as he leaned over him, dragging his lips across his shoulders, nipping the back of his neck. He scissored his fingers, preparing Brantley for his cock.

"Now," Brantley urged, his ass rising, hips pushing back to take more of his fingers. "Fuck me, Reese."

Because he couldn't wait another minute, Reese guided his cock into the tight, blazing-hot hole, pushing in as far as he could go before stopping.

He nipped Brantley's shoulder once more. "You can't come," he ground out. "Not until I've got you in my mouth again."

This time Brantley's groan sounded tormented and it made Reese smile. That smile faded, turning into pure bliss as he began moving inside Brantley, pushing in deep, retreating slowly, loving the way his tight ass stroked every nerve ending.

When Brantley began rocking against him, Reese dug his fingers into his hips and held him in place, pushing in deeper, harder, faster until he was fucking him in earnest, the sheer ecstasy rocking him from all angles. Time warped. He wasn't sure if it had been seconds, minutes, or even days as Brantley's body gripped him like a vise.

"Oh, fuck, yes," Brantley said, his hands fisting the comforter. "Oh, fuck … Reese. It's too good. I…"

"Don't you dare come," he warned. "Not yet."

A tortured growl sounded and Reese gave himself over to the overwhelming pleasure. He let Brantley's ass stroke him several more times before he groaned long and low, coming so hard he thought for a second his head would come off his shoulders.

But he didn't waste time, didn't let the high of release stop him. He pulled out, manhandling Brantley until he was on his back, then took him in his mouth once again. There was no exploration this time. He simply offered up his mouth, letting Brantley fuck himself into his throat. Reese moaned around the thick cock tunneling in deeper with each frantic thrust. And when Brantley came, he closed his eyes and drank him down.

The emotion that overcame him was surprising. Not fear, not anxiety. Something equally powerful though.

It was in that moment, right there in Brantley's bed, that Reese realized what he felt for Brantley was so much more than desire.

It was love. He was falling in love with this man.

And not surprisingly, the acknowledgement scared him. But not nearly as much as he'd expected.

Chapter Six

THE NEXT DAY STARTED OUT WITH BRANTLEY agreeing to meet Professor William Dugan, the former principal of Coyote Ridge High School, back when Lauren Tyler had gone missing, at a Starbucks near the UT campus.

Professor Dugan had since left his position in secondary education, taking a job at the University of Texas teaching English or some shit. He had been a high priority on their list of people to speak to considering, according to the notes in Lauren's file, the man had been a huge part of the investigation back then.

"I remember that day," William said, his eyes bouncing around the room. "God, I remember that day. I saw Lauren when she was leaving the school. If one of her teachers hadn't stopped me to chat, I would've been gone already."

"You saw her?"

He nodded, his eyes settling on his coffee cup. "Yeah. She stayed after to work on a project. I was talking to Ms. Jenkins, her English teacher, when the group broke up. Waved when Lauren passed. Next thing I know, she's gone."

Brantley continued to watch Professor Dugan, the way his hand trembled only slightly when he reached for his cup, the way his eyes darted from one person to another. He seemed nervous.

"Did you know Lauren?" Reese inquired. "See her often?"

The guy's eyes cut over to Reese quickly. "Not any better than I knew the rest of the students. As you both probably know, Coyote Ridge isn't a big town. The entire population of the school was roughly the same size as the senior classes in Austin's schools. Plus, I lived there at the time, tended to run into a students and parents all the time. So, yeah, I knew her like I knew the rest of them."

"Can you walk us through what happened that day?" Brantley prompted.

Dugan's eyes snapped to his. "What … do you mean?"

"Was it a normal school day? Was there anything going on? Special events? That sort of thing."

"Normal," he stated, once again looking at his cup. "A lot of the teachers were prepping for final exams. They tended to stay later during that time. I remember there were quite a few teachers around that evening."

Interesting thing for him to remember.

"There might've been a basketball game scheduled that night, but it would've been at the other school's campus." Dugan sipped his coffee, lifted his gaze. "We had no events going on that day."

Brantley noticed the subtle shift in Dugan's posture. His shoulders squared, his chin lifted only slightly. It was like he was getting more confident in his answers. A strange reaction to this conversation.

"Do you know if Lauren spent her time with anyone?" Reese asked. "I mean, more time than usual?"

"Corinne Greenwood," William answered, holding Reese's gaze now. "They were close. I believe they were neighbors."

"They were," Brantley confirmed. "Did she have any other close friends?"

William shook his head in that relaxed way that said he really didn't know. "Like I said, I didn't know her all that well. Besides Corinne, I couldn't really tell you who she hung around with."

"What about boyfriends? Did she have any?"

William watched them as though he was thinking back. "Not that I remember. There were some couples we encountered all the time." He smiled, his eyes flashing with what Brantley assumed was amusement. "The ones who were a bit too touchy-feely in the hallway. But I don't recall Lauren having a boyfriend. Then again, I didn't know most of them all that well. Have you had a chance to talk to Corinne?"

Guy seemed rather adamant he didn't know them well.

"Not yet," Brantley admitted, still gauging his reactions. "We're gonna meet up with her soon."

William nodded. "If anyone knows what Lauren was up to at the time, it would be Corinne."

"We're hopin' she'll give us some insight," Reese said.

William's forehead wrinkled. "Now that I think about it, there was this one boy Lauren was spending time with. I recall seeing them talking in the hallway from time to time."

Really? The guy was going to pull an about-face now?

Brantley waited for him to continue.

"Jason ... Jason Montgomery. Yes. He was a senior. Took a real liking to Lauren."

Interesting. A minute ago, the good professor said he hadn't known his student body that well. Now he was offering up gossip?

William's eyes widened as he glanced between Brantley and Reese. "I heard Jason was arrested a couple of years after he graduated. Assault, I think. On a woman."

Brantley fought the urge to look at Reese. Last thing he wanted was for William Dugan to think he was suspicious, although he most definitely was. But not of Jason Montgomery. Well, not only of Jason Montgomery.

"Definitely worth lookin' into," Reese noted. "We appreciate you agreein' to meet with us, Professor Dugan. If you happen to remember anything else, please give us a call."

"Absolutely." William's dark eyes held a hint of concern. "I do hope you can get some answers. This tragedy has plagued that town for far too long."

"Was that as weird for you as it was for me?" Reese asked as Brantley drove back to his house.

"There was definitely somethin' up with that guy."

"I can't help but think we're stirrin' up a hornet's nest."

Brantley was inclined to agree.

William Dugan was the last of the people they'd talked to this week, with more lined up for next week. Friends, family, teachers, neighbors. Surprisingly, or maybe not so surprisingly, those who'd been closest to Lauren remembered that day clearly. At least what they were doing after she went missing. Interesting how people tended to notice what was going on around them after something horrific happened rather than before.

But one thing that stood out, no one remembered seeing Lauren leave the school that day. Not even Rachel Conway, formerly Jenkins, the English teacher Dugan had referred to. Because Brantley had already spoken with her, he gave her a call to confirm what Dugan had said. And though Mrs. Conway wouldn't swear to it, she was almost positive whatever project Lauren had been working on hadn't pertained to her class because she very rarely kept kids after school. Dugan hadn't specified that it had, but he'd certainly alluded to it, which was why Brantley had inquired.

"At least for the rest of the night, we won't be talkin' about this case," Reese said, pulling Brantley from his thoughts.

He glanced over. "We won't?"

"No."

"You have somethin' better to do?"

"I'm takin' you out, remember?"

Brantley's eyes cut back to the road. "Oh, shit. It's Friday."

"It's Friday."

"Where're you takin' me?"

"It's true, I haven't been on a date in a while, and I've never been on a date with a man, but I know how to seduce with the best of 'em, Navy boy. Tonight's not for you to worry about."

He smiled as he pulled into his driveway. "Well, heavens to Betsy, what ever will I wear if I don't know where we're goin'?"

Reese laughed, as Brantley'd meant for him to.

"Nothin' too fancy but not too casual," Reese said. "Jeans and a T-shirt'll do."

Brantley frowned, feigning indignation. "Jeans and a T-shirt? That's what I've got to look forward to for our first date?" He glanced over. "More importantly, you consider that not too casual?"

The smile Reese shot at him was filled with promise. "Not all you have to look forward to."

He pulled the truck to a stop in his driveway beside Reese's new truck. "You comin' in?"

"Nope. But I'll be back to pick you up at seven."

"I'll be ready," he said, grinning. "Bring flowers."

Reese rolled his eyes, hopped out of the truck. There were no lingering goodbyes, not even a quick peck on the lips before Reese was in his truck and heading out. Brantley wondered if that would ever be something Reese was okay with.

Because he had a couple of hours and required only ten minutes to get ready, Brantley headed for the barn.

Rather than sit at his desk, he marched to the bank of monitors he'd had originally, keyed in a few things, and pulled up information on William Dugan. There was something about the professor that didn't sit right with him.

Of course, on paper the guy looked perfect.

Too perfect, in fact.

He was raised by a two-parent household in north Dallas, and both parents were dead, having been married for fifty-eight years. Dugan fast-tracked it through his secondary education, finishing high school early at the age of sixteen with a GPA of 4.1. Went on to the University of Texas. Bachelor's degree in education with a minor in English. Worked as a tenth grade English teacher at two Austin high schools while getting his master's degree in school administration. Hired as principal at Coyote Ridge High School at the below-average age of thirty-eight. Started one year before Lauren Tyler went missing, stayed on for another four years. Transitioned to English professor at UT, where he was currently employed.

"And where do you live now, Professor Dugan?" Brantley muttered as he keyed in a few more commands.

Hmm.

Seemed as though Dugan wasn't a fan of staying in one place for too long. He'd bought and sold six houses in the past nine years. Looked as though he waited a little more than the required eighteen months to avoid paying capital gains taxes at each residence. Now lived in a historic home in Taylor, just a few miles northeast of Coyote Ridge.

Perhaps they should pay Professor Dugan a visit at home. Drop in unannounced, see how the man reacted.

In the meantime, Brantley would also look into this Jason Montgomery just so he could check off the box and say he had. He doubted it would lead him anywhere, but he wasn't going to leave it to chance. Last thing he wanted was to leave any stone unturned.

CHRIST ALMIGHTY, HE WAS NERVOUS.

As Reese pulled down Brantley's drive just a few minutes shy of seven, he couldn't deny his stomach was pitching left and right. It didn't necessarily bother him as much as it intrigued him. When was the last time he'd been on a date and had any reservations whatsoever going into it? More importantly, why would he? He knew Brantley, knew what to expect from the man.

"Maybe you wanna impress the guy," he muttered as he pulled his truck in behind Brantley's.

Snagging his Resistol hat from the passenger seat, Reese put it on his head and climbed out. He found himself standing taller as he made his way to the porch. His boots were clean, his jeans starched, and the navy blue button-down he wore was ironed. He looked good, if he did say so himself. In fact, he'd even sprayed on some cologne with the hopes of catching Brantley's attention. Of course, he had also fought the urge to take another shower because he didn't want to overdo it, either.

Dates sucked.

Rather than waltz into Brantley's house like he was wont to do, Reese rapped his knuckles on the screen door, stepped back.

Once more, he smoothed down his shirt, took a deep breath.

From inside the house, he heard the sound of footsteps, Brantley making his way to the door. He heard the knob turn, the creak as the door opened.

At that point, when Brantley appeared framed in the doorway, Reese was pretty sure his heart stopped. He had no idea why. Brantley looked not much different than usual. He'd gone with a white button-down shirt, sleeves rolled up over his muscular forearms, unbuttoned at the throat. The Stetson on his head was a nice touch.

Very nice touch.

"I'm nervous," he blurted as Brantley pushed open the screen.

Brantley's smirk was slow and sexy. "Yeah?"

"Oh, yeah. You look … edible."

Brantley chuckled. "You look pretty damn good yourself."

When the man took a step closer, canting his head to the side, Reese held his breath.

"Smell good, too," Brantley whispered. "Almost too good to go out."

"Almost?" Reese rasped.

Brantley took a step back. "Although gettin' you naked's definitely at the very, very top of my priority list, I'm hungry."

Some of the tension eased, even as his nerves continued to riot. "You ready?"

"Yep." Brantley pulled the door shut behind him, didn't bother locking it. "Gonna tell me where we're goin'?"

"Nope."

They started for the truck. "Gonna tell me why you're nervous?"

"No idea," Reese admitted as he climbed in behind the wheel.

"You know I've had your cock in my mouth, don't you?" Brantley said, the words whispered in that dark, seductive tone.

Reese's cock remembered, the damn thing coming to attention at the reminder.

A gruff chuckle sounded from Brantley and then Reese found his free hand being shifted, their fingers twining when Brantley took his hand.

"Better?"

"Surprisingly, yes," he said, realizing it was true.

"You have nothin' to be nervous about. I'm a sure thing, cowboy."

Reese laughed, more tension draining away.

Half an hour later, Reese was heading down Sixth Street toward their destination. He should've known Brantley would guess where they were headed the closer they got.

"Goin' all out, are ya?"

"I was in the mood for steak," he said, playing it off.

"Yeah? I can think of half a dozen steak houses near Coyote Ridge."

"None of them as good as this one."

"I don't doubt that."

Reese pulled to the curb for the valet, got out of the truck, passing over the keys. When he stepped up beside Brantley, his nerves returned. Only this time, it was a little more than simply being in Brantley's presence. He could feel eyes on them and once more that unsettled feeling began to choke him.

Brantley opened the door, held it. Reese swallowed past the lump forming in his throat, stepped inside. He made it to the hostess stand, relayed they had a reservation, gave his name.

The woman smiled kindly, then led the way back to a table in the back.

There was nothing unusual about the interactions, but Reese felt as though every eye in the room was on him, everyone was questioning why he was here, why he was with a man. On a date.

Oh, shit.

"Breathe," Brantley said firmly from behind him.

Easier said than done, Reese thought as he allowed the hostess to take his hat and hang it on a rack in their section. Brantley did the same, then took his seat across from him.

Reese tried not to look around, didn't want to see all the eyes surely staring at them. Two men out together, having dinner in a fancy restaurant. He couldn't stop himself from peering over his shoulder and oddly didn't feel any better when he noticed no one was paying them any mind.

Christ. He was sweating and he was almost sure his hands were trembling. If he wasn't careful, he'd be in a full-blown panic attack.

"What can I get you to drink?" the waiter asked, stepping up to the white-linen-draped table all prim and proper.

"Two beers. Whatever you've got on tap," Brantley said, his tone edged with irritation.

"Of course."

When the man left, Brantley leaned in. "You wanna leave? Say the word."

"No," he said adamantly, exhaled. "I don't."

"Coulda fooled me."

"I'm sorry," he said quickly. "I just…"

"Don't apologize. Just two guys out enjoyin' the best steak in Austin."

Right. Two guys. Fancy restaurant. Tablecloths and candlelight. They might as well have had a rainbow flag flying overhead.

"Now tell me about Z," Brantley prompted. "What's your brother up to these days?"

Reese stared at Brantley, the words not making any sense although he knew they should. "What?"

"Let's get your mind off it. Tell me about Z or Jensyn. Or your parents. They're up in Dallas, right?"

"Yes," he answered, reaching for the glass of water in front of him.

"You said Z works for Sniper 1 Security. Why didn't you go that route when you got out?"

Reese shrugged. "Don't know."

The waiter returned, setting two beers on the table, then asking if they were ready to order.

Brantley was the one to speak up. "Can you give us a few minutes?"

"Of course."

Reese reached for his beer, did his best not to down it in one gulp. He took a couple of sips, set it back down, barely managed not to spill it, met Brantley's gaze.

"What're you worried about?"

Reese frowned. "What?"

"Somethin's got you on edge. What is it? This place? These people? You think someone you know'll see you here with me?"

Reese stared back at Brantley. He could hear the wariness in his tone, knew he was offended by Reese's reaction but was doing his best to pretend otherwise.

"I don't know," he said, going for the truth. "It just … it feels weird."

Brantley nodded. "Perhaps we should go."

"No." Reese didn't want to go. He wanted to spend the evening with Brantley. He wanted to enjoy a nice dinner, go to the range like he'd planned, because he had reserved it specifically for tonight. He damn sure couldn't hide out in Brantley's house for the duration of their relationship.

"The last thing I want is for you to be uncomfortable," Brantley said softly. "If goin' out isn't your thing…"

Then what? Reese wanted to ask him to finish that sentence, but he wasn't sure he wanted to know the answer. If he couldn't handle going out in public with Brantley, would it mean they were doomed? Was it wrong that he was self-conscious? It sure felt that way.

"I'm good," he told Brantley, forcing himself to believe it.

Reese opened the menu, scanned the selection. He could feel Brantley's eyes on him, but thankfully, he didn't say anything. A few minutes passed, the waiter returned, they placed their orders, Reese added an appetizer. And then they were left in peace.

"Focus on me," Brantley said softly. "Forget everyone else in this place."

Reese nodded. It wouldn't be too difficult considering his back was to the room. That and he happened to enjoy looking at Brantley. If he forgot the fact they were in a restaurant full of people, it would've been ideal. He'd had dinner with Brantley many times. Both as friends back in the beginning and at Brantley's house in a more intimate setting.

So why couldn't he settle now? What was it about this setting that left him … well, unsettled?

IT WAS SAFE TO SAY THIS WOULD likely be their first and last date.

Brantley could see by the sweat beading on Reese's brow that it was taking everything in him to get through this meal.

And they hadn't even gotten their food yet.

"I'll be right back," he told Reese, getting to his feet and heading over to where their waiter stood near the drink station, waiting for a table to tend to. "Excuse me."

"Yes?" the man said, eyes wide, a hint of fear glittering there. Clearly he thought he'd somehow done something wrong.

"My friend … he's not feelin' well. I'd like to ask for our food to go."

The waiter nodded.

"Here's my credit card," he said, pulling his wallet out of his back pocket. "Add something for dessert. Whatever you suggest."

"Yes, sir. Gladly."

Brantley returned to the table to find Reese with his head in his hands, staring down at the tablecloth.

Clearing his throat, he took a seat. "You okay?"

"I will be."

Yeah, Brantley seriously doubted that. But if he had anything to say about it, they'd get back on track soon. Although he didn't claim to know what Reese was going through, he knew it was natural. For many, being gay meant remaining in the closet. Sometimes because they were nervous about what others would think, sometimes because they knew what others would think. Sure, there were communities that encouraged open and proud lifestyles, but those were few and far between.

He'd been out with a handful of guys in his time, mostly going to sports bars. But this didn't feel at all awkward to him. Then again, he didn't much give a damn what people saw when they looked his way. Brantley'd never been the sort to flaunt his sexuality, but he wasn't ashamed of who he was, nor was he concerned what others thought about him.

Didn't mean Reese was going to feel the same or that Brantley could even fathom what this felt like to him. The guy was going out on his first date with a man. That alone probably had his stomach twisted in knots. He damn sure wasn't going to hold it against Reese, either.

"Shoulda gone the Tex-Mex route," he said, reaching for his water, "got a couple margaritas down you. You'd liven up the party."

"I really am sorry," Reese said, his voice so low Brantley only heard because he was sitting so close.

"Don't apologize. I've got a plan."

Reese's forehead creased in a frown. "What?"

"We're takin' our meal to go."

Reese's back straightened, his eyes narrowed. "That's not necessary."

"Maybe not, but it's how I want it."

"No, you don't."

"You really wanna argue with me here?"

"Brantley…"

"Done deal." He nodded in the direction of the waiter, who was carrying two large paper sacks their way.

Brantley took the check, signed the receipt, added a generous tip, then pocketed his credit card.

"Come on. We've got somewhere to be."

He could tell Reese wanted to argue on sheer principle, but underneath, he could sense his relief.

They grabbed their hats, had the valet bring the truck around, but before Reese could take the wheel, Brantley grabbed the keys and made his way to the driver's side. He deposited the food bags in the backseat, and a minute later, he was heading out of downtown Austin, back toward Coyote Ridge.

By the time he made it back to his house, he knew Reese was preparing an argument. Rather than let him, he ordered the man to go around to the back, take a seat at the patio table.

The night could be salvaged. Just because Reese wasn't ready to be seen out in public with him didn't mean they couldn't enjoy their time together. Brantley would simply have to make some adjustments. And he would. For Reese.

Inside the house, Brantley dished everything onto plates, tucked the cheesecake in the refrigerator for later, added real silverware, snagged some napkins, and carried it out. After he set everything on the table, he returned, grabbed a couple of beers before sitting down to enjoy their meal.

They shared their first-date meal on his back porch, Brantley carrying most of the conversation. It was obvious Reese was uncomfortable, but why, Brantley wasn't entirely sure. Could've been because he'd panicked at the restaurant, or because Brantley had taken the lead and made the decision for them to leave. Since it was over and done, he didn't want to dwell on it.

When they were finished, Brantley took the dishes inside, grabbed a couple more beers, and rejoined Reese.

"I'm sorry about how I reacted," Reese began.

"There's nothin' to apologize for."

"That's not true and you know it."

Brantley exhaled his frustration, leaned back in his chair. "If you spend all your time apologizin', this isn't gonna work."

That seemed to shut Reese up.

"So intimate steakhouse dinners aren't your thing. That's fine. You live and learn, Reese. Next time we'll try my idea. Sports bar. Tex-Mex. There's always somewhere we can go where you won't feel out of place."

"I was gonna take you to the gun range after."

He grinned. "Yeah? You romantic, you."

Reese chuckled, although there was still an edge to it. "I suck at this."

"There's nothin' to suck at, Reese. Do you wanna be with me?"

"Yes. More than anything."

"Then it's just a matter of figurin' out where we fit in."

"You didn't seem to mind the restaurant."

"I was there for the food," he admitted. "And the company. I couldn't give a shit less what other people think of me. And no, I don't go around flauntin' the fact I'm gay. I don't feel the need to hold your hand in public to assure myself we're together. If I want to hold your hand, it's because I want to touch you. But I wouldn't do that to you, Reese. I wouldn't put you in that position."

"I feel like I'm fuckin' this all up."

Brantley stared out into the night. No amount of words was going to reassure Reese. He had it in his head that this was more difficult than it really was. Unfortunately, Brantley's gut told him things weren't going to get any easier for a while. The only thing he knew to do was give Reese space.

"You deserve better than that," Reese whispered.

Brantley jerked his gaze to Reese, held his breath because that sounded a hell of a lot like Reese walking away.

"I want to be those things for you, Brantley. The guy who can take you out, meet your folks, hang out with your friends. I'm not sure I can do that." Reese exhaled. "Try as I might, I can't wrap my head around this. Bein' attracted to you, wantin' to be with you … none of it makes sense. I'm straight, Brantley."

Technically, he wasn't, but Brantley didn't feel the need to point that out.

"I don't know what I want," Reese continued. "I thought I did. When I'm with you, it's easy. Or I thought it was. Then tonight happened…"

There was a boulder sitting on his chest, but Brantley breathed through it.

"Maybe it's best we take a step back," Reese said softly.

"Maybe." There was no conviction behind his agreement, but he figured Reese had made up his mind, so it didn't really matter.

It didn't surprise him when Reese pushed back his chair, got to his feet. Brantley stared out into the night, refusing to look at him. If Reese wanted this, there wasn't a damn thing Brantley could do. He would suck it up, let him walk away. Wasn't like he could sweet-talk the guy.

Truth was, he didn't want to.

Brantley did not want to be the guy groveling, begging. He refused to do it. Reese would either be with him or he wouldn't.

His choice.

Chapter Seven

"ALL RIGHT, WHAT'S WRONG?" TREY ASKED, HIS lips puckered like a fish, eyes squinted as though this would help him see into Brantley's soul.

"Nothin'," Brantley answered easily. "What's wrong with you?"

Trey's chin dipped down, eyes narrowing even more. "Liar."

Brantley chuckled, forcing a lightness he didn't feel. Last thing he intended to do was to tell Trey about Reese, about how their date last night had come to a tragic end. That wasn't the reason he'd invited his brother out tonight. Okay, maybe not entirely true. Reese was part of the reason Brantley was here at Moonshiners. This was his way of pretending the man didn't exist, that last night hadn't happened, that his whole fucking world hadn't been upended in a matter of hours.

Nope.

Not thinking about that.

Brantley grabbed a handful of peanuts, tossed them back, reached for his beer. "If you do insist on starin' at me like that, I will have to leave."

Trey leaned back, schooled his expression. "How's the governor gig goin'?"

"Eh. It's underway. We're workin' on a case."

"Lauren Tyler," Trey noted. "The girl who went missin' from here."

"Yeah." Brantley took a long pull on his beer. "How'd you know?"

"Saw the whiteboard in the barn."

"Why were you in my barn?"

"Stopped by to check in. JJ was there."

"When was this?"

"Last night."

Shit.

Trey smirked. "Which is why I know somethin's wrong, otherwise you would be out on another date with Reese. Or still recoverin' from the first one."

"Next time, I'm invitin' Killian," Brantley told his brother. "At least he won't give me shit."

That got him a grin. "Killian? Seriously?"

"What's wrong with Killian?" he asked, curious as to what Trey had to say about their brother-in-law.

"Nothin'." Trey took a drink of his beer. "And that's the problem."

Killian Thornburg had been part of their family for the past seven years, ever since he tied the knot with their sister Tori. He also happened to be the guy standing directly behind Trey at the moment, but Brantley didn't bother to make Trey aware of that fact.

"I mean, for starters, the guy's hot. And he's straight. That's certainly a problem," Trey grumbled.

"Not only does he have the looks, he's got the brains, too," Killian added, stepping around Trey to join them at the table.

Trey glared at Brantley. "Fucker."

Brantley laughed. "Hey, it's important that family knows how much you care about them."

Trey shot him the finger.

"What's up?" Brantley asked Killian. "Where's Tori?"

"Hangin' with Bryn and Sadie. Somethin' about a sisters' night. Eric's with your folks." He thanked the waitress when she delivered his beer. "Where's Cal and Griffin?"

"I hit them up," Brantley told him. "They said they'd stop in if they could."

"I saw Sawyer and Kaleb out in the parkin' lot," Killian supplied. "They were waitin' for one of their brothers."

Perhaps they'd make it a party. Brantley wasn't about to complain. The Walkers could fill up the bar and he'd be quite content. Considering this was purely a distraction, the more the merrier.

Two hours later, Brantley wasn't so sure more and merrier went together all that well.

Turned out, Brantley's text had turned into a mass invitation and what looked to be half the family had descended on the only bar in town. Travis and five of his six brothers had arrived along with some of their significant others. Griffin and Cal had both showed up solo and were now three sheets to the wind. Some of his cousins had joined the festivities: Rex Sharpe and his husband, Jack, were there. Rex's brother, Rafe, was working the bar. Jaxson Briggs was rolling solo, as were Kaden and Keegan. And those were just the ones Brantley had stopped to chat with.

Of course, his mingling had ended abruptly when Reese arrived not too long ago. At that point, Brantley had opted to chill in the corner by his lonesome, pretending it didn't bother the shit out of him that the man had crashed his party. Not that it was really a party. Nor was it his because this was a public place, after all.

But still.

"All right, spill," Cyrus said, taking a seat in the vacant chair to Brantley's right. "Who pissed in your Cheerios?"

Brantley offered him a glare, tossed back the rest of his beer before signaling to the waitress for another one.

"You two are somethin' else," Cyrus said, a huge grin planted on his face.

Brantley knew he was attempting to get a rise out of Reese, who happened to be paying attention now that Cyrus had wandered over. The smile belied every ounce of concern in Cyrus's tone, yet it was there all the same. Thankfully, Cyrus was keeping a safe distance, the blinding smile meant to infuriate Reese as much as if Cyrus had saddled up on Brantley's lap.

"Why's that?" Brantley asked, his gaze connecting with Reese's across the room.

"What's it been? Two months? Three? And the bottom's already dropped out."

"It didn't drop out," Brantley argued, holding Reese's gaze. "It never fully formed."

"Wouldn't know it by the way you two are mopin' around here."

"Not mopin'," Brantley countered, turning his attention to Cyrus.

"Well, I would play it up for your audience, but I'm a reformed man." Cyrus sat up straight, ran a hand over the front of his shirt.

"Is that right? Who's the lucky guy?"

"Hint: you're related to him."

Brantley grinned. He was already well aware that there was something going on with Trey and Cyrus. He'd given Trey a hard time about it earlier, when Cyrus appeared and both men got a little taller in the other's presence. It was an interesting combo, but Brantley could see how they might make a good pair.

"I'm happy to hear it," Brantley said, grinning back. Might as well let Reese think what he would. "But do me a favor," he said quietly, leaning in near Cyrus's ear. "Spare me the details of your sex life. Unless, of course, you want me to punch you in the face."

Cyrus barked a laugh, still smiling.

They sat there for a few minutes, chatting about mundane bullshit when the door opened and a newcomer drew Brantley's attention. All eyes seemed to shift to the entrance, but he doubted anyone else saw what Brantley did.

A fucker who was going to get a beatdown.

Dante Greenwood stepped into the bar, his gaze doing a quick skim. No sooner did their eyes meet across the room than Dante turned and walked right back outside.

Brantley might've taken offense to his hasty retreat if he hadn't seen the woman Dante had on his arm.

A woman who was not JJ.

He was quick on his feet, marching past the waitress on his way out the door. He didn't slow down, not even when he slammed through the doors and out into the night. Behind him, he heard the conversation dim, a couple of shouts directed at him, then footsteps in his wake.

Brantley ignored everyone except for the motherfucker making a quick dash to his car.

"Dante," he shouted.

Dante stopped at his fancy BMW, but not before tucking away the redhead he'd brought with him. Before she was practically shoved into the car, Brantley met her surprised eyes. She had no idea what was going on, clearly. Or perhaps she was that good of an actress.

Not that it fucking mattered.

"Look, man, I've got no beef with you," Dante said, his voice low. "We're leaving."

"Where's JJ?" Brantley inquired, holding the other man's stare.

Dante started to open his mouth, closed it quickly as he peered over Brantley's shoulder. "Could we do this another time?"

Brantley glanced back to see some of his cousins and all three of his brothers had stepped outside.

"Where's JJ?" he repeated, turning back to Dante.

"I don't know. Probably at home."

"Who's she?" he asked, nodding his head toward the car.

"My assistant."

"Your assistant?" Brantley nodded. "Do you always take your assistants out on Saturday night?"

Dante swallowed hard. "That's none of your business, Brantley."

"So that's a yes?"

Before he could stop himself, Brantley's hand shot out, taking a handful of Dante's shirt in his fist. He yanked the fucker forward, got nearly nose to nose with him.

"You fucking bastard," he growled. "You son of a bitch."

"It's not what you think," Dante stammered.

"No? Then why the fuck'd you run outta the bar before you came in? In fact, why the fuck are you here at all? You don't live in Coyote Ridge, Dante. This isn't your stompin' ground anymore. Were you hopin' JJ would find out?"

Dante's eyes narrowed. "Mine and JJ's relationship is none of your business."

"It is when you make it my fuckin' business. You're whorin' around on her again." Brantley shoved him back, sending Dante careening into the car.

Before Brantley could descend, two sets of hands landed on him, both pulling him back.

"Not here," Trey said firmly.

Brantley tried to shrug him off. It didn't work.

"You stay away from JJ," Brantley snapped, lunging forward. "You hurt her, Dante, I will come after you. That's a fuckin' promise."

"Might take this as the opportunity to get the hell on," Trey told Dante. "Now."

Dante moved around the car, yanked open the door, and all but dove inside.

Brantley was seething. Enough that he hadn't realized the other set of hands attempting to hold him back belonged to Reese. When he turned and came face-to-face with the man, he nearly snarled. Instead, he shoved Reese back and stomped back toward the bar.

"Let me take you home," Killian offered. "Designated driver and all."

"Need to close out my tab," he muttered.

"Got it taken care of," Trey said, stepping up to his side. "Head home. And don't you dare fuckin' go after that asshole, Brantley. You do and I'll kick your ass myself."

For Trey to think that was even a possibility would've been amusing, if, you know, he wasn't seeing red.

REESE PROBABLY SHOULD'VE LEFT WHEN HE ARRIVED at Moonshiners and realized Brantley was there.

He definitely should've minded his own fucking business when Brantley went after Dante.

Yet here he was, in Moonshiners, his mind on the fierce expression on Brantley's face when he realized Reese had been out there with him.

No doubt about it, that had hurt.

Not so much the shove but the disdain he'd seen in Brantley's eyes… That was a knife to the chest. Then again, what the hell did he expect? He was the one who'd walked out last night, calling a halt to what they'd had between them. He was an idiot, no one would dispute that. He had panicked and given up on the best damn thing he'd found in … perhaps ever. It killed him that he didn't have the balls to own up to that relationship, to give Brantley what he truly deserved. If he could—

"What's up, bro?"

Reese glanced over to his left, noticed Zane Walker had stepped up to the bar. The other man rested his forearms on the top, hung his boot heel on the bar at the bottom, and waved Rafe over to order another beer.

"Not a whole helluva lot," Reese answered.

"I just figured the world was comin' to an end or some shit," Zane said. "What with you all doom and gloom over here. It's like a toxic cloud emanating around you, man."

Reese smiled because that was what Zane expected him to do. Laugh at his attempt at a joke.

Too bad Reese didn't find it all that funny.

He and Zane had been friends since middle school. They'd never been as good of friends as Zane and Beau were, but Reese had felt included from time to time. The same went for when he'd returned to Coyote Ridge a few years ago. Zane had welcomed him back as though years hadn't slipped by in between Reese's appearances.

When Rafe passed over Zane's beer, the man thanked him, then turned and faced away from the bar, leaning his back against it. Casual as you may, Zane stretched out his long body, crossed his ankles, and drank his beer while observing everyone around them.

Or so he pretended.

"What's really up with you? How's that new detective thing you've got goin'?"

Because he didn't feel like getting into the details, Reese offered an unenthusiastic "Fine."

"Yeah? Didn't look all that fine. You and your boss on the outs?"

Reese caught himself before he blurted out that they weren't a thing. "It's complicated."

"Aren't all good things?" Zane smirked.

"You wouldn't understand."

"Try me."

Reese was tempted. Damn it, he was truly tempted to tell someone what was going on, to find a sounding board, because keeping this shit inside was killing him. He could usually hash these things out with his brother, but right now Z was off doing God knew what, God knew where, and Reese wasn't about to lay his problems at his brother's feet. Not to mention, the complication of the whole thing. He wasn't sure he was ready for his family to find out he wasn't who he'd thought he was all this time.

"I know all about complicated," Zane said sincerely, turning to face him as he propped himself on a stool.

"Not like this, you don't."

"No?" Zane huffed a laugh, set his beer on the bar. "You probably don't know this because you hightailed it right after high school and didn't bother to check in all that often, but things aren't always what they seem."

Not the first time Zane had told him that.

"You know how close Beau and I were growin' up?"

Reese nodded, took a drink.

"Well, turned out, Beau had a thing for me." Zane chuckled. "Me. Of all fuckin' people. Guy was clearly delusional. Wasted a whole helluva lot of time on the likes of me when he coulda had so much better."

That got Reese's attention.

"Anyway," Zane continued. "We were close. Close enough we shared some of the chicks I dated."

Reese was aware of that. He'd heard the stories.

"Wasn't until I started chasin' V that things changed between us. He came out and told me he was in love with me."

Although the details were curiously entertaining, it was the ease with which Zane relayed them that held Reese's attention.

"At V's urging, and thanks to the heat of some rather intense moments, I let the man explore, if you know what I mean. We ended up gettin' intimate."

"Seriously?"

"Yep." Zane's eyes were serious, something that wasn't common for the man. "An experience, I tell ya. Didn't do much for me, but I don't regret what happened. Not even a little."

Reese wasn't sure where he was going with this.

"Granted, I don't tell that story to just anyone. Nobody's business and all."

"So why me?"

"Because it doesn't take a fuckin' genius to see somethin's goin' on with you and my cousin."

Reese looked back at his beer, dug at the label with his fingernail.

"Nothin' to be ashamed of, Reese. The heart wants what it wants."

"Evidently, so does the body," he mumbled.

Zane laughed. "Yes, it most certainly does. And you could do a helluva lot worse than Brantley. I mean, come on, the guy's a fuckin' SEAL."

Reese had nothing to say to that.

"What I'm tryin' to tell you is you don't have to be ashamed of who you are. You spend all your time pretendin' to be someone you're not, life's gonna pass you right on by. Look what happened to Beau once he finally stopped hidin' who he was. He hooked up with my brother. Now they're livin' their very own happily ever after."

He wanted to tell Zane he had no clue what Reese was going through, but it sounded as though the man might have some idea. He had had sex with a man, after all. Or at least that was what Reese was getting from all this.

"Did you enjoy it?" he found himself asking.

Zane took a long pull on his beer. "What? Bein' with Beau?"

"Yeah."

"Let's just say it wasn't horrible. And don't get me wrong, if it had been somethin' I thought would make us both happy, I would've pulled on that thread. I've got no shame."

Reese laughed because that was true.

"You shouldn't, either," Zane added.

"What are you two whisperin' about?"

Reese glanced to his right, saw Beau had joined them.

"That night," Zane said simply.

If Reese hadn't been looking at the man, he probably wouldn't have noticed the blush that infused Beau's face. The big man's response belied his body's reaction though.

"Best night of his life," Beau joked. "Don't let him tell you otherwise."

Zane barked a laugh.

Reese figured this was the hardest part about being friends with the Walkers. They truly were a special group. They didn't make excuses for who they were and they had no shame. They lived their lives out and proud, whether it be Travis, who was married to a man and a woman, or Beau and Ethan, who were happily married, Kaden and Keegan, who were open with the fact that they fully intended to end up with one woman eventually. Or even Zane, who'd had a fling with a man although he was happily married to a woman now.

Reese envied them that.

But it wasn't that he was ashamed of what he felt for Brantley. When he thought about it rationally, he didn't feel the need to explain it to anyone. However, he did seem to have a problem being open about it. Probably could keep things going with Brantley like that, too. But where would that get them? And how would that make Brantley feel? Reese didn't want to do that to him.

He didn't want Brantley to have to hide who he was, and right now, Reese wasn't sure he had even accepted the fact he was falling in love with a man.

Chapter Eight

MONDAY MORNING CAME QUICKLY.

When Brantley arrived at the barn shortly after eight, he didn't expect to find Reese already there, his head buried in his laptop, fingers pecking over the keys. He'd honestly figured the guy to leave him hanging, to gracefully resign from his position on the task force and go back to living his regular life working for Travis at Walker Demolition.

It surprised him so much, he couldn't even bring himself to greet the man.

Then again, his attention was on JJ, who was smiling up at him from her desk as though her world hadn't been tipped on its axis this weekend.

"Good mornin', sunshine," she greeted. "Was startin' to think you'd abandoned us."

"I'm here," he grumbled, making a beeline for the coffeepot.

"How was your weekend?" she asked, her voice carrying through the open space.

He grunted, not intending to get into it. The truth was, Brantley didn't really remember much of his weekend. Not after Killian had dropped him off at his house. He'd spent all of Sunday buried in that bottle of Jack Daniels Reese had found in his liquor cabinet. Finished the damn thing off, then broke the seal on a bottle of Jim Beam. At that point, he could've been drinking moonshine for all his taste buds cared. But it had cured what ailed him.

Temporarily.

"What about you?" Brantley asked when he rejoined them. "How was your weekend?"

"Good." Her smile was oddly sincere.

"Yeah?"

"Yep. Went out with a couple of friends Saturday night."

"No Dante?" he asked pointedly.

Another smile. "Just because I'm datin' someone doesn't mean I've got to spend all my time with them."

She didn't know.

Son of a bitch.

"So, what's on the agenda for today?" she inquired, her gaze bouncing between him and Reese.

Brantley debated on whether or not he wanted to spring the news on her now. The easy decision was to let it lie. No one said he had to be the one to tell her. The thought of breaking her heart because of Dante… It was enough to have him turning away and heading for his desk.

"I was gonna call Corinne, see if she's got time to talk to us."

"She doesn't. I reached out to her a little while ago," JJ added quickly. "She replied almost instantly. She's focused on school right now, asked if we could give her a few more days. She'd let us know."

"Well, then I guess we'll tackle the rest of the list. Split it evenly," he told her without bothering to look at Reese. "I'll take half, Reese can take the other."

JJ nodded. "Um … okay."

He could feel Reese's eyes on him, but he managed to ignore him. They would eventually have to learn to work together, but right now, Brantley needed space from him.

"Shoot my list to my phone," he told JJ, then slipped out of the barn and headed for his truck.

Part of him expected Reese to come after him, to confront him. Brantley wasn't sure what was worse: the fact he had hoped Reese would or that he didn't.

By the time night fell, Brantley found himself back at the house. He had bypassed the barn when he saw Reese's truck outside. When he eventually heard the soft rumble of the truck's engine a short time later, more disappointment came over him. And yes, he was a dumb ass for thinking Reese might have the balls to come talk to him about what had happened. Didn't matter that there really wasn't anything more for Reese to say. But Brantley had a shit ton he wanted to tell the man.

Thankfully, Brantley had fought the urge to swing by the liquor store to get something else to erase the discomfort. No way would he get completely lost in a bottle. Not for anyone and certainly not for a guy he'd had a fling with for a couple of months. It was time he pushed it all aside, focused on the task at hand. He didn't need Reese in his life to make him happy.

If he said it enough, perhaps it would be true.

A knock on his sliding glass door had his head jerking up. JJ's face was distorted against the glass. Clearly her way of trying to cheer him up.

"It's open," he called out.

"Didn't realize you were back," she said, joining him at the kitchen island, her smile instantly fading.

"Haven't been here long."

"You doin' all right?"

"Peachy," he said, though even he knew he didn't sound it.

"What happened with you two?"

Brantley lifted his eyes to hers. "If it's all the same to you, I'd prefer to talk about anything else. Doesn't matter what. Just not Reese."

"Okay."

They were silent for a few minutes. While JJ stared at him, Brantley threw together a turkey sandwich, piling it high with meat and cheese before he realized it was rude not to offer one to her. She accepted gratefully, so he went to work making her one.

"How're things with Dante?" he asked, attempting to make conversation.

"Good." She sounded genuinely sincere. "He's busy this week, but he promised we'd catch up next weekend."

Brantley paused what he was doing, staring at his best friend. "You really don't know, do you?"

JJ frowned. "Know what?"

"About Saturday night?"

"What about it? I hung out with my friends down in Austin."

"Where was Dante during all this?"

Her expression didn't change, confusion angling her brows downward. "I didn't ask him. He does his thing, I do mine. He said he was gonna hang with the guys. Why?"

The guys. Right.

"He came to Moonshiners," he blurted, passing over her sandwich before grabbing two bottles of water from the refrigerator.

Her eyes narrowed and Brantley could tell she was curious where this was going.

"You and him clear the air?" she asked, although it was obviously not the question she wanted to ask.

"I think it's safe to say we're clear," he grumbled.

Because he didn't know how to tell her Dante was stepping out on her, Brantley took a bite of his sandwich, chewed.

"What's goin' on, B?"

He shook his head, took another bite, ensuring there wasn't any room in his mouth for words to slip out.

JJ's eyes narrowed on his face.

This truly fucking sucked. Brantley did not want to be the one to tell her that her boyfriend was still a cheating asshole. Maybe the guy hadn't hit her all those years ago the way Brantley had thought he had. But that didn't mean he hadn't treated her like shit. And here he was, repeating history.

"Brantley Walker, you better tell me what the hell's goin' on. Right now."

He huffed, setting the rest of his sandwich on his plate and grabbing his water bottle.

"He wasn't alone when he came to Moonshiners," he finally said after washing down his food with water.

JJ had her sandwich halfway to her mouth but she paused. "What?"

"He wasn't alone. And he wasn't with the guys."

"Who was he with?"

Brantley shrugged, not wanting to tell her the bastard was banging his assistant.

"Are you serious right now?" JJ's eyes blazed with anger. "You're seriously gonna do this?"

Frowning, Brantley set the bottle down, stared at JJ. "Do what?"

"I get that you and Reese are havin' a hard time, but that doesn't mean you've got to instill your insecurities in me."

"That's not what I'm doin'," he argued, his own ire rising. "You think I wanna tell you that Dante was at Moonshiners with some fuckin' chick? That he took one step inside, realized who was there, and walked right back out with that redhead on his arm?"

Her eyes widened and he saw the hurt.

Son of a bitch.

"Why the hell didn't you tell me?" she demanded.

He motioned between them. "This is why. Your immediate response is to think I'm tryin' to sabotage you, JJ. I don't like Dante. I've never liked the asshole. Not since you started datin' him, anyway. But I've stayed outta your business."

"Who was she?" JJ inquired, her voice softer.

"Said she was his assistant. I confronted him in the parking lot, but she was in the car." Brantley exhaled. "I'm so fuckin' sorry, JJ."

She shot to her feet, turned around as though she wasn't sure what she was doing.

"Please don't leave," he urged. "Stay for a while. We'll have a beer."

"I don't want a beer," she countered, her green eyes lifting to his face.

Yeah, Brantley saw the hurt and anger. Problem was, he suspected some of it was aimed at him. No, he hadn't told her what happened sooner, but he thought for sure someone would have.

He fucking hated having to always be the bad guy.

A minute later, JJ stormed out of the house and Brantley's first thought was: would she be coming to work tomorrow?

He was a truly shitty friend.

WHEN JJ LEFT BRANTLEY'S HOUSE, HER ENTIRE world had been encased in a red haze. Everywhere she looked, the red film of anger clouded her vision. Still did as she pulled into her driveway.

How could Dante do this to her? He was the one who had pursued her, and despite her reluctance, he was the one who had insisted on exclusivity. She hadn't wanted any of this.

He was such a fucking asshole.

Storming into her house, she threw her purse and keys on the coffee table, marched into the kitchen. She flung open the refrigerator, stared inside. She had no idea what she was looking for, but was certain something would ease the fiery anger that blazed through her. Wine, beer, whiskey. Something.

Only she didn't want to get drunk. It never turned out well for her. She and booze were a toxic combination.

She would be the first to admit she had a temper. It was something that Dante had always been able to incite in her. And she suspected he did it on purpose. Back when they'd dated in high school, she'd been angry all the time. Back then, her anger had been joined by a need to hurt someone. She could still remember the night the shit had hit the fan with Dante. She'd been so pissed that he was cheating, JJ had lost complete control. Whaling on him had been the answer and it resulted in her getting a black eye. To his credit, Dante hadn't hit her. It had been an honest accident, something she had pretty much done to herself. He'd gotten shit for it from everyone, and at the time, JJ hadn't cared.

The shithead.

Of course, that had been the very last time she had ever hit anyone. She'd been so overcome with remorse, confused by how she could do such a thing. To a degree, she figured she had deserved the black eye she had sported for a week and a half. Then they had gone their separate ways.

Years later, Dante would come back into her life, requesting her help with his work. JJ had figured she owed him for that little outburst. Having intended only to help him the one time, she was still confused how she had allowed that to continue. How she had even started considering dating Dante on a permanent basis.

What she didn't understand was why Dante insisted on chasing her when he clearly wanted to be with other women. They'd been doing fine these past few months. Sex, nothing more. Casual encounters, no entanglements. But he could never let it go, always claiming he wanted more. And when she'd stopped fighting…

The fucker.

JJ slammed the refrigerator shut, marched across the kitchen. She pivoted at the back door, headed the opposite direction, then continued. Again and again, she paced the length of her kitchen, hoping it would settle her.

It didn't.

Although she would prefer simply never talking to Dante again, she knew she had to confront him. Otherwise, he would continue to pretend nothing had happened. After all, she had talked to him last night and he hadn't bothered to mention he'd brought his slutty assistant to Moonshiners and gotten into an altercation with Brantley. No, he had conveniently left that part out.

The bastard.

Grabbing her phone, JJ resumed her pacing, tried to relax her shoulders and breathe. She couldn't call him in this state; it wouldn't do any good. She needed to calm down.

In the grand scheme of things, Dante didn't matter to her. She had known all along that this thing between them wasn't going anywhere. He was a means of passing the time. Her in-between. JJ had always figured she could use him until she found someone better. After all, that was what he was doing to her.

However, she was not going to fuck him while he was parading other women around. If he wanted to be discreet, more power to him.

But he'd fucked up by trying to make this serious between them.

Finally calm enough to dial, she pulled up Dante's contact information, hit the button to place the call.

"Hey," he greeted.

It was then she realized he was hesitant, the same as he'd been last night when he called. Dante wasn't sure if she knew and he was preparing for her wrath.

The dickhead.

"Is there somethin' you wanna tell me?" she asked by way of greeting.

"I'm sorry."

Great, now he had that haughty air he took on when he knew she was upset.

"It's been brought to my attention you're spendin' quite a bit of time with your new assistant."

"Who told you that?"

"Come on, Dante. Don't be a douche. You brought her to Coyote Ridge. Surely you expected me to find out. Otherwise, why bring her here? You've got no business in Coyote Ridge."

Then it hit her.

He had hoped she would find out. It had been his plan all along. She was his in-between.

"Oh, my God, Dante. You are such a fuckin' dick. Seriously? Where the fuck are your balls?" JJ seethed. "Are they in her goddamn purse? You couldn't just text me to say you've changed your mind? That this assistant was the love of your life?"

"JJ—"

"No, fuck you. I'm done, Dante. Go fuck your assistant. I don't care. I've never cared. You're the one who wants this to be somethin' it's not."

"I never meant to hurt you."

"And that's a load of bullshit. We both know it. That's exactly what you meant to do. You want me to hurt, Dante. You want me to hurt."

"Fine," he hissed. "You're right. I do. I want you to act like you give a damn, JJ. It's all I've ever wanted."

"And what better way to do it than to flaunt all your women in my face. You're tryin' to make me jealous."

"Did it work?"

JJ stopped pacing, stared up at the blinds on her window. "No, Dante. It doesn't make me jealous."

And that much was true. It pissed her off that he could disrespect her that way, but beneath it all, JJ simply didn't care about Dante the way he wanted her to. She wished she could love him because he was familiar to her, he was a security from her past, but she didn't love him.

"I didn't think so."

"We're done, Dante," she said, her voice level once more. "Don't call me for a date, don't hit me up for a hookup. Don't ask me to help with a job. It's over between us."

"What about friends?"

"No." JJ shook her head although he couldn't see her. "No, I don't think we can be friends, either. My friends wouldn't disrespect me like this."

"JJ, I'm sorry."

"Save it," she said easily, then disconnected the call.

JJ figured she should've still been upset about it all. Oddly enough, it actually felt as though a weight had been lifted. She didn't love Dante, doubted she ever had. Granted, her safety net was now gone, but was that really a problem?

Perhaps she could find the answer in a pint of Ben and Jerry's.

REESE WAS UP HOURS EARLY FOR WORK on Tuesday.

Rather than go straight over to Brantley's and risk running into the man, he sat on his couch in the dark, staring at nothing. He didn't get up to get coffee, to take a leak, to shower. He simply sat there, his head pounding because he couldn't fucking sleep, he couldn't fucking eat. His heart actually ached—which he knew wasn't even possible—and it was all his own damn fault.

He was an idiot.

On a positive note, this was the first time in his thirty years that he'd felt true heartbreak.

And the first time ever he'd felt anything for a man.

Why? Why was that such a problem for him? Reese didn't understand it. So Brantley was a man. He was also a human. A very smart, sexy, funny human. Never had he been so comfortable around someone, so interested in them, and never had anyone made Reese feel the way Brantley could. And he wasn't only referring to the sexual chemistry although they had that in spades.

It was in the way Brantley looked at him, the way he smiled. The gruff tone of his voice that reminded him of melted chocolate, smooth and warm. His touch, desperate but gentle, so sure of himself, yet hesitant at the same time. His laugh, rare, but so open when he let himself.

What he enjoyed most, missed the most? Sleeping beside Brantley.

Reese ran a hand over his face.

Fucking idiot.

Was he seriously willing to give it up because of what other people might possibly think? So what if they knew him, knew he'd dated dozens of women, slept with just as many? Did it fucking matter that they might question why he'd switched teams at this point in his life?

Did it really. Fucking. Matter?

Reese groaned, pushing to his feet and heading for the shower.

Half an hour later, after grabbing scones from the bakery and a cup of coffee, he was strolling into the barn. It was still too damn early for anyone to be there, and Reese was glad for it.

After setting the box of pastries on JJ's desk, he started back to his own but paused when he noticed a piece of paper stapled to one of the walls. He recognized Brantley's neat handwriting, the measurements noted beside the rather impressive sketch of a set of stairs.

Glancing up, Reese checked out the loft, looked back at the paper.

Brantley was going to install stairs to the second floor. He hadn't mentioned it, but it made sense. A lot of space being wasted.

Hmm.

He snagged the paper from the wall, headed for his desk, set his coffee cup down.

Roughly twenty minutes later, he'd added the true dimensions necessary to install the stairs, taking into account the required width, depth, and height of the risers according to building code. He took out another sheet of paper, jotted down the building materials needed to make it happen.

After checking the time, he grabbed his shopping list, went back to his truck, and headed to the closest Home Depot. Thankfully, they opened early for contractors, so Reese went inside, retrieved the items he needed, had one of the employees help him cut down some of the boards to size because it was easier and because he had time to kill.

An hour after he'd entered the store, he was leaving, heading back to Brantley's. Still no JJ, but he did notice there were lights on in Brantley's house. Pretending not to be thinking about what Brantley was doing inside, he backed his truck closer to the barn and began unloading the materials.

It was on a return trip to his truck when he ran into Brantley.

"What're you doin'?"

Reese considered ignoring the question but figured it was rude.

"Saw your design for stairs. Went and got the materials," he said casually, as though it made perfect sense.

Thankfully, Brantley didn't bombard him with questions, just set his coffee cup down and began helping to unload the material, dragging it into the barn.

"You got the equipment to build this?" Reese asked, hoping he sounded nonchalant. "Saws and shit?"

"Yeah. In the back storage room."

Once they'd gotten everything inside, Reese poured another cup of coffee, then stood beside Brantley and stared at all the lumber he'd acquired.

"I could help you knock it out if you want."

"Why?"

He glanced over at Brantley. "Why what?"

"Why do you wanna help?"

"Why not?"

That seemed to appease Brantley because he eventually nodded, although he didn't glance over at him.

Reese wished like hell he'd make eye contact, but he wasn't going to push it. This was good enough for him. The two of them working side by side. It would do.

For now.

They spent the entire morning working on the new staircase. Measuring, cutting, stacking.

It wasn't until noon that he realized JJ hadn't come in.

"She okay?" Reese asked, nodding to JJ's empty desk as he grabbed a bottle of water.

Brantley looked over at her desk, his expression impassive. "She's pissed at me."

"Dante?"

"Yeah."

Figured.

Sucked that Brantley had been the one to break the news to her, but Reese had expected no less. Wasn't like Dante was going to tell her he'd been stepping out. Of course, that meant JJ was going to blame Brantley in some way. That was the way it worked, right? The messenger took the brunt of the anger.

"How much do I owe you for the material?" Brantley asked, getting to his feet and dusting his hands on his jeans.

"Nothin'," he grumbled. "It's my contribution to the business."

He expected an argument, could even see the storm brewing in Brantley's eyes, but it never came.

"I'm meetin' with one of Lauren's teachers," Brantley explained, turning away from him. "I'll grab lunch while I'm out."

Because he could add nothing, Reese said nothing.

A few minutes later, he was alone in the barn.

After carrying his water to his desk, he flopped down, stared at the pile of wood that would eventually give them access to the loft. He had no idea what Brantley intended to do with the space, wasn't sure it was even his place to ask.

Rather than worry about it, Reese grabbed his phone, pulled up JJ's number, shot her a text.

You doing all right? Just checking in.

He didn't expect a response, certainly not for her to call him rather than message him back.

"Hey," he greeted. "You slackin' off today?"

"Workin' from home," she said, her voice huskier than usual.

"Everything all right?"

"Actually, yes. Where're you at?"

"HQ," he said, using her term for the barn. "Helpin' Brantley put in stairs. You should come by. Another set of hands'll be good."

"Stairs?"

"To the loft," he explained.

"Oh. Sounds fun."

It wasn't, but Reese didn't say as much. Truth was, he was spending time with Brantley, and right now, that was all that mattered. He knew once the project was complete, they'd go back to working solo until it was absolutely necessary. Hell, Reese wouldn't be surprised if Brantley hired on a couple more people just so they didn't have to work together ever again.

"Anyway," he told JJ. "If you need to get outta the house, I'll be here."

"Where's B?"

"He went to meet with one of Lauren's teachers, then he's grabbin' lunch."

A soft grunt was her only response.

"JJ?"

"Hmm?"

"Don't be mad at him. You should've seen him on Saturday night. It took me and Trey to hold him back when he saw Dante. He's got your back. Don't think he doesn't."

"I know." She cleared her throat. "You're right. I know you are."

"Dante's not worth it. You deserve so much better than him."

"I really do," she agreed and he was almost positive he could hear the smile in her voice.

"Like I said, if you wanna swing by, I'll be here."

"'Kay. Talk to you later."

Setting his phone on his desk, Reese leaned back in his chair and stared around.

How the hell had everything gotten so fucked up so quickly?

Chapter Nine

By the time Saturday rolled around, Brantley could see the light at the end of the tunnel for the project they'd spent the week working on. Hadn't taken much to get the stairs installed. From there, they'd added a railing to the loft level, manufactured hardwood to the plywood floors, then installed a window because JJ said some natural light would be good.

Turned out, the two of them worked well together when it came to building projects. Brantley was rather impressed with how well they'd done for amateurs. And he knew they'd done a damn fine job when JJ had given her approval. Granted, she wasn't talking to him much, but she had stopped by on Wednesday to check in. She hadn't stuck around long, insisting she was working from home until they were finished. He took it as a good sign that she'd come by every day after that.

Brantley was giving her a wide berth, not sure where they stood but hoping like hell they'd find their way soon enough.

And while the work had gone smoothly, the interactions between him and Reese hadn't. No conversations had taken place, the barn filled with music in an attempt to avoid having to talk. That had been Brantley's doing. He could tell Reese wanted to talk, and as much as he wanted to clear the air between them, Brantley wasn't ready yet. However, he did hold out hope that they would eventually be friends again.

One day.

Not that he wanted to think about that. He was exhausted, both body and mind. It had been a successful week with the exception of one more migraine last night. Once the pain had subsided, he should've been able to catch some z's but sleep eluded him.

If Brantley had to guess, he had managed at least three hours of shut-eye every night since Reese walked off his back porch and right to his truck. It had been enough to keep him functioning on a physical level, but his brain was getting foggy. He needed a good eight hours, preferably ten to catch up and reboot his system.

Since he'd tossed and turned all last night, too, he would have to wait until tonight to try again.

If only his fucking brain would shut off. If thoughts of Reese didn't plague him at all times. When he was lucid, he could easily tell himself he was damn tired of this roller coaster ride with Reese. He should've expected it would come down to this.

But in the dark of night, he longed for those stolen moments. Hell, he would've been content to simply have Reese there with him.

He hated himself for wanting the man so damn much. And he got the feeling he could easily convince Reese on a do-over. He'd spent the week working alongside him, knew a conversation was in order. Brantley could've instigated a chat, forgiven him for what had happened. Reese would likely be in his bed right now, waking up beside him.

Temporarily.

It all boiled down to one thing. Reese was curious, not committed.

And that, Brantley knew, was only a recipe for disaster. There was no way anything could come of this unless Reese was all in, the way he'd said he was. The guy had lied. All there was to it.

But Brantley wasn't going to sit around and mope about it. He had shit to do, starting with a five-mile run.

After setting a new personal best for five miles, Brantley hit the shower, got dressed, and headed into town. He called JJ, invited her for breakfast. If she wasn't going to make the effort to clear the air between them, he had to. And he would do it by treating her to breakfast and pretending all was well between them.

"Uh-oh, what's wrong?" she said as she approached the booth he'd secured for them.

"Nothin'," he lied. "Why should somethin' be wrong?"

Her gaze was unsettling, bouncing over his face as she took a seat across from him. "Did you sleep at all last night?"

He offered a shrug, glanced down at the menu. "Headache. Got a coupla hours. You?"

She laughed, the sound a bit too forced. "More than you."

Brantley met her gaze, held it. "You talk to Dante?"

Her eyes narrowed. "I wouldn't call it talkin', but yes, we managed to settle things. Or rather, end things. It was inevitable."

He couldn't quite gauge her mood, but he sensed she was not too upset over the loss.

JJ motioned the waitress over. "Can we get two coffees and two waters?"

The waitress nodded in response, sauntered off.

"Where's Reese?"

"Not his keeper," he grumbled.

JJ nodded, giving him that look that said she had it all figured out. "Y'all have another fight?"

"Nope. Nothin' to fight about."

Her green eyes narrowed. "All right, Walker. Enough of this shit. You invited me here. I came. We're gonna hash this out right now. No way are we lettin' our love lives come between us."

Although he would prefer to talk about anything but Reese, it wasn't like Brantley could refuse JJ. He did want to clear the air between them. He needed her right now. She was his best friend and he could sure as shit use one.

However, he wasn't going to make it easy on her. "I didn't ask you here so we could talk about Reese."

"Then why did you ask me here?"

"Because I miss your company."

"You've seen me nearly every day."

"That's work. This … is not."

JJ thanked the waitress when she set down two mugs and poured coffee into them.

"Y'all ready to order?"

"Go ahead," JJ urged.

Brantley rattled off his order—scrambled eggs, sausage, bacon, ham, hashed browns, and a side of pancakes. When he was done, JJ stared at him as though he'd lost his mind. He had. No way he could eat all that, but he was damn sure going to try. He'd been eating healthy since he started hanging out with Reese. No time like the present to make up for all that lost time.

"So what happened with you and Reese last weekend? Bottom obviously fell out. Why?" JJ asked after she'd ordered a fruit plate and a southern biscuit.

He considered brushing her off, telling her it didn't matter because it was all in the past, but Brantley knew JJ was like a dog with a bone. She was not going to give up easily.

"We went out to dinner. Nice restaurant. Lasted about twenty minutes. He was havin' a panic attack over bein' out in public with me."

He could see the sympathy in her eyes.

"I don't need your pity, JJ. It's done. He decided it was best to call things off."

"He did?" She took a sip of her orange juice.

"I've been pretty damn patient with him," he bit out. "Woulda continued on. It's too much for him."

JJ sighed. "That sucks, B."

"Better now than later. Happens once, chalk it up to the situation. Twice?" Brantley shook his head. "He's not gonna be able to handle it."

"It happened more than once?"

He went on to tell her how he'd found Reese at Moonshiners, the guy ignoring his texts while he had drinks with a woman.

"He's straight, JJ. Curious but straight. Now it's outta his system. He can move on and not have any regrets. He knows it's not like I'll go off runnin' my mouth. No one'll be the wiser. As long as he can do his job, we'll be fine."

"You considered maybe seein' it from his point of view?" JJ asked, her eyes boring into him. "Reese is thirty years old, Brantley. Thirty. All that time, he's been passin' time with women. Then you come along and shake the foundation of his life. All those years, he was playin' tonsil hockey and doin' the horizontal mambo with women and suddenly he's got the hots for a man. Think about that. You've never been with a woman, right?"

She knew he hadn't.

"Pretend you woke up this mornin' and suddenly you've got this thing for a woman. How would you feel? Awkward? Scared? Confused."

Brantley couldn't imagine it, but he certainly understood where JJ was coming from.

"I've seen the way he looks at you," she tacked on.

"You saw what you hoped to see," he countered. He knew because he'd done the same.

"Maybe he needs some time."

"Maybe," he agreed. "But I'm not gonna sit around and wait."

"Please tell me you're not gonna hook up with Cyrus."

"And what if I do?"

"Brantley…"

"Don't, JJ. Just … don't. I'm done with this shit. I'd rather be single for the rest of my fucking life than find myself caring about someone who can't handle it. Now it's your turn. What happened with Dante?"

Her gaze instantly dropped to her coffee cup. "I'm not ready to talk about it."

He grunted.

JJ's eyes shot up to his. "I will though. I promise. For now, all you need to know is that I've told him to stay far away from me."

It was something, at least.

"Fine. Then let's find a neutral topic."

"Good idea." She took a sip of her coffee, set it down. "I hear we've got storms rollin' in tonight."

"It's what I hear," he muttered. "Not lookin' forward to it."

"Don't tell me you developed a fear of thunder and lightnin'," she teased.

"No. But the sounds…" Brantley stared down at his hand on his coffee mug. "Seems to be a trigger for flashbacks. Nightmares."

"That sucks."

"It is what it is."

"What do you say we hit the range after this?" She offered when he said nothing more on the subject. "Might be busy, but we can get in an hour or so."

"Sounds like a perfect plan."

And that was what they did.

After breakfast, Brantley followed JJ back to her house so she could get her range bag. They managed to get two lanes for an hour in the main gallery. When they were leaving, Brantley saw Reese's truck in the parking lot, swallowed down the pain that came with it. Thankfully, JJ didn't say anything.

At that point, he wasn't feeling up for company, so he dropped JJ back at her place, then headed home. He contemplated hitting Cyrus up because his kind of company was different. The thought was fleeting, more of a thought on how he could get back at Reese for hurting him. And yes, Reese had hurt him. Irrevocably. At that point, Brantley decided to swear off any sort of sexual relationship for the foreseeable future. Right now, he needed to work on the task force. It was a damn good place for him to direct his attention. Hell, he could likely spend day and night working on cases. They definitely had enough of them.

As he pulled into his driveway, Brantley heard thunder rolling in the distance. He was prepared for it this time. No way would some storm send him reeling into the past again. It had happened numerous times since he'd come back home, but he had a good handle on it now.

Or so he wanted to believe.

The storm rolled in shortly before midnight, and because he'd slept so little all week, Brantley had drifted off, sucked under into the recurring nightmare.

"We go on my command," Brantley stated, standing at the ready while the rest of his team was in position surrounding the single-story house where the American scientist was said to be held in an underground bunker.

The recon was completed, and if all went well, they'd be in and out, getting the hostage to safety so he could, no doubt, find his way back into the hot seat. Seemed to be a trend for this guy.

"Copy that," came the response from his team.

Waiting for the confirmation from his command, Brantley remained silent, still. They just needed one final check on the number of tangos inside. The last report had contradicted the one prior, leading them to believe there were six inside, versus the original three they'd seen from the eye in the sky.

"Phantom One, you're cleared to go. We've got six heat signatures coming from inside. Repeat, there are six."

Brantley glanced at his second-in-command, silently communicating that they were a go. They were going in pairs, his 2IC at his side while the rest of his team were storming in secondary doors.

"Move," he ordered over the comms, leading the way.

Sticking close to the structure, he made his way to the front doors. No hesitation. He had a job to do and a damn good plan. They would stick to it, be out in under five minutes.

He paused, glanced around the side of the building. Nothing moved. He nodded, continued.

"Phantom Three, location?"

"In position," came the response.

"Phantom Five?"

"In position."

Brantley took a deep breath. "Go, go, go!"

No sooner had they stormed the building than the shouts began. Gunfire followed, the tangos panicking while Brantley's team took them out one by one.

Brantley tossed and turned on the bed, his brain taking him back to that day. It didn't matter that he was fighting the nightmare; it was taking root, dragging him deeper. His team moving in, taking out four of the six from the front.

"Clear the rooms!" Brantley shouted.

They split up then, moving from room to room to ensure they'd eliminated the tangos so they could retrieve the package.

"Moving," he announced, continuing toward the target.

That was the moment the op went from routine to FUBAR.

After getting a visual on the room that would lead to the bunker beneath, Brantley stepped forward and—

In his bed, Brantley thrashed, the feel of the wire against his leg, the sound of the blast that obliterated the floor beneath him.

Falling.

Crashing.

The ground opened up, swallowed him down. Rock and debris fell as fast as he did, none of it giving a shit that he couldn't keep his footing. Chunks of rock landed, pinning his leg, shattering the bone.

Pain.

So much fucking pain.

Outside the house, thunder rolled, lightning crashed, dragging him deeper and deeper into the hell of that night. For a moment, Brantley couldn't breathe in, his lungs filled with the dust and dirt raining down on him. He couldn't decipher reality from the dream. More thunder crashed outside, lightning flashing.

The sound of footsteps alerted him to the tango.

Within seconds, Brantley had his SIG in hand.

"Brantley! Wake. Up."

The bark of words shot him from unconscious to conscious in seconds. He blinked his eyes open, saw the silhouette of a man standing in the doorway. It took a second to recognize his brother.

Lowering his weapon, he fought the fogginess that surrounded his brain.

Home.

In bed.

Not buried beneath rubble.

No broken bones, no explosions to come, no building rattling, getting ready to cave in on him.

"Hey, man," Trey said softly, stepping into the room.

"I could've shot you," Brantley bit out.

"Could've, yes. Won't keep me from checkin' on you though."

"What're you doin' here?" he grumbled, wiping his forehead with the back of his hand before dropping his feet to the floor, pretending not to notice the way his hands trembled. He remained where he was for a minute, got his bearings before getting to his feet. The SIG went on the nightstand when his brother passed over a bottle of water.

"Thought I'd check on you."

"Yeah? Just outta the blue?" Brantley padded to the bathroom, splashed water on his face.

Thankfully, Trey gave him space, didn't try to baby him while he pulled himself together. When he left the bathroom, he realized he was limping. The pain in his left leg was only a ghost ache. Not real yet it hurt all the same.

By the time he made it to the kitchen, he'd lost the limp, forced some steel into his spine, and headed for the refrigerator to get another bottle of water.

Trey was sitting on a stool at the island, watching him closely.

"Why're you really here?" he asked, downing half the bottle of water in one pull.

"Cyrus told me. About the nightmares." Trey gestured toward the ceiling. "The storm."

Brantley nodded, looked away from Trey. "Cyrus shoulda kept his fuckin' mouth shut."

As it was, Cyrus was the only one who'd witnessed one of Brantley's nightmares. The night he'd learned of them, Cyrus had woken up with Brantley's hand around his throat. Thankfully, his weapon had been secured at the time, otherwise… No, he didn't want to think about what might've happened if he'd had access to his gun.

And though they didn't talk about it, he knew Cyrus remembered it well. Brantley damn sure did.

"Where's Reese?" Trey inquired, watching him like an animal on a frayed leash.

"Don't know. Don't care."

If he said it enough, maybe it would be true.

REESE SAT AT THE BAR AT MOONSHINERS, his phone faceup in front of him, his gaze continuously scanning the screen as though that might possibly make the fucking thing ring.

"Problem?"

The gruff question came from behind the bar, drawing Reese's attention to Mack.

"No problem," he answered, tipping his beer bottle to his lips.

"Then why're you avoidin' him?"

"How do you know it's a him I'm avoidin'?" Reese shot back, wincing as soon as the words were out of his mouth. "Sorry, Mack. I'm just…"

Truth was, Reese didn't know what he was. Confused seemed to be the adjective that could explain it all away, but having a diagnosis didn't seem to be solving the problem.

"Figured it had to be since you shrugged off the last two ladies who attempted to catch your eye."

Reese stared back at the man. "It's not supposed to be obvious, Mack."

The older man stood tall after dragging a rag over the bar top. "It's not. Even if it was, why're you worried about it?"

Million-dollar question.

"I'm not."

"Keep tellin' yourself that, boy. But until you start livin' for your own happiness, you'll just be miserable."

Speaking from experience, Mack was.

Reese took another pull on his beer, glanced at his phone once more.

It would've made more sense for him to go home, get some sleep. He was exhausted and the storm raging outside would've made it easy for him to hunker down on his lumpy couch and drift off into the ether.

Instead, he was keeping this fucking barstool warm, listening to the din of conversation, the clack of pool balls from the tables in the back, and George Strait crooning from the jukebox.

"Well, fancy seein' you here, cowboy."

The familiar voice had Reese glancing over. JJ stood at his side, her elbow resting on the bar, a smile as big as Texas on her face.

"Hey," he muttered, turning his attention back to his beer.

Evidently taking his response as an invitation to hang out, JJ grabbed the stool on his right, hopped up on it. She waved Mack over, ordered a beer.

"You doin' all right?"

Frowning at his beer bottle, Reese nodded. "Good as can be expected."

"I saw Brantley today."

The admission had him looking over at her. It was then he saw the concern glittering in her eyes. He wasn't sure what she expected him to say, so he didn't say anything.

"I know what it's like," JJ said softly.

"What?" he asked, digging his fingernail under the label on the bottle.

"To want to be with someone, but not want others to know. Mine was a little different than yours, and way in the past, but the feelin's all the same, I figure."

He cut his eyes her way. "Is that what you think it is?"

"Isn't it?"

Reese huffed a laugh, took another pull on his beer to finish it off. "I don't know what it is, JJ."

"If it's any consolation, he's just as fucked up."

"It's not," he countered hotly. "I didn't mean for this shit to happen."

"What shit is that, Reese? To fall for him? To not know how to deal with those feelings?"

"Christ Almighty," he bit out, turning toward her. "I don't wanna talk about this."

"Maybe not. But I do," she declared.

It was the first time he'd ever heard her raise her voice. JJ was one of the most laid-back people he'd ever met. The kind who eased into any situation, blending as though she belonged. Sure, she was feisty, quick to joke, tease, pick on someone, but it was always in fun. He liked her, he really did, but right now, he didn't need someone trying to poke and prod at his psyche.

"There's no need to rip me a new one," he informed her. "I'm good at doin' that myself."

"I also heard you're good at speakin' your mind. Did you happen to tell Brantley that you were in love with him?"

"I'm not—" Reese sighed, turning away from her. "JJ, while I appreciate your good intentions, I don't—"

"Wanna talk about this. I know," she said snarkily. "You said as much. But I do. You're my friend, Reese. Say whatever you want, but we've become friends. And Brantley's my best friend. I care about both of you. Damn sure don't want to sit back and watch the two of you fuck up somethin' that could be good."

"He deserves better," Reese said, some of the heat leaving his words.

"I disagree."

She said it so easily, he couldn't help looking her way again.

"What? I do. I think you and Brantley are meant for each other. And trust me when I tell you, I don't think of myself as any sort of relationship expert. But I've seen you together."

"I've never been with a man before him," he admitted.

"So? And maybe you'll never be with a man again. It's not about his gender, Reese. Or yours, for that matter. The two of you found somethin' together. Yeah, I'm sure it's weird for you. Unexplored terrain. Doesn't mean it's wrong."

"I didn't say it was wrong," he said defensively.

"No. But you're thinkin' it."

"I am not. I'm think—"

"He has nightmares," she stated, effectively cutting him off.

"What?"

"Nightmares. Flashbacks." She gestured toward the ceiling as thunder rolled above them. "Storms trigger them."

Reese hated that he wanted to race to his truck and speed over to Brantley's just to check on him, make sure he was all right. It pained him to know that it was no longer his place to do so.

"I've never seen him like this with anyone," JJ said, her voice taking on a sympathetic tone. "He was happy for the first time. Without you, he's miserable."

"I can't give him what he needs."

"Actually, you already did. But then you went and jerked it out from under him."

Frowning, he peered over. "What?"

"You, Reese. You're what he needs. I'm not even sure how you don't see it. That man ... God love him." JJ smiled. "Brantley's an intense man on a good day. With you ... he's someone else entirely. Too bad you didn't feel the same."

He knew what she was doing. JJ and her mind games. He'd seen her perform them before. And as much as he wanted to ignore her, he found himself drawn into the conversation, desperate to argue his point.

"Trust me, I felt the same." Probably more.

"Then I suggest you get your happy ass on up and go over there. Check on him, Reese. Someone needs to."

"Why's that someone need to be me?"

"Because if I know Brantley, and trust me when I say that I do, you're the only person he'd be okay with seein' him like that."

The way she said it had his worry intensifying. He wasn't sure what it was about Brantley that drew out the nurturing side of him, but Reese couldn't deny his desire to keep the man safe, to take care of him. He'd learned of that need after that first headache he'd witnessed.

Mack returned with another beer, but before Reese could reach for it, JJ got her hand around it, dragging it away.

"I'll take this. You go check on Brantley." She flashed him a bright smile. "I'll even cover your tab."

"Figures," he grunted. "I only had one."

"I know." She grinned widely. "Mack told me."

He told himself the only reason he was going was because JJ wouldn't stop harping on him until he did.

Twenty minutes later, Reese was pulling in behind Brantley's truck. For some stupid fucking reason, he was relieved to see that no one was there. Especially not Cyrus. He wasn't sure why he'd thought Brantley would rebound right back to that man, but it had crossed his mind. Numerous times.

Because he'd made the trek, he decided to see it through. Once he confirmed that Brantley was okay, he would be on his way.

He counted down before making his exit from his truck. Hauling ass to the porch, he still ended up drenched from the deluge. He shook off the excess water, then turned to the door to find it was open, the screen the only separation between him and the interior. While Brantley rarely locked his doors, he wasn't the type to leave them open. Certainly not in the middle of the damn night.

An unsettling feeling came over him, and for a second, he considered going back to his truck to retrieve his gun.

Instead, he opened the screen door, stepped inside.

"Brantley?"

Grumbling came from the direction of the kitchen, drawing him deeper into the house.

He found Brantley perched on the kitchen island, wearing only a pair of shorts and a frown, staring out the sliding glass doors, the night pitch-black beyond, lit up every now and again by a flash of lightning.

Their eyes met as Reese made his way around the island.

"What are you doin' here? Goddamn Trey. Did my brother call you?"

"No. Ran into JJ at Moonshiners."

"Did you now? Couldn't talk her into goin' home with you, so you thought you'd come over here for a pity fuck?"

He could hear the anger, knew Brantley was trying to piss him off. But beneath that, he could hear something else. Hurt.

And while he wanted to argue and fight, anything to keep Brantley talking, he held his tongue.

"I'm sorry," Brantley said quickly. "That was uncalled for."

"It was," Reese agreed. "You're more than welcome to take a swing at me. I definitely deserve it. But not JJ."

Brantley's head lifted and he was doing that stare-down-his-nose thing that signaled he was shoring himself up for a blow.

"I just wanted to check on you. She told me…" He exhaled slowly. "She told me you have nightmares triggered by storms."

"Trey's already stopped by, so I'm covered, thanks." Those steel-blue eyes flashed with anger. "It's not your duty to take care of me, Reese. In case you forgot, you gave up the right to give a damn."

"You're right," he conceded, backing away because the urge to go to Brantley was too great. "I did."

He hadn't made it three steps when the thud of feet hitting the floor had him bracing for an attack.

"Why?" Brantley demanded, stomping in his direction. "Why the fuck do you pretend to give a shit, Reese?"

Spinning around, he found himself nose to nose with one very pissed-off Navy SEAL.

"I'm not pretendin'," he declared, holding his ground.

"No? All this back-and-forth bullshit. You want to fuck but you don't want anyone to know?"

Now his ire was rising. Although there was some truth to Brantley's statement, it was much more complicated than that and they both knew it.

As they faced off, Reese could see Brantley's muscles coiling tighter. He was gearing up for a fight and Reese didn't blame him one bit.

"You wanna take a swing at me?" he taunted, stepping back. "Go for it. God knows I deserve it."

For a second, he thought Brantley would take him up on the offer.

"I don't wanna hit you," Brantley snarled. "I wanna fuckin' understand."

His words were clipped, tipped in fury but laced in pain.

"Understand what?"

"Why? Why the fuck did you string me along, Reese? I was so damn close… Fuck. I coulda fallen in love you, goddammit."

Reese's jaw snapped shut as he tried to hold back the words that threatened to come out. He failed at holding them back because that was what he did. He spoke the truth. Even when it would cause him pain.

"Well, lucky for you…"

"Lucky for me?" Brantley barked a mirthless laugh. "How the fuck does that make me lucky?"

Reese stepped forward, lowered his voice. "Because unlike you, I wasn't close. I already fell."

Chapter Ten

VENOMOUS WORDS WERE ON THE TIP OF his tongue, but the instant his brain processed Reese's admission, he pulled up short, his breath coming to a halt in his lungs.

"What?"

"I'm not gonna repeat it," Reese bit out.

"Yes, you are," he demanded, stepping forward.

His chest heaved as he stood there, waiting. Desperately waiting for Reese to say it again.

"It doesn't change anything, Brantley." There was a hint of defeat in his tone. "Still doesn't make me the man you deserve."

"Tell me," he insisted, moving closer. "Say. The. Words."

Those beautiful brown eyes flashed with both defiance and what looked a hell of a lot like fear. "I can't."

"Say. It."

"It doesn't chan—"

Brantley reached for Reese, gripping the sides of his neck with both hands. "It changes every fuckin' thing, Reese. Say. It."

He watched as Reese swallowed, his Adam's apple sliding down, then back up slowly. "I fuckin' love you, all right?" he whispered.

If the sun were to rise in his chest, there wouldn't be more warmth than there was now.

Brantley wanted to echo the sentiment, to tell Reese that he'd been lying earlier, that he wasn't simply close, but he'd fallen in love already. For the first time in his goddamn life. Something had him biting them back. Not because he didn't want to say them. More so because he didn't want to diminish this moment.

No one had ever loved him. Not since Jeremy, and looking back on that now, Brantley wasn't so sure Jeremy had loved him. More that he'd been looking for an anchor in the chaos. Brantley had failed him in that regard, but he damn sure wouldn't fail Reese.

"You confuse me," Reese continued, as though he had to fill the space. "I left the other night and … I felt like there was a hole in my chest. It felt like the right thing to do because I only want to protect you. I continue to fail you and—"

"You haven't failed me," he cut in. "I told you, you can't."

"Just because I love you, Brantley, doesn't mean I know how to be with you."

"But I do," he countered. "I know enough for the both of us."

Unable to resist, Brantley drew Reese in, his lips hovering over Reese's mouth. They stood like that, breaths coming in deep pants, neither taking that final step. There was a warmth churning in his chest, a strange quiver in his stomach. His entire body was hard, so fucking hard.

Goddamn. Brantley wanted this man with every ounce of his being. The pain in his chest had lessened, replaced by a glimmer of hope.

"Brantley…"

Unable to resist, Brantley leaned in, meeting Reese's lips, brushing them softly with his own. He didn't inhale him the way he wanted, but rather kissed him as though the world might end tomorrow. Long, deep, slow. And Reese kissed him back. For a man who claimed he didn't know how to be with him, he sure knew how to be vulnerable to him.

Warm hands curled around his sides, sliding slowly up, down. No rush.

Reese's touch was all he needed. It was more than he'd ever expected. And while he was terrified that this would ultimately end badly, Brantley had never lived his life running from what scared him. He was the one who did the recon, led the charge. He had no doubts Reese wanted him, loved him, even. It was because of that, he knew he could get them where they needed to go. Together.

"I need you," Reese whispered.

Those words had Brantley jerking Reese to him, crushing their mouths together as hands began to roam. The need to get as close to him as possible was so intense it threatened to steal the air from his lungs.

He wasn't sure how it happened, but they managed to fumble their way to his bedroom. But rather than let Reese take control, Brantley maintained a firm grip on the reins. He took Reese down to the mattress, crawling over him, covering him with his body. He was aware of Reese's wet clothes, but the heat from his skin made the chill bearable.

Their tongues danced and dueled while they managed to get rid of the clothes keeping them apart.

Brantley produced a condom, lube, kept them close at hand while their bodies continued to grind in the most exquisite places.

"Let me have you, Reese," Brantley whispered.

He felt Reese tense beneath him, but neither of them moved. Brantley wouldn't push the issue, but he wasn't going to back down easily, either. Not anymore.

"Let me have you," he repeated. "Let me love you, Reese."

A strangled moan escaped the man beneath him as strong arms banded around his back, holding him tightly.

"Yes," Reese mumbled. "Love me."

Brantley's cock throbbed. The aching need to slide inside the man was so strong, it robbed him of air. But he knew this wasn't going to be quick. No way he would take Reese without working him damn close to the edge first.

He managed to work himself out of Reese's hold, sliding down his body, letting his lips and tongue trail over his warm skin, pausing to kiss his shoulder, to nip his bicep, back to his chest, lower. He teased Reese's nipples with his teeth, loving the way Reese reared up to meet him, begging for more. There was an urgency to Reese's movements, a similar one building inside Brantley, but he ignored both, taking his time. He gave Reese what he asked for, licking, sucking, working his way lower. When he took his cock in his mouth, Reese's hips shot up off the bed. Brantley solved the problem, easing him back down, then curling his arms beneath Reese's knees, holding his thighs in place, making him vulnerable in every way.

He worked him for long minutes, sucking, laving, inching lower. He took Reese's heavy sac into his mouth, sucking his balls, listening to the tortured groans, feeling the thrash of Reese's big body. And when he licked over Reese's taint, that enormous body went stone still. Brantley didn't stop. He shouldered Reese's knees toward his chest, bending him in half, then used his hands to hold him in place before he dragged his tongue over his anus.

"Oh, fuck," Reese hissed.

Yeah, he was just getting started.

Brantley rimmed him first, exciting the nerve endings before he stabbed his tongue deep. Reese cried out, pulling his knees closer to his chest. Brantley took that as encouragement, parting Reese's ass cheeks and working him over until Reese was warning him he would come.

He forced himself to pull back, to sit on his haunches, fumbling for the condom, finding the lubricant.

Kneeling at Reese's side, Brantley was shocked when Reese propped himself up and leaned over to take Brantley's cock in his mouth. While the man's skilled mouth did glorious things to him, Brantley slicked two fingers and worked them into Reese's ass. Slowly, gently. He let Reese set the pace, gauging by the moans, the subtle vibrations that shot through his cock thanks to the blessed heat of Reese's mouth still wrapped firmly around him.

When Reese flopped back down, his hips pumping against the fingers impaling him, Brantley repositioned so he could align their bodies in the most intimate of ways. He rolled on the condom, lubed himself by stroking firmly, his eyes on Reese.

"You want me, Reese?" Brantley generously lubed Reese's asshole again, pushing two fingers in deep, scissoring them. "You want to feel me inside you?"

A shudder racked Reese's body even as he nodded. "God, yes."

Knowing he had to go slow, Brantley recalled every ounce of control he possessed, replacing his fingers with the head of his cock.

Reese groaned.

"Relax," he urged, leaning forward, forcing Reese's legs toward his chest once more.

Brantley held himself over this sexy, beautiful man, palms planted firmly by his head so he could watch every expression.

Seconds turned to minutes until time became obsolete. The only thing that mattered was the wicked heat that engulfed him as he inched deeper inside the man. He was careful, so fucking careful. The goal was pleasure, not pain.

"More?"

"Yes … fuck yes. More." Reese's hands came up, curling around Brantley's wrists as their eyes met, held. "Everything."

Brantley had a feeling Reese Tavoularis was going to be the death of him, but fuck if he could bring himself to care.

If this was the end for him, what a hell of a way to go.

BREATH-STEALING PAIN MORPHED WITH MIND-NUMBING pleasure as Reese forced himself to relax, to take Brantley deep inside his body.

He was panting, his heart pounding, but he didn't want to stop. He could see the tension in the corded muscles of Brantley's neck, knew he was holding back, intent to make it good for him. Reese focused on breathing, inhale, exhale, until the pleasure choked out the pain, his body acclimating to the intrusion.

And while it didn't exactly feel good—yet—Reese was overwhelmed by a pleasure he'd never known. Here with Brantley … it was the only place he wanted to be. Their eyes connecting … it was more than sex, more than Reese giving his body to this man. He was giving himself. In every way.

Brantley grunted and groaned as his hips reversed, his cock retreating before sinking in once more.

"More," Reese pleaded, attempting to rock his hips. "Don't need slow."

He felt Brantley's gaze boring into him, the man's face hovering over his as they stared back at one another. It was intense, the eye contact. It was a connection he hadn't felt before, one he wanted to feel again and again. Today, tomorrow, forever. Reese never wanted this to stop.

And it didn't. The intensity increased as Brantley began fucking him. Harder, deeper.

It was then that the pleasure came. The sensations rocking him, making his skin feel too small for his body. Every so often, Brantley's cock would brush something sensitive inside him, making him light-headed from the pleasure of it all. His cock was rock hard.

"Reese…"

God, he loved the way Brantley said his name. More so, he loved the way Brantley's tight leash on his control seemed to snap when they were together. It was dangerously close now even as the man continued to make love to him. He knew that was what this was. Making love. Not sex for the sake of sex. Not fucking. It was deeper, and quite frankly, so much hotter. But making love didn't mean slow and gentle and Reese was ready for him to unleash.

"Fuck me," he ground out, pulling his knees back, shifting his hips, changing the angle of penetration. "Fuck … oh, yes … fuck me."

Brantley's guttural growl made his cock pulse. Reese reached between his legs, fisting his cock, jerking it in time to Brantley's thrusts.

When Brantley caught sight of what he was doing, he sat back, his hands on Reese's knees, holding his legs in place so he could drive into him again and again.

"I want to watch you come," Brantley groaned. "Come for me, Reese."

He stroked himself in rhythm to Brantley's thrusts. As they increased, so did their breaths. Sweat covered his skin as he sought the release that was lingering just out of reach.

"More," he ground out. "Brantley … need more."

Another grunt before Brantley surged into him, their bodies rocking as they united in a cataclysmic explosion of sensation.

"Come for me so I can come inside you," Brantley demanded.

That was enough to have his back bowing, his cock jerking in his fist. He came with a startled cry, the tension within him shattering. Not long after, Brantley drove into him one final time, his head falling back as he groaned low and deep in his throat.

When Brantley pulled out, Reese grabbed for him, not letting him get away. Brantley was deadweight over him, but Reese didn't mind. He held him, arms wrapped around his back as they both sucked in air.

They remained like that for a few minutes. Brantley was the one to move first, hoisting himself up, staring down at him.

"You okay?"

"Better than okay," he said, remembering the first time Brantley had asked him that. It was after their first kiss, right here in this very same bed.

Seemingly content with his answer, Brantley crawled out of bed, headed for the bathroom. Reese heard the sink running, then when the shower came on, he decided to join Brantley.

There was minimal washing that ensued. More kissing and touching than anything.

Before the water could go cold, Reese flipped it off, grabbed two towels, tossing one to Brantley. They dried off, but before Brantley could leave the bathroom, Reese stepped in front of him, reached up, and cupped his face.

"Don't let me fuck this up," he whispered, more of a plea than a request. "I don't wanna fuck this up."

He couldn't. Not again. Reese wanted to be what this man needed. Screw his own insecurities. But he needed Brantley's help.

"You won't." Brantley's hand curled around his cheek in a similar manner, pulling him forward until their foreheads touched. "No more games, Reese. This is it. No more back-and-forth."

"No more," he agreed. "But you'll have to be patient with me."

Brantley pulled back, grinned. "I've got you, baby. Of that you can be certain."

Reese watched Brantley saunter out of the bathroom. Baby. Brantley had called him baby. Probably should've sounded strange. Oddly, it didn't. In fact, it felt … right.

His heart slammed against his ribs, warmth consuming him.

CORINNE GREENWOOD STEPPED INTO HER APARTMENT AND immediately sighed. It was the middle of the night, she'd had a few drinks, was almost certain she was tired, but the instant she closed her door behind her, she was invigorated.

What was it about coming home? Didn't matter what kind of day—or night, as was the case here—that she'd had, didn't matter how many times she'd done it, coming home to her apartment in the heart of downtown Austin always gave her a sense of both pride and relief. Smiling, she admired all her things, once again proud to have a place of her own.

She kicked off her heeled sandals at the door, slipped the little clutch she'd taken with her to the bar into her coat pocket before hanging it up in the little closet. Her cell phone buzzed in her hand, a smile instantly forming on her lips.

Nope, she wasn't quite ready to get to bed. Not when she was in the middle of a rather lovely chat conversation with the man she'd met a couple of hours ago at the wine bar. Felt almost wrong that she was excited to talk to him considering she'd already been talking to another man on Facebook.

But, hey, she was young, she was single, and she was letting fate dictate the way her life played out. Who was she to intervene if the universe wanted to send another handsome, charming man into her life. Who knew? He could possibly be the one.

While she waited for him to respond to her last message, Cori pulled a glass down from the cabinet, retrieved the opened bottle of wine from her refrigerator. Perfect night to sit out on the patio. Now that the storm had passed, the evening was cooler and she loved to watch the sky as the clouds moved out.

With glass and bottle in hand, she picked up her phone and headed outside. The sky was bright thanks to the lights of the city, no stars overhead, all hidden by the lingering clouds. It wasn't like Coyote Ridge, where the sky seemed to go on forever, the stars somehow brighter because of the lack of lights. But she didn't mind the difference between the two. Living in Austin was what she wanted to do. For now, anyway. In the future… well, Cori didn't know what the future held for her, but she was excited about the prospects. Only a few more months and she would graduate from the University of Texas, armed with a degree that would hopefully land her an exciting job.

Her phone buzzed again as she retrieved her chair cushions from the patio closet, where she'd tucked them away that afternoon to keep them from getting drenched. Using a towel she kept in the closet, she made a quick pass over the wicker to dry it and the chair was as good as new.

Cori smiled down at the phone as she settled into the thick cushion, relaxing as she read the text that came back. This guy seemed too good to be true, if she did say so herself. The corporate type, Andrew was well-dressed, well-spoken. Not to mention, movie-star handsome with a bright smile and those eyes. So very blue, they glowed like the waters of the Caribbean in the sun.

Forcing herself not to giggle like a schoolgirl, she responded to his next question, shooting back one of her own, letting the minutes tick by as she finished off her wine and sleep began to look like a better and better idea.

She was in the middle of typing when she heard her doorbell. The sound had her sitting upright, turning as though she might be able to see through her apartment and out into the hall. Since clearly that wasn't going to work, she set her phone and glass down on the table, hopped to her feet.

Probably Leah, stopping by to talk. She'd been out of sorts tonight, on the outs with her boyfriend of five years. Cori had tried to tell her she was far too young to think about settling down with a man she'd been dating since she was a teenager, but Leah never listened.

"Coming," she shouted when the doorbell sounded again.

Pressing her eye to the security hole, she peeked out, saw a familiar face, and frowned.

After unlatching the door locks, she slowly pulled the door open only to realize the mistake, but it was too late.

He stepped forward, making a retreat impossible, filling her doorway while aiming a gun directly at her.

"Good to see you again, Corinne. I think it's time we take a little trip."

"What are you doing here?" she asked, wishing like hell she hadn't unlocked the door. "How'd you know where I live?"

"I keep track of the pretty ones," he said, his voice almost as creepy as his words.

He waved the gun in the direction of the floor.

"Shoes. Now, Corinne. Don't make me shoot you."

He was serious. She could see the intent in his eyes, her entire body trembling as fear lit a fire in her veins.

"Now!" he barked.

The violent sound had her jumping, even as she stepped back and grabbed her shoes off the floor. He held the door open with his foot, remained in the hallway while she pulled them on.

"Where are we going?"

"You'll find out soon enough. Where's your cell phone?"

Shit. She'd left her cell on the back porch.

"I left it inside," she told him.

"Good. Now be a good little girl," he crooned, sliding his arm over her shoulder as he let the apartment door swing shut behind them. "Don't make me kill you, Corinne. Such a waste if I have to."

It was sheer terror that had her moving with him, letting him guide her to the elevators. She knew this was a mistake. If he got her to a secondary location, he would kill her, right? That was the way this always played out?

Swallowing the cold lump of fear, Cori turned and peered up at the camera while they waited for the elevator. Not sure what else to do, praying someone was watching, she mouthed the words help me.

Unfortunately, no one did.

Chapter Eleven

THE HARSH RING OF HIS CELL PHONE roused Brantley from a deep sleep, had him rolling over, dragging the pillow over his head in an attempt to block out the sound and the light filtering in through the blinds.

A big hand smacked him on the chest. "Phone."

"I know," he mumbled into the pillow.

"Answer it?"

"It'll stop."

Only it didn't. Damn thing kept right on ringing. One second there'd be blessed silence, then the harsh shrill sound would start again. He really needed to change that fucking ringer. Or better yet, put the damn thing on silent.

Tossing the pillow to the floor, Brantley threw out an arm, snagged the phone, and punched the button, not bothering to open his eyes.

"Walker," he grumbled.

"Brantley. Oh, thank God you answered. We need your help."

The agitated voice had sleep vanishing as he forced his eyes open, focused on the ceiling fan making a slow turn. "What's wrong, JJ?"

"It's Cori. Dante's mom can't get ahold of her. She went out last night with some of her friends, never came home. He called me. Said his mother's freaking out. She thinks… Oh, God, Brantley, she thinks somethin' happened."

Sitting up, he came fully awake, dropping his legs over the side of the bed. "Calm down, JJ. Tell me what happened."

While she rattled off more fear than details, the words managed to clear the fog from Brantley's brain.

"And Dante called you?" he asked.

"He didn't know who else to call. Asked that I reach out to you."

"Okay. Where are you?"

"I'm at home. I told him I'd call you. Please tell me you'll help."

"Of course, yes," Brantley assured her, because what else was he going to do? While he wanted to put Dante through a wall for the shit he pulled with JJ, it wasn't like he could refuse to help the man's family. "I'll call him, give you a call back."

"Okay."

Squinting, he pulled up Dante's number, which he'd logged a couple of months ago when he'd reached out to the man. He hit the button to dial.

Dante answered immediately. "I tried her cell phone," he blurted, his voice trembling. "But it just rings. Says the voicemail's full. Something's wrong, Brantley. I know how much you hate me, how—"

"This isn't about you," Brantley bit out. "It's about Corinne."

"I know."

"So let's keep it that way," he said. "Give me a few minutes and Reese and I'll head over."

"I'm with my mother," Dante said quickly.

"At the governor's mansion?" he asked incredulously.

"Yes."

Fan-fucking-tastic. "Okay, fine. We'll come there. It'll be about thirty. Maybe forty-five. Keep your phone nearby."

"Thanks, Brantley. Please help … my sister. You've got to find my sister."

"I will," he assured him, dragging his ass out of bed.

Reese was sitting up, watching him intently as Brantley disconnected the call, tossed the phone on the bed.

"Dante's sister went out last night, didn't come home. They can't get in touch with her. Let's get dressed. Head over there."

Brantley marched to the bathroom. In order to wash the rest of the sleep from his brain, he opted for a quick shower. Ten minutes later, alternating in the bathroom, they'd both shaved, showered, and dressed, then headed out the door. He snatched his truck keys on the way.

Reese was silent, taking cues from him, getting into the passenger seat.

Brantley's truck started with a rumble, followed by the scrape of rubber on gravel as he reversed onto the grass, then swung around and headed down his driveway. Neither of them spoke, nor did they bother with the radio, opting for silence as Brantley navigated through the small town on his way to the toll road that would take him into Austin.

Because it was Sunday and there weren't too many cars on the road this early, it took only forty minutes to wind his way downtown. He pulled up to the governor's mansion in what was likely record time, but probably felt like an eternity to the anxious family waiting inside. At the gates, Brantley flashed his ID at the guard, who gave him a bland smile before waving him through.

Unlike many visitors who traipsed across these grounds, Brantley and Reese weren't there to admire the Greek Revival style architecture, the six twenty-nine-foot Ionic columns lining the front porch, the floor-to-ceiling windows, or even the priceless art and antique collections that were housed within the governor's mansion. Nope, today they would be using the back entrance to gain access to the house, since only visitors and tour groups came in through the front doors.

He parked his truck and let his gaze scan his surroundings. He couldn't count the number of residences he'd visited over the years during his time as a SEAL, hunting down a target, or on some sort of protection or extraction mission in which one official or another had pissed off the wrong people. He prayed that wasn't the case here and that Corinne Greenwood had decided to make it a late night and perhaps her phone had simply died.

Taking a deep breath, Brantley resigned himself to this new mission.

Somewhere in the back of his mind, he was thinking that this could be something else entirely. They were currently investigating the disappearance of Corinne's childhood friend and now they were looking into Corinne's whereabouts? Coincidence? He didn't think so.

He shot a quick look at Reese before he knocked on the back door. The door flew open and a petite woman stared up at him, her face wrought with concern.

"Oh, thank God!" Trina exclaimed, greeting him when he stepped into the house.

Brantley accepted Dante's mother's panicked hug, taking a step back when she released him. "Katrina Greenwood, I'd like you to meet my partner, Reese Tavoularis. Reese, Trina."

Reese held out his hand, Trina taking it firmly within both of hers. "Thank you. Thank you for coming to help."

"Hey," Dante said, thrusting out a hand in Brantley's direction. "Thanks for comin'."

Brantley looked at the hand, up at Dante's face. The only reason he shook it was because Trina was there. Had she not been, he probably would've simply punched Dante in the face, which would've been nothing less than he deserved.

Stepping back, Brantley turned his full attention to Trina. Though he did his best to hide it, he couldn't deny it felt a bit awkward to be here. Not only in the governor's mansion but around Dante and his mother. Yeah, it was true, Dante had been his friend throughout his younger years, but there had been tension between them ever since the black-eye incident with JJ. None of that mattered now, he reminded himself. This was about Corinne, not Brantley's comfort level.

"Dante said you could help us," Trina said, her voice pitched a little high.

"Considerin' I'm on the governor's task force..." Brantley glanced at Dante, curious as to why the governor hadn't been the one to call.

Obviously understanding, Dante nodded. "We haven't told my dad yet. Until we know for sure she's missing..."

He didn't like the sound of that. If they truly believed Corinne was missing, they needed to call in the cavalry.

"Is this somethin' she does often?" he asked, curious as to why they might hold off.

"Not often," Trina said. "But there's been a couple of times…"

Yeah, okay. So a whole lot of nothing being said.

"But you don't think this is one of those times?"

"No. Cori's supposed to have breakfast with me. And that's not something she ever misses. We have a standing reservation, every Sunday for brunch. She always calls me to let me know she's up and getting ready." Trina's eyes turned glassy. "I haven't heard from her this morning. I've called and texted since I woke up, but she hasn't responded. Now her voicemail's full. Probably from me."

"Do you know where she was goin' last night?" he asked, dividing his attention between Trina and Dante, who was pouring coffee from the pot on the warmer.

"Out with friends. She mentioned a wine bar."

"The Grove," Dante supplied. "She loves that place."

"Cori called me last night. Before they went out," Trina explained. "Said it was just a few of them. They were going to hang out for a bit." Trina set her phone down, ran her hand through her thick red hair. "She promised to text me when she got home. This morning, when I woke up, the first thing I did was check my phone. No text.

"Again, not entirely unusual. I get it, she's young, out having fun with her friends. Gets home late, forgets to text her mother."

Brantley could see that.

"But she always texts me back. When she didn't call about brunch, I started to panic."

Leaning a hip against the counter, Brantley accepted the coffee cup Dante passed over. In an effort to get his bearings on the situation, he watched Trina pace, waited to see if Dante would contribute.

He didn't.

"Thanks," Reese mumbled when Dante passed him a cup of coffee.

Brantley continued with, "And she hasn't called Gerard?"

Trina shook her head. "No. I checked his phone before he left, but I didn't want to worry him. Not yet."

"Where's he at now?"

"His office at the capitol," Dante supplied. "He usually goes in on Sunday mornings. Says it's quiet then."

A broken sob came from Trina, drawing Dante to his mother's side. Katrina Greenwood's face was pale, eyes wild, her fear prominent, but they all avoided offering her placating words.

"Have you notified APD?" There was no way the police could ignore this. They wouldn't put it off until she'd been gone for forty-eight hours, which was sometimes the case for missing persons. All rules and regulations went out the window when the governor's daughter went missing. At this point, they'd likely have every law enforcement agency in Texas on high alert.

"Not yet. I…" Trina swallowed. "I don't want to look like a panicked mom in the event she simply stayed with a friend. Or maybe left her phone."

"Does she usually do either?" Reese asked.

"No. Cori prefers her own space, doesn't stay at other people's houses. And her phone is her lifeline. If she left it anywhere, it would be completely by accident."

"Have you received any calls? From anyone else?" Brantley inquired.

Her light blue eyes were solemn as she shook her head. "You mean someone asking for a ransom?"

Yes, that was what he meant, but he knew better than to say the word. Trina was hovering on the fringes of a panic attack and the last thing he needed was for her to get hysterical.

"No. No phone calls. Not yet."

"Okay. We need a list of her friends," he told them both. "The ones she was going out with."

"I don't know exactly who," she said, her words rushed. "She didn't tell me."

"Then a list of all her friends," he said calmly.

Trina spun around, snatched a spiral-bound notebook off the counter, passed it over. "Already did that. I knew someone would ask."

Brantley scanned the names, noticed she had a few phone numbers listed. They would call them all, track down those she didn't have contact info for.

For simplicity, Brantley snapped a picture of the names, gave her what was meant to be a reassuring hug, then promised he would be in touch as soon as he learned something.

"Can I talk to you for a minute?" he prompted Dante on his way to the door.

Dante nodded, then followed them outside.

"I'd like to check out her place. See if it'll give us any insight."

"Of course." Dante dug in his pocket, retrieved a key. "I was planning to stop by there, but I didn't want to leave my mom…"

"She's understandably upset," Reese noted. "We'll see what we can do to get some answers."

"Yeah. Thanks." Dante's blue eyes bounced between the two of them. "Keep us in the loop."

"Of course," Brantley said, motioning for Reese to lead the way down the steps.

Once back in the truck, Brantley let his phone connect to Bluetooth, then dialed JJ's number.

"Hey," she said, her tone rushed. "Please tell me you found her."

"Not yet, no. I've got a list of names. Need you to track them down, find out where they are. Sending it to you now." He passed the phone to Reese so he could send over the image of the names.

There was a brief pause, followed by, "Got it. Lot of names here."

"It's a list of Cori's friends. I suspect some of them were out with her last night."

"Gotcha. Give me half an hour. I'll hit you back when I've located them. Where're you headed?"

"Gonna stop by Cori's apartment. Call me when you know somethin'."

"Will do."

Brantley disconnected the call, let Reese key in the address Dante had sent via text.

Reese still wasn't saying much and Brantley had to wonder if it was because of their abrupt wakeup call or if it had something to do with last night.

Last night.

Holy fuck.

The memory was still vivid in his mind. He could practically feel the heat of Reese's body. Had it not been for that wakeup call, he probably would've been balls deep inside the man again now. As it was, it was an ache he hoped to quench again in the very near future. Thinking about it damn sure wasn't going to help though, so he made a mental note not to bring it up. Not even to himself.

Once they reached San Antonio Street, Brantley parked the truck in the garage closest to Corinne's apartment complex. With Reese in tow, they headed into the building. The lobby was empty but there was movement in the leasing office off to the left. Rather than stop to chat with anyone, they got into the elevator, up to the third floor. Unit 3810 wasn't too far down the hall. He entered using the key Dante had given him.

Admittedly, it was rare for him to visit a woman's apartment. Well, a woman who was not one of his sisters. The only real female friend he'd ever had was JJ and he'd yet to make his way inside her place now that she'd grown up and gotten one of her own. Last time he'd been in her personal space was when she'd lived at home with her parents and rocked boy band posters on her walls.

As he stepped inside, the first thing he noticed was the powdery floral scent. He assumed it was Corinne's perfume lingering even though she wasn't. Two thousand square feet of luxury overlooking Lady Bird Lake in the heart of downtown Austin. As was the design of most things these days, Corinne's apartment boasted hardwood floors, cream and tan tones on the walls and trim. The appliances were stainless steel, the countertops white quartz, cabinets a high-gloss brown. But that was where the simplicity stopped. Corinne had an eye for color and she'd designed the space to draw one's attention where she wanted it to go. A decorative mirror framed in faux brick, a large silver clock, jewel-toned throw pillows on the overstuffed sofa, a beige rug with turquoise stripes running through it.

He glanced around, noticing everything had a place and it hadn't been disturbed. It appeared as though Corinne was as meticulous as her brother, and her apartment reflected the same obsession with cleanliness and distaste for clutter that he'd witnessed with Dante.

They went their separate ways, perusing the space. The first of two bedrooms was for guests, the bed made, closet and drawers empty. Next bedroom was hers. Queen-size bed with an antique iron headboard and footboard, nine-drawer dresser with mirror, a couple of nightstands, and a cheval mirror in the corner. Only decorative lamps on the nightstands and a charging cord for her phone. The bathroom was equally tidy, towel hanging on a bar near the shower, dry to the touch. The countertops were wiped down, nothing on top except for a lighted makeup mirror and a vase holding a single orchid. The small bench was tucked out of the way between the two cabinets holding the sinks.

Brantley opened the closet door and smiled. This was where the disarray was. The seventy-five-or-so-square-foot space looked as though it had been hit by a tornado.

Corinne had more clothes than any one person should and it looked as though she'd tried on a large majority of them last night. A couple of dresses were haphazardly tossed over one of the hanging rods, three pairs of shoes scattered on the floor, boots tucked under a row of jeans, one on its side. And the jewelry chest was open, a variety of earrings and necklaces sparkling in the overhead lights, tossed about as though she could not make up her mind.

Considering all the sparkling baubles, he had to believe nothing was missing. Well, other than Corinne.

Reese joined him, coming to a stop in the closet doorway. "It doesn't look like she came home last night."

That was what Brantley was thinking.

"I know what her mother said, but there's plenty of places a twenty-four-year-old college student could go," Reese mused. "She could've crashed at a friend's place, or maybe she met someone, went back to his place."

It was certainly possible. From what he'd learned about her from JJ, she was a normal twenty-something who'd been pinned down beneath her parents' thumb all her life. It made sense that she would want to have some fun.

It would've been ideal if he could really believe that was all this was. Unfortunately, he couldn't.

"You find a cell phone?" Reese asked as they headed back toward the living room.

"No. You?"

"Not anywhere in here that I can tell."

"What do you think?"

Reese stopped in the kitchen, looked around before his gaze settled on Brantley. "I don't know. Right now, I'm more curious about who saw her at the wine bar. Who did she hang out with? Did she meet up with anyone else? How'd she get home?"

"Good questions. Let's hope JJ'll get some answers. In the meantime, I say we head over to the Grove, see what we can find."

After locking up Corinne's apartment, Brantley and Reese made a quick pass through the recreational areas. Fitness center, pool, club house, media room, community grill, and outdoor congregation area. No signs of her or that she'd been around recently.

"Holy shit, this place makes mine look like the projects," Reese muttered.

"Your apartment's nice," he argued.

"This is nice. Mine's simply shelter."

On their way back to the truck, Brantley followed Reese when he stopped at the leasing office, approached the guy reclining at the desk.

"Question for ya," Reese told the man. "Have you seen Corinne Greenwood around today? She lives in 3810."

The man sat up straight, smiled. "No, sir. But I saw her yesterday. Stopped in to secure one of the cabanas for later in the week. Something wrong?"

"What time did you see her?"

"I work eight to five," he mused. "I'd been here a couple of hours, I figure. Maybe ten or eleven. Close to lunch, I think."

Reese nodded, clearly ignoring the man's previous question. "Thanks. If you happen to see her, would you have her give her brother a call?"

"That you?" the man inquired.

"No. We're just friends."

The guy scribbled down the note. "Of course."

Leading the way, Brantley exited the building the way they'd come.

"A lot of security cameras in there," he noted.

"In the lobby, anyway. I only saw a couple on the floors we were on."

But it was something. Worst case, they'd get the apartment complex to provide the footage.

He was pulling out of the parking garage when his phone rang. He hit the button on the steering wheel to take the call through Bluetooth.

"Tell me you've got somethin', JJ."

"Unless you consider me freakin' out a bunch of society princesses, no. Unfortunately. Three of the girls on the list went out with her last night, said she left the Grove in an Uber around one. She was headin' home, they claim."

"Any of the others see her recently? Maybe before last night? Mention if she had a boyfriend?"

"One of the girls ... Michelle Breeland. She said she saw Cori a week ago. According to her, they get together to have coffee a couple of times a week. Michelle's been out of town on vacation, but she did mention Cori'd recently started talking about some guy."

"She say who?"

"Nope. But I've got an address for her. I told her you might wanna ask some questions."

"Great. Shoot it over. We'll stop by, see if we can get more details."

"Will do. And Brantley?"

"Hmm?"

"Let me know when you hear somethin', would ya? Also hit me up if I can help with anything else."

"Sure thing. Thanks for this, JJ. Appreciate it."

When the text came in, Reese programed the address in the navigation. Getting a bead on where they were going, Brantley headed west and did his best to ignore the concern roiling in his gut.

MICHELLE BREELAND LIVED IN A QUAINT LITTLE neighborhood just west of downtown Austin. Prime location for the young and hip, those who preferred to walk to and from the variety of eclectic shops that dotted the landscape. The street she lived on was quiet, or appeared that way. No cars parked at the curb, each house well-manicured, looking as though they'd been spruced up at least once in the past decade.

Granted, Reese wasn't much on the Austin scene. He preferred small towns to big cities, hence the reason he'd opted to stay in Coyote Ridge versus follow his parents and siblings up to Dallas.

"There it is," Reese called out. "Blue house, white shutters."

Brantley pulled the truck over to the curb, parked, both of them staring up at the house.

"Either she's got two rides or she's got company," he noted before getting out of the truck.

Reese waited for Brantley to join him, wondering exactly how this woman would react to the two of them crowding her front porch. Because of their sizes, they weren't the unassuming sort. Because he didn't want to freak out a woman who might live alone, Reese opted to hang back, remaining at the bottom of the steps while Brantley knocked on the door.

It took a minute before he heard the sound of locks disengaging. The door opened and a brunette appeared, her hair pulled back in a ponytail, workout leggings and a sparkly sports bra giving the clue she might've come from the gym. Then again, it could've been her relaxing-on-the-weekend attire, Reese didn't know. Didn't really care, either.

"Michelle Breeland?" Brantley asked, holding up his badge for her to see.

"Yes?"

"You spoke with JJ earlier? She's a friend of ours."

"Oh, yes," Michelle said, eyes widening. "Please. Come in."

Brantley peered back at Reese, cocked an eyebrow, clearly as surprised as he was that this woman would simply invite two strangers into her house. Granted, they had badges, but she hadn't bothered to look all that closely at them.

"If you'll excuse me for just a minute … I'll be right back."

"If she's smart, she's gettin' a Taser."

"Or a can of mace," Reese muttered as he peered around.

The inside of the house was as small as the outside, but clean and uncluttered like Corinne's apartment. Little color on the walls, offset by jewel tones throughout.

"Can I get you something to drink?" Michelle offered, coming back into the room and glancing between the two of them.

Didn't look like she'd gotten a weapon, but she had put on a jacket, effectively covering herself.

"We're fine," Brantley said, pulling his sunglasses off and tucking them into the neck of his T-shirt. "If you don't mind, we'd just like to ask you a few questions."

"Of course." Michelle motioned toward the couch, although no one took a seat.

"I'm a friend of Corinne's family," Brantley explained. "From what I've been told, she went out with some friends last night. Met at the Grove, left there around one this morning. No one's seen her since."

"The Grove's a wine bar," Michelle said. "I know Cori likes to hang out there. Like I told the woman who called, I've been out of town for a week. Last time I saw Cori was the Thursday before last. We had coffee. Met at Starbucks near campus as is our routine. I mean, I'm not sure what I can tell you. We don't usually talk on the phone or text, just catch up in person."

"Anything you can tell us would be beneficial."

"Did you go by her apartment?" Michelle asked, big brown eyes darting back and forth between them.

"We did. Doesn't look like she came home last night." He tucked his hands in his pockets. "Do you know if she was seein' anyone?"

"Cori mentioned a guy she met online a couple of months ago." Michelle shook her head as though answering a silent question. "She never told me his name. Said it was nothing serious, and she hadn't met him in person. They were just messaging back and forth. I tried to get details, but she said she didn't want to jinx it."

"Did she mention what he looked like?" Reese asked. "If they have anything in common? Restaurants, museums?"

"Museums?" Brantley asked, casting an amused look his way.

Thankfully Michelle ignored his question. "No. I got the impression he was older though."

"Older?" Reese asked. "Like college-grad older? Or tenured CEO older?"

Michelle chuckled. "She said he's been married before. Has a kid, I think."

Reese watched Brantley, observing the way the man processed the information. Probably asking himself if this guy was legit or some online predator. The same questions were going through his mind, but until they had more to go on, none of them could be answered.

Brantley's phone rang and he reached in his back pocket, pulled it out. "Excuse me. I need to take this."

"Of course," Michelle said quickly.

"Whatcha got, JJ?"

Reese watched Brantley, curious as to what JJ might've found in the few minutes since they last spoke with her. He couldn't hear what was being said, but whatever it was sparked Brantley's attention.

"Thanks, JJ. You're a godsend," he said quickly. "Shoot me the address. We'll check it out."

"A lead?" Reese inquired when Brantley pocketed his phone.

"Yeah." Brantley turned back to Michelle. "Thank you, Ms. Breeland. We appreciate your help."

"I'm not sure I did much. But if there's anything else, please let me know. Cori's my friend and now I'm worried about her."

Brantley pulled his sunglasses off his shirt, then headed for the door.

Reese followed, curious as to what JJ had told him, but smart enough to hold off asking until they were back in the truck. Evidently it was enough to cut their questioning short, which hopefully meant good things for Corinne Greenwood.

A minute later, he was riding shotgun.

Chapter Twelve

ONCE THEY WERE BACK IN THE TRUCK, Brantley keyed in the address JJ had sent over, surprised when Reese didn't ask where they were going.

Glancing over, he noticed Reese was staring out the window, seemingly lost in thought.

"Somethin' on your mind?"

Reese peered over. "JJ said Corinne left the bar at one in the morning. Took an Uber. You think she could reach out, pinpoint the driver?"

"Good question. Why don't you call her and ask?"

Dragging his phone out of his pocket, Reese dialed. A second later, JJ's voice sounded on the phone's speaker.

"What's up, cowboy?"

Brantley smirked. Why she referred to Reese that way, he wasn't sure, but he kind of liked it.

Reese grinned. "I need a favor."

"Hit me."

"Corinne left the bar last night in an Uber. Could you get me a line on the driver? Maybe they'll know something."

"Already done," JJ came back. "When her friend told me, I started looking into it. Driver's name is Suzy Dumonde. Single mom of two teenagers, runs Uber and Lyft on the weekends for extra money. Clean as far as I can tell."

"Perfect. You got a number?"

"Got it and already called. Suzy remembers Cori. Said she dropped her at the Northshore apartments at half past one, waited until Cori went through the door, and then drove off. She took two more rides after that. I verified. One took her up to Round Rock, the other back toward the Domain."

Which meant Suzy was a dead end. "Son of a bitch."

"I'm sorry, guys."

"Yeah." He was, too.

Reese spoke up. "Hey, JJ? Any chance you can dump Corinne's phone? See if she got any calls after she was dropped off?"

"Uh … it's a big possibility, if it's still turned on. Would be easier if I had it. Hold tight. Let me see what I can do."

"Pretty damn smart for a cowboy," Brantley teased while they waited for JJ to pull up what she could.

Reese rolled his eyes, but there was a smile that pulled at his mouth.

While JJ muttered on the phone, Brantley focused on getting them to their destination. He was curious to talk to this supposed boyfriend, figure out what he knew. If they were lucky, Corinne had spent the night with the guy, keeping it on the down low. She'd told her friend she didn't want to jinx it, so maybe this was her way of ensuring she didn't.

"All right, boys. Had to move to the offline system, but I found that there were no calls to or from Cori after one this morning. Not until her mom started callin'. She used her phone to secure an Uber, and there are a handful of text messages to someone named Andrew, who it appears she met at the bar last night. Seem innocent, questions back and forth. Like they're gettin' to know each other. They end with Andrew asking a question and Cori never responding."

"Maybe he followed her from the bar?" Reese asked.

"It's possible. Let me pull up what I can on him. See if I can track him down. Did you find anything at her apartment?"

Reese took point on answering. "No evident signs she'd been there since before she went out last night. We'll see how this lead pans out, then it might be worth a second look."

"Like I said, let me know if I can help."

"You talk to Dante?" Reese inquired.

"Yeah. Trina's in a panic now. She broke down and called Gerard. He insisted they call us. Dante assured him we were already looking into it."

"They notify APD?"

"Yeah. He let them know we were lookin' into it, too."

Good thing. They'd yet to encounter being up against law enforcement. Last thing they needed was a road block or red tape.

"Hey, JJ. We'll hit you back in a few," Brantley told her. "We're about to exit Burnet."

"Sure. No problem. Keep me updated."

"Will do." Brantley flipped on his turn signal and exited.

"Whose house are we goin' to?" Reese inquired as he pulled out his weapon, checked it.

"JJ scanned Corinne's social media accounts. Found this guy friended her a couple of months back. Name's Tyler Murphy. Thirty-six, divorced, a six-year-old daughter. Sounds a lot like the guy Michelle described."

"Yep. You buyin' the story? Or think he's probably married and lookin' for a little somethin' on the side?"

"Damn," he said, grinning. "Went down that rabbit hole awfully quick. Jaded, are you?"

"Realistic," Reese countered.

Brantley turned down the street the guy lived on, glanced at the numbers painted on the curb. He steered past a few houses, pulled the truck to the side of the road. "That's it. Two doors down. Red Malibu in the driveway."

"Got it. What's the plan?"

Resting his hands on the steering wheel, Brantley cocked his head toward Reese. "I'm not one to cop to shortcomings," he said easily, "but this is outta my wheelhouse. I'm a SEAL, not a cop."

"Ah." Reese nodded as though that made sense. "You'd be more suited if we needed to blow shit up."

He cocked an eyebrow. "Damn straight."

Reese chuckled. "I guess we're gonna test that whole immunity and means thing then, huh?"

Brantley grinned. "I like the way you think."

With that, Brantley got out and strolled across the street, past a couple of houses that looked like mirror images of those across from them. It was a cookie-cutter neighborhood, one filled with families. Kids, dogs, hamsters. Playscapes and trampolines likely dotted the backyards, bikes littering the front when the kids were let out to play. Which meant there was a good chance Reese was right. This joker was probably married.

He fought the urge to pull his gun and go in hot. He did, however, make sure his badge was visible on his hip.

Taking a deep breath, he stuck to the sidewalk, sneaking a peek in the Malibu as he passed by, noting a phone charger in the center console, a couple of toys in the backseat.

Brantley shot a quick look over his shoulder to see Reese ambling along behind him, looking casual, like he belonged strolling the streets of this neighborhood.

When Reese joined him on the concrete porch, Brantley banged on the door, waited.

"I told you, I'm not interested," the male voice sounded as the door opened.

A man appeared, eyes widening when he took in Brantley. Guy was clean-cut, if not a bit uppity with his plaid shorts, V-neck T-shirt, feet bare. He looked as though he'd been camping out on the couch, chilling on a Sunday.

"Uh ... sorry 'bout that. Thought you were those solar guys coming back. Been hassling me since I moved in."

"You Tyler Murphy?" Brantley prompted, foregoing the social niceties.

"Yeah." The guy frowned, glanced past him to Reese. "What's going on?"

"We're lookin' for Corinne Greenwood. You seen her lately?"

"Corinne—you mean Cori?"

Brantley pulled off his sunglasses, cocked an eyebrow. "Have you seen her lately?"

"No. Actually, I've never seen her. Not in person. We just started talking online. Why? What's—"

"You mind if we come in to talk?" Reese asked, holding up his badge as he stepped up beside Brantley.

The guy's gaze shot from the badge to the gun on Reese's hip. "You're police?"

"Governor's task force," Brantley confirmed.

Based on the confused expression, Brantley was starting to think maybe JJ was right. They needed a name, something that didn't sound so … fake. Something that would hopefully start getting around so they didn't look like a bunch of imposters.

"We just wanna talk," Reese said, his voice lower, almost comforting.

"Sure. Yeah. Come in." Tyler stepped back, motioned them inside. "Is Cori okay?"

The scent of bacon and coffee lingered in the air, the sound of a television coming from the room at the back of the house. Brantley scoped what he could see. Sparse on furniture, a couple of boxes stacked in the formal dining room, a pogo stick leaning against a closet door. No one else in view.

When Tyler closed the front door, Brantley turned his attention to the man. "When's the last time you talked to her?"

"We just IM. You know, instant message?" Tyler's gaze bounced back and forth between them. "We're taking our time getting to the meet-in-person phase. I think I chatted with her yesterday. She said she was going out with friends last night. I haven't heard from her today. Would you please tell me what's going on?"

"Corinne's missing, Mr. Murphy," Reese supplied. "She went out with some friends last night, but she never came home."

Brantley watched closely as the man's eyes dilated, true fear forming on his face. Question was, was the fear from guilt or concern?

"Where were you at one o'clock this morning?" Reese questioned.

"Here. Asleep."

"Anyone confirm that?"

"My daughter," he said simply. "But she's six. She was asleep, too. It's my weekend to have her."

"Is she here now?"

Now Tyler's fear shifted, morphing into something protective. "She is. She's playing in her room, but I'd prefer you leave her alone. Like I said, she was asleep."

As much as he wanted to rough this guy up, Brantley knew then that Tyler Murphy had nothing to do with Corinne's disappearance. He could also sense the guy's worry, but it wasn't that of a man who'd developed feelings for her. More like that of a parent, or maybe of a Good Samaritan. Whatever the relationship he had with Corinne, it hadn't taken root yet.

"If you hear from her, you mind giving me a call?"

"You got a card?"

No, actually, he did not.

Another thing they needed to work on.

Reese reached for his wallet, pulled out a card, passed it over.

Curious, Brantley peered down, noticed it was a Walker Demolition card.

"I thought you said—"

"Previous job," Reese stated. "Haven't gotten new cards yet. But that's my cell."

Tyler's gaze scanned the card briefly, then held it up. "I'll call if I hear from her."

"Thanks." Brantley motioned for Reese to go out before him.

Once they were back in the truck, Brantley turned over the engine. He relaxed against the seat, stared out the window.

Where the fuck was Corinne?

"Where to next?" Reese inquired, the click of his seat belt catching Brantley's attention.

"I suppose a quick stop at the house so I could get you naked and beneath me's outta the question?"

When he glanced over, he saw the surprise on Reese's face. Clearly hadn't expected that.

"Please tell me that's a yes," he teased.

Reese sighed. "One-track mind, Navy boy. Here I was thinkin' you got more than enough last night."

"Not by a long shot. Probably take ten, twenty … thousand more times before I'm sated enough to start takin' it slow with you. Now that you gave me the green light…"

"Great. Just promise you don't intend to knock all that out in a week."

Chuckling, Brantley reached for the gearshift, put the truck in drive. "Won't make promises I can't keep."

REESE TRIED TO IGNORE THE FACT HIS cock had decided to imitate a steel beam thanks to Brantley's revelation. It wasn't easy. Definitely not in Wranglers while sitting in a truck. But the discomfort did keep his imagination from running away from him.

Determined to stay on track, Reese released a breath when Brantley pulled out of Tyler Murphy's neighborhood and headed back south on the interstate.

"Where's the Grove?"

"She went to the one downtown," Brantley answered, his tone reflecting his amusement. Evidently he was still thinking about that off-topic conversation.

"We should head over there," Reese suggested. "Check it out. Maybe someone'll remember seeing her."

"Couldn't hurt."

So that was what they did. Brantley drove them downtown and together they questioned the wine bar's manager, getting the name and number of the bartender who'd been on duty last night. No one currently working had remembered seeing Corinne the night before, although they'd admitted the place had been packed, which evidently wasn't unusual for a Saturday night.

While Brantley tied up the conversation with the manager, Reese walked out the front door. He peered down the steps to the street, glanced over the bushes on the right. He imagined he was Corinne, walking out, maybe a little tipsy from indulging, smiling because she'd met someone new. He imagined her glancing at her phone, maybe checking the Uber app. Figuring she was a smart woman, he guessed she would've double-checked the vehicle information, the tags, ensured they matched the information the app had given her.

From there, she would've gotten into Suzy Dumonde's light blue Camry. Alone. The backseat. She would've relaxed a bit. Maybe Suzy chatted her up, asked how her night was, if she'd had fun. Corinne would've smiled, nodded. She was tired though. Ready to go home, kick off her shoes.

Reese stepped down to the sidewalk, did a three-sixty as he took it all in. Had someone been waiting for her out here? Watched her leave? Or had someone been inside, waiting? This Andrew guy. Had he followed her home? Intercepted her before she could get into her apartment? They would definitely have to check out the security cameras.

He glanced down the road, imagining Suzy's car heading away from the bar before making the trek toward Corinne's apartment.

Footsteps sounded, drawing Reese out of his thoughts. He turned to see Brantley sliding his sunglasses on, pulling his truck keys out of his pocket.

"Can we go back to her apartment?" Reese asked.

Brantley didn't say a word, simply nodded and led the way to the truck.

Not long after, the two of them were walking up to the front of the Northshore building. Reese paused in front, saw Suzy's car in his mind, parked at the curb waiting for Corinne to go inside. He could sense Brantley watching him, but the man didn't ask questions and Reese felt no need to explain.

Once he was satisfied he'd rehashed Corinne's steps outside, Reese followed Brantley into the building.

From the left, the leasing agent they'd talked to earlier called out, greeting them. The guy stood up, walked over, his face reflecting concern.

"Please tell me you've found her."

Seemed rather anxious for a man who simply worked in the building where she lived. Did he know her? Maybe on a more personal level?

Reese peered over at Brantley, watched as he tucked the arm of his sunglasses into the neck of his T-shirt.

"Not yet."

The guy gestured to another woman. "I asked Sylvia if she's talked to Cori recently. She said no."

"What about the security cameras?" Reese asked, motioning toward the ceiling. "You have the footage from last night? Early this morning?"

The man's expression changed. It was subtle.

"I can look."

Interesting. Usually the answer to that would be yes or no, Reese figured. It was almost as though this guy didn't expect to find footage. Coincidence?

"We'd appreciate it," Brantley said, then motioned for Reese to head toward the elevators. "We'll check with you on our way out."

"Oh," the man called out behind them. "There's a detective up there now. APD, I think he said."

Once again, Reese glanced at Brantley.

Brantley nodded. "Thanks."

This time, as they made their way up to Cori's apartment, Reese took it all in as Brantley led the way. Although they had the key, it wasn't necessary because the door was unlocked. Out of courtesy, Brantley rapped his knuckles on it as he pushed it open.

"Can I help you?" a man greeted, approaching them slowly.

Interesting look for a detective, Reese thought. He was dressed in a pair of well-worn jeans, equally worn shitkickers, and a T-shirt that looked as though he'd slept in it. Of course, somehow he managed to pull the look off, probably because he was nicely built with the face of a model. Blond hair, midnight blue eyes, chiseled jaw. Despite the laid-back appearance, there was a look in his eyes that said he missed nothing. Perhaps this was a disguise, something meant to throw people off.

Brantley approached, held out his hand. "Brantley Walker. This is my partner, Reese Tavoularis. With the governor's task force."

The man's gaze was steady, assessing. It moved over them both as though attempting to determine if they were telling the truth.

"And you are?" Brantley prompted.

"Sebastian Buchanan." The man held up his detective shield.

"Came by earlier," Brantley informed him, "but Reese wanted to have a second look. Mind if we take another look around?"

Detective Buchanan motioned around him. "Be my guest. I just got here. Haven't started poking around yet."

Reese left the two men to chat. He moved past them, pausing to take in the living room. A closer look this time. He wanted to view it from Corinne's perspective, then as a cop might. Brantley and Detective Buchanan continued their conversation in the kitchen while he made his way through each room, peering in drawers, cabinets, looking at the washer and dryer tucked into a closet.

Like earlier, he came up with nothing. No cell phone, no lead as to whether she had come home or not.

He paused to check out the view through the door to the balcony, which they hadn't bothered with during their earlier visit.

The blinds were encased in a glass frame that fastened to the door. He pushed the handle upward, opening the blinds so he could see out. He'd expected a small space, surprised to find that the outdoor patio was almost as large as the living room. Reese went to unlock the door, found it wasn't locked, then looked down as he reached for the doorknob. Something flashed on the floor, caught by the light and the angle. He squatted to get a closer look, noticed an earring. Single teardrop diamond dangling from what reminded him of a fish hook.

Rather than pick it up, Reese pulled out his phone. He took a quick picture just to have it, then pulled up his Facebook app. The last thing he'd viewed had been Corinne Greenwood's profile, which was exactly what he was looking for. Scrolling down her timeline, he found the images taken the night before. Most of them had been by her friends, who had tagged Corinne.

"Find something?" Detective Buchanan asked.

"She was wearin' this last night," Reese said, peering up at the man.

Footsteps sounded as Brantley joined him. Reese passed over his phone.

"Here," the detective offered, handing over a small evidence bag.

Using the bag to pick it up, he sealed the earring inside and passed it back, taking the phone that was traded before opening the door.

"Have you been out here yet?" he asked Detective Buchanan. "No."

Reese nodded toward the door handle. "It wasn't locked."

Perhaps Corinne didn't feel the need to lock her balcony door because of the location of her apartment. She was used to living in Coyote Ridge, where it still wasn't necessary to lock your doors, so it was possible.

When he opened the door, Reese was hit with a gust of wind that made the lightweight curtains hanging from a rod overhead flap. Looked as though Corinne could shield a portion of the patio from the sun if she chose. Probably wouldn't do a lot of good with the wind though.

The patio was decorated with a large turquoise rug made for the outdoors. On the left, tucked into an indention in the railing, were two rattan chairs, a small table between them. To the right, a wicker barrel chair with a turquoise-colored cushion that looked as though it could seat five full-size adults. There were a few throw pillows, none of which were faded by the sun, suggesting either they were new or Corinne kept them stored.

"Notice the chair's dry," Detective Buchanan stated. "And everything else is still wet from last night's rain."

That was a good observation. And the detective was right. It would mean that Corinne would've had to come home after she left the bar, taken the cushion out from wherever she kept it. If it had been left out while she was at the bar, it would've been soaked.

Reese stepped around the chair to see what was on the other side. There on a small side table was a dark bottle, a wineglass with maybe a swallow left in it. Beside it, a cell phone.

"Detective, you might wanna check this out."

The man stepped forward, clearly sensing Reese's concern.

Pulling on a latex glove, the detective picked up the phone, tapped the screen, bringing it to life.

"This is Ms. Greenwood's phone," he muttered.

Reese didn't bother to mention they'd overlooked this earlier. The look on Brantley's face said it all. He'd likely been hoping to find exactly what they'd found earlier. Nothing to show Corinne had come here after her night out. Because the blinds were all closed, the doors shut, Reese hadn't even thought to come outside.

He watched as Detective Buchanan skimmed through what appeared to be a bunch of missed calls. Likely from her mother. Maybe some additional ones from family and friends having heard the news, hoping to ping the phone and get Corinne to answer.

A phone rang, but it wasn't the one in the detective's hand.

Brantley stepped away as he took the call. Reese listened as Brantley greeted JJ, then the silence that followed.

"Yeah," was the response, the inflection noting Brantley's disappointment. "I know. We're here. Reese found it, actually. No. She's not here. Just the phone."

More silence, followed by a quick goodbye.

"That was JJ. She was calling to tell me she'd gotten a bead on the phone."

Reese nodded.

"If she met with someone after she came home," Detective Buchanan said, "they didn't call her and she didn't call them. Looks like the missed ones are from Mom."

"Yeah," Reese agreed. "We've already checked all the numbers."

That seemed to catch the detective's attention.

"We've had a little more time to look into it," Reese explained. "We got the call from Corinne's mother this morning."

Turning back to the outdoor furniture, Reese imagined Corinne coming home after a night out with friends. Grabbing another glass of wine, stepping outside. She probably enjoyed sitting out here. Perhaps it had been one of the reasons she'd picked this place. The view, the solitude.

But the storm had blown through sometime around midnight. Maybe it had already passed when she got back? Maybe she was drawn out here by the sound of thunder rumbling in the distance? In his mind's eye, he saw her curling up on the chair with her wineglass, reflecting on her night? Thinking about her friends, what she'd be doing today when she woke up? Texting the man she'd met at the bar.

"Someone came here," Reese pondered. "She was sittin' out here, drinkin' wine, texting. Someone knocks on the front door, she sets her glass down, goes to see who it is. Explains why the back door was left unlocked."

Brantley watched him, looking as though he was turning the words over to figure them out.

"Which means it was unexpected," the detective mused. "She didn't plan to leave."

Brantley sighed and Reese could feel the man's tension.

"We should check the security cameras in the building," Reese told them, glancing down at his watch.

Thirteen hours since Corinne Greenwood was last seen by Suzy Dumonde walking into this building.

Thirteen and a half since her friends had bid her a good night.

He wouldn't say it aloud, but he knew they were likely thinking the same thing: They were running out of time.

CORI CAME AWAKE WITH A HEADACHE THAT throbbed behind her eyes. It took a minute to realize where she was, remember how she got there. The knock on her door, the gun, being forced out of the building and into a dark blue car. She'd caught a glimpse of the license plate but couldn't remember what it was anymore. Not that it would do her any good now.

From the looks of it, there wouldn't be anyone to tell about her ordeal. No one who would care, anyway.

Didn't mean she wasn't going to find a way out of here.

She stared around the small room, taking stock. Concrete walls and floor, both of which had seen better days, a small window high up on the wall, too small for her to fit through and too high for her to get to. Without getting to her feet, she strained to look out. The sun was still up, which meant it was daytime, although she wasn't sure what day it was. It didn't take long to realize she couldn't see anything except for the grimy glass and what appeared to be weeds on the other side. So she was in a basement? What else had that sort of view?

Probably not a good escape route option.

Continuing on, she noticed a set of stairs leading up, presumably into the house. It was visible through the bars that kept her contained to this side of the room. It looked as though the space had been split down the middle, a cheap metal cot and a portable toilet on this side, nothing but the stairs on the other. The door wasn't made of bars, though. It was solid, with a couple of slots—one at the bottom, another in the middle. Like a pass-thru for bigger things than what might fit through the bars.

The stairs would be her only option, the door her biggest obstacle.

Above her head, she heard footsteps. Every now and then, she could almost make out someone talking, but it wasn't the man who had taken her. No, she knew his voice, remembered it. This was a woman.

Oh, God. Please, someone help me.

Cori didn't dare speak the words aloud. The last thing she wanted was to anger her captors in any way. He'd already hit her once, told her to sit down and shut up or he would smash her head in. The rage she'd heard had convinced her he wasn't lying. It had taken her completely by surprise considering she'd known him for what felt like her entire life, and never had she seen him angry. Not like that. And the look in his eyes... Definitely not the same treatment she'd encountered when he had been the principal of her high school. But it was definitely Principal Dugan who had knocked on her door, held a gun to her face, and forced her to leave with him.

What she couldn't understand was why.

A clanking sound had her looking up from the cot she'd been on since he had tossed her into this cell. He must've used something to knock her out, because she'd been drowsy, drifting in and out during the car ride, more when she'd arrived here. She had no idea where he'd taken her, how long the drive had been.

The door at the top of the stairs creaked open, followed by footsteps. They were lighter than his, which meant this was the woman coming down. Cori hadn't yet seen her face. The one and only time she'd been down here before, her long, stringy hair had been hanging down, shielding her face.

There was a clank as the pass-thru at the bottom of the door was opened. The scrape of plastic on concrete drew Cori to a sitting position even as the woman slammed the little door closed, locked it as though Cori might possibly be able to squeeze out of that tiny opening. It was hardly big enough for the tray of food to pass through.

When the woman started up the stairs, Cori was on her feet in an instant, racing over to the bars, gripping them tightly. "Please let me out! I need to go home! Please!"

The shuffle of feet was the only sound she heard, but even that was drowned out by the sobs that escaped as she let herself slide down to her butt.

That woman wasn't going to save her.

Chapter Thirteen

THE SECURITY CAMERAS WERE A BUST, BUT with the way their luck was going, Brantley had expected no less.

"Kinda convenient, don't you think?" Reese said as Brantley steered his way toward the capitol building.

"Too damn convenient." No way it was a coincidence, and Brantley was almost positive the squirrelly leasing agent had something to do with the recording's vanishing act. There was something up with him, Brantley just wasn't sure exactly what. Yet.

"I'm not sure I've ever seen a grown man turn that shade of pink before," Reese muttered. "I thought he was gonna piss himself when you told him you'd be lookin' into why the complex was having such problems."

Brantley grinned, although he didn't find it funny. However, the leasing agent had gone some interesting shades of color when Brantley started asking questions about the footage after the woman agent explained they'd been having issues for months, a lot of the footage was disappearing. And it was random.

"Where're we headed?" Reese asked.

Peering over at the man who'd uncovered clues that they should've unearthed during their first pass at the apartment, he exhaled. "Figured we'd stop in, give the governor an update."

"Good idea. Though we don't have much to go on."

More than they'd had. Thanks to Reese wanting a second pass.

Back at Cori's apartment, he'd had an opportunity to observe Reese, see him in action, so to speak. He'd been intrigued watching him move from place to place, taking it all in. He had a different approach to things than Brantley, that was for sure. While Reese was the contemplative sort, Brantley was more of a brute-force kind of guy. It was the first time he'd really seen Reese dig in. With their last case, it had been personal for all of them, which had made their actions a bit more … reactive, rather than proactive.

He could admit, he liked to watch Reese work.

Of course, it was possible Detective Buchanan would've uncovered what they'd missed. As it was, he'd taken the phone and had a crime scene unit coming by to dust the place for prints. If they were lucky—which was sincerely doubtful—they'd find something that would give a clue as to who Corinne had left with. No doubt in Brantley's mind, she'd left. Whether on her own accord or by force, he didn't know.

"What I wanna know is when we're gonna stop for food," Reese grumbled. "I'm even willin' to eat the crap food you're so fond of."

Just the word made Brantley's stomach rumble. "Next stop. Deal?"

Reese offered a nod, his attention out the window as they made their way to the parking for the capitol.

Brantley remembered the last time they'd come here. It had been when Kate Walker had disappeared from these very halls. Brantley and Reese had come to do their own check of the premises. Despite the fact they hadn't found the little girl, the trip had provided them with much-needed clues as to her location.

Fifteen minutes later, Brantley was pacing the governor's outer office while Governor Greenwood's secretary announced their presence.

As he was on another return from the small window, he paused, looking at Reese. The man was smoothing down his shirt, then staring down at the boots on his feet.

"You look pretty enough," Brantley told him with a smile.

He earned a glare in return.

"Coulda warned a guy he'd be payin' a visit to the governor of Texas today."

"Woulda worn a suit?" he teased.

"Maybe."

Brantley would definitely like to see the man in a suit.

The door to the office opened. "Governor Greenwood will see you now."

When the governor's secretary stepped out of the way, Brantley offered a nod, slipped past her, Reese right on his heels.

"Please tell us you've got news," Gerard said, his tone only reflecting a hint of his concern but the lines around his eyes and mouth speaking volumes.

Trina was standing at his side, her eyes rimmed with red, her face grim. She looked like she'd aged a decade since he'd seen her a few hours ago.

"Not much, but I figured I'd relay what we do have."

"Please, have a seat," Gerard offered.

Trina headed for the cushioned bench near the window, clutching the tissues she was holding on to like a lifeline. Reese eased into one of the guest chairs near the desk.

Despite the offer, Brantley was too keyed up to sit, so he returned to pacing. Trina's face was pinched in pain, her fear evident. He'd give Gerard some credit, he was hiding his own emotions relatively well. Granted, he couldn't make a living as an actor, but Brantley figured he was maintaining his composure in an effort to keep his wife from losing it entirely.

Resigning himself to giving them what little they'd learned, Brantley relayed the information he had thus far. Confirmation that Corinne had gone out, come back home, appeared to have left after that, though likely not willingly. He explained how they'd looked into the man she was interested in, the Uber driver who'd dropped her off, and the friends. He was still debating as to whether he wanted to tell them he believed Corinne's disappearance was directly related to their investigation into Lauren Tyler's disappearance. Last thing he wanted was for them to think Corinne would end up suffering the same fate as Lauren.

"While we were at her apartment, we ran into Detective Buchanan."

"Baz." Governor Greenwood nodded. "Yes. He's assigned to her case. I hope you'll utilize his skill set to help."

"So you know him?"

"I know of him," the governor said. "He's a damn fine detective. Been with the department for ten years now. Started out on patrol. When I asked for the best they had, his name was offered first."

Although Brantley didn't have a problem with Baz, as he was referred to by his friends, he would certainly be doing some background checks on the man. He'd already passed along the detective's information to JJ, asking that she contact him so they could sync up with what they'd all learned, ensure they were keeping everyone in the loop.

"I've also reached out to the Texas Rangers to assist," Governor Greenwood noted, then looked up at Brantley. "But I've informed them all that you're leading the investigation. They're to contact you if they come up with anything."

Brantley nodded. "I'd like to give them a call, let them know what we have so far. No reason to work in a vacuum here. More people looking for her, better our chances of finding her."

"Understood."

What worried him the most was the fact that Corinne had disappeared without a trace. Simply vanished. And from where Brantley stood, there were no more leads to follow, no clues to unearth. Brantley felt as though they'd gone headlong into a brick wall and he didn't know how to get around it.

"I heard you've been looking into Lauren Tyler's case," Governor Greenwood noted. "Do you think this has anything to do with that?"

Well, that made the decision as to whether he wanted to share or not.

"It's possible," Brantley told him, maintaining eye contact. "Anything's possible. We haven't spoken to Corinne yet, but we've reached out to her. We did sit down with Lauren's mother and father, and I've had some discussions with the teachers and the principal of Coyote Ridge High School."

"Anything worth mentioning?" Gerard probed.

"Not yet." Brantley sighed, deciding on full disclosure. "I have to believe I might've tipped someone off and because Corinne is possibly the one who can solve the case, even if she doesn't realize it, whoever took Lauren has decided to tie up loose ends."

Brantley and Reese would have to go back through, look into anyone and everyone they'd spoken with about Lauren's case, see where they were at the time of Corinne's disappearance.

"So what now?" Trina asked, her voice trembling.

"We've still got a few avenues to go down," Brantley lied, intent they would have them by the time night fell. He damn sure wasn't giving up. If he had to personally visit every single person Corinne had come into contact with in the whole of her twenty-four years, he damn sure would. "I assure you, we'll work every angle we have until we find her."

"Find my baby, Brantley," Gerard pleaded. "Bring her home to us."

He was damn sure gonna try.

And pray like hell, to boot.

Half an hour later, they were sitting at a table at Wendy's.

Brantley was staring at his phone, exchanging texts with JJ, waiting for her to hit him back.

"What next?" Reese asked.

Lifting his gaze, he peered at his partner. "Did you get the feelin' that leasing agent was keepin' somethin' from us?"

"You think? Guy's hands were shakin'. Couldn't get us outta there fast enough."

"I noticed that, too." Brantley drew on the straw of his drink. "I want to know what else is on those videos. The other ones that vanished."

Reese leaned back, seemed to ponder his statement. "Good thing is, they maintain their recordings in the cloud."

"Which means?"

"Means they're accessible." Reese nodded to Brantley's phone.

"Not through legal channels," Brantley noted.

"No. That's where immunity and means comes in."

"True. But then comes the problem with convicting the bastard responsible. Whoever it may be."

Reese stared back at him. "Good point."

"If JJ hacks those cameras, anything we find won't be admissible."

Reese leaned in, expression turning icy. "Right now, the only thing we need to find is Corinne. Fuck how we get to that point. That's our job, right? The police and the DAs can figure out the rest."

Brantley knew he was right. Deep in his gut, he knew it. But he couldn't help thinking about Juliet Prince, the woman who had kidnapped Travis's daughter. He'd been keeping track of the FBI's investigation. Unfortunately, Juliet's trail had gone cold, which meant they were no closer to bringing that woman to justice.

"Look," Reese said, voice low. "I figure there's a reason the governor wants us to take point on this. Corinne's his daughter. He doesn't give a shit how you find her. Leave it to APD and the state troopers or the Texas Rangers to skim the textbook on how to cover our asses later."

"Off the books," he said, thinking about Travis's comment when they'd discussed the task force originally.

"Exactly."

Well, as long as they were on the same page.

"Then I say we head back to the barn, see what else JJ's dug up," Brantley suggested.

Reese snagged the Frosty he'd set aside. "And I'll take this for the road."

GETTING BACK TO COYOTE RIDGE TOOK ROUGHLY half an hour thanks to Sunday afternoon traffic, or the lack thereof. They'd both remained relatively quiet, the weight of this case beginning to add to the tension. When they'd been looking for Lauren Tyler, there hadn't been a sense of urgency. Being that she'd been gone for nine years, the hurry-up-and-solve mentality wasn't there. But with Corinne … Reese knew they couldn't slow their momentum. They had to continue to pursue any and all leads, pull on threads until they unraveled the mystery behind who took the governor's daughter.

As Brantley steered the truck down his driveway, Reese looked at the property. Really looked at it. He had to assume Brantley owned roughly ten acres, maybe a little more. There were no neighbors on either side. Not that he could see, anyway. More farmland, most of which was being utilized, unlike Brantley's land.

But it was the house that caught his attention like it usually did. From the outside, it looked much like a lot of the white farmhouses in the area. Two stories, wraparound porch complete with swing. It was the second story that made him curious since he'd never gone up there before, despite the fact he'd been staying over at Brantley's for weeks now.

"Just curious, but how much space do you have in that house?"

"Too much. I use the kitchen, the bedroom, and the bathroom. Why?"

"You don't even go upstairs."

"Nothin' up there but some bedrooms, a game room, and a coupla baths."

"No furniture? Really?"

"What?" Brantley smirked. "You think I'm hidin' a couch and dining table up there?"

Reese chuckled. Funny how he'd never really paid much attention to the house. Now that he was, he had to admit, he liked the charm of it. Didn't necessarily suit Brantley, but it was nice.

"How many square feet?" he asked, curious.

"Thirty-nine hundred or somethin' like that."

Wow. That was a lot.

"And no, to answer your silent question, I didn't need all that space. I bought it because it was the only thing on the market at the time."

Reese fully understood that. Coyote Ridge real estate was in high demand.

"You plan to do anything with the upstairs?"

Brantley shrugged, putting the truck in park. "One day. Maybe."

Reese climbed out of the truck, followed Reese to the porch.

"Gonna make some coffee," Brantley said as they walked into the house. "Want some?"

"More than my next breath," he admitted.

While Brantley set the pot to brew, Reese moved to the refrigerator, snagged the carton of milk, then took two mugs from the cabinet.

When he turned back, he found Brantley leaning against the island, arms crossed over his chest.

"What?"

"Nothin'."

Reese grinned. "That's not your nothin' face."

Brantley laughed, dropping his arms and stepping toward him.

Reese didn't back up, didn't try to get away. No, when Brantley was close enough, Reese reached for him, curling a hand behind his neck, pulling him in closer.

"I didn't get to wake you appropriately this mornin'," Brantley muttered, their lips brushing.

"I'm sure there'll be plenty of mornin's for you to do so."

Brantley pulled back, locked eyes with him. Reese could see something brewing, wasn't sure what it was.

Unfortunately, he didn't get to find out because rather than speak, Brantley leaned in, their mouths melding together. Not that he cared to talk when they could be doing this. It probably should've been a simple kiss considering the task they were tackling, but it wasn't. Then again, nothing about Brantley was simple.

Next thing he knew, Reese was pinned between Brantley's body and the island, the hard ridge of Brantley's erection grinding against his own. A groan escaped when Brantley rolled his hips, more friction applied to Reese's straining cock. This man could so easily work him up. A look, a touch. But this ... having Brantley's weight pressed against him was almost too much to bear.

"Keep that up, I'm gonna get you naked," Brantley warned.

"Me?" Reese nipped his lower lip. "I'm pretty sure you're the one humpin' me right now."

Brantley's deep groan signaled another kiss, this one heating more than the last, hands beginning to wander.

"Brantley..."

"Hmm?"

"JJ's waitin' for us."

"Let her wait."

"She won't. She'll come lookin'." Reese remembered the time she'd come to find them when Reese had been kissing Brantley in the truck.

"True." Brantley eased back, sucking on Reese's lower lip. "Bedroom door's got a lock on it. Or better yet, I'll take you upstairs. We can hide out while we christen all those empty rooms."

Reese knew it was wrong to be thinking that was a damn good idea. It was wrong because they had a case to deal with. And finding Corinne was more important than them exploring one another.

"Fine," Brantley said gruffly, obviously thinking the same thing Reese was.

When the man took a step back and dropped his hands with a dissatisfied grunt, Reese laughed, letting him go.

"I'll pour the coffee, you add the crap to yours, then we'll head over to the barn."

"You say it like you need a plan, Navy boy."

Brantley adjusted himself. "Trust me, I do. Otherwise, I'm just gonna get you naked and say fuck it to everything else."

Reese felt himself blush, hated that he did.

He put the milk away, stirred his coffee. He was just about to follow Brantley out to the barn when there was a knock on the door.

"Expectin' someone?" they both asked at the same time.

Clearly not.

"Detective Buchanan," Brantley greeted as he opened the door. "Didn't realize you'd be makin' house calls."

"Please, call me Baz," he said easily. "And I'm here to talk to … JJ?"

Interesting.

"Sure thing. She's actually in our office," Brantley explained. "The barn in the back. Follow me."

"You got news for us?" Reese asked, hopeful he'd come bearing gifts of the detective variety.

"Unfortunately, no. JJ mentioned she had some thoughts, figured it would be best for me to come here."

The three of them fell into step, Reese pulling up the rear as they made the trek to the barn. Brantley keyed in the code, opened the door, and some old-school Blake Shelton escaped, the man singing about Austin still loving someone.

Reese stepped inside first.

"'Bout time you boys showed up," JJ announced once Brantley had instructed Alexa to turn down the music. "Thought for sure you'd gotten waylaid in the house."

"Coffee," Reese said, lifting his cup as though she might need proof.

"I believe you. And even if I didn't, I promise I won't be comin' to check on y'all in the—" Her eyes widened as she took in their guest. "Sorry. Didn't realize we had company."

Clearly not seeing JJ's interest was more than the man's job description, Brantley made the introductions.

Reese watched as JJ's face transformed into a soft smile. It was likely the first time he'd seen her … shy. She stepped out from behind her desk to greet the detective, shaking his hand when he offered it.

"It's a pleasure to meet you," Baz said, lingering a little longer than he had when he'd introduced himself to them earlier in the day.

And Reese was almost certain JJ blushed.

He glanced over at Brantley, smirked.

"Let's get to it, shall we?" Brantley stated.

Reese followed Brantley around behind the bank of monitors when JJ did. Baz joined on the other side.

"Like you suspected," she began, "your guy at the apartments was hidin' somethin'."

Reese watched as her fingers flew over the keyboard before an image appeared on the center monitor.

"I was able to get into their security feed. When he said they no longer had the videos, he was tellin' the truth. Someone deleted the footage. In fact, someone deletes a lot of the footage." She glanced over her shoulder. "I'm pretty sure the guy's a perv and he's manipulatin' the cameras. What I uncovered was mostly close-ups of the women in the building, mostly by the pool and in the gym. Probably deletes it so no one asks why they're gettin' up close and personal with a set of breasts. Kinda creepy."

Definitely creepy. Then again, Reese hadn't been impressed with the guy.

"Could you find last night's footage?"

"It hurts my feelin's that you'd even ask that," she said easily. "It was deleted from the server early this mornin'." She leaned in. "A few minutes before eight to be exact." JJ sat back, sighed. "You're probably not gonna like what I found."

Reese watched as a video began to play. The timestamp in the bottom left reflected 0207 this morning.

Guy appeared in the hallway, but his face was obscured by the cowboy hat on his head. Despite the fact it wasn't quite cold enough, he was wearing a heavy coat that covered his arms, hiding any chance of them getting a look at some sort of identifying mark.

"He seems a bit overdressed for the weather," Baz noted.

"My thoughts exactly," JJ agreed.

The four of them watched as the man on the screen knocked on Corinne's apartment door then poked the doorbell. The camera was at the end of the hall, so it didn't provide a good angle.

"Any way you can get closer?"

JJ clicked a few keys; the camera zoomed in. A minute later, the door opened, a few words were exchanged, but that was where the friendly encounter ended.

"That's a gun," JJ said, pointing to the spot on the screen where the weapon was.

The man was doing his best to conceal the handgun beneath his jacket, motioning with it. Without audio, there was no way to tell what he was saying. Corinne's face never appeared, but it was clear she went back inside. The man stepped forward, part of his body hidden from the angle of the camera, but the light was still spilling out into the hallway, which meant the door was still open.

Next thing the camera captured was Corinne stepping out into the hall. She looked nervous as the man put his arm around her shoulder in a casual move, tugging her against him, the other hand pinning the gun to her side. The video showed them walking down the hall, back toward the elevators.

JJ keyed in something again, the image flipping to another camera, a different angle, this one in the hall with the elevators. Guy pushed the button, stepped back. A few seconds later, he was urging her forward, into the elevator. Right before she slipped inside, Cori's face lifted, her eyes locking on the camera she obviously knew was there. She mouthed the words help me, stark terror reflected in her stare.

Reese winced, fury igniting in his veins, made worse by the fact they couldn't find this bastard and make him pay for taking her.

"Son of a bitch," Brantley muttered.

"That's the last we get of them," JJ explained. "Based on the feeds from the lobby cameras, they didn't go out that way."

"Or someone managed to erase their exit," Brantley grunted.

Yep. And there wasn't a single inch of the guy's face revealed, which meant he knew where all the cameras were. In order to know that, he would've had to be familiar with the place. Or cased it before hand. Ruled out the guy she met at the wine bar. Wouldn't have had enough time to do that.

"Could you go back?" Baz suggested. "To when the guy gets to the door."

More keying, then the feed started again with the man stepping up to the door, raising his hand to knock.

"Pause it there," Baz instructed.

JJ did.

"Back just a little."

More adjusting

"There. Can you zoom in on his hand?"

JJ dragged the image closer, but it obscured as she did. The four of them leaned in at the same time.

"Looks like a tattoo," JJ noted.

Yeah. Problem was, the image was too grainy to make it out. There was something inked on the guy's right hand, peeking out from beneath the cuff of the jacket.

"I can play with it," JJ stated. "It may take some time, but I'll see if I can clean it up."

Reese glanced over at Brantley, noticed the man was still staring at the screen.

"Son of a bitch," Brantley muttered again.

Yeah. His sentiments exactly.

JJ HADN'T EXPECTED HER DAY TO GO this way, but she couldn't deny it was a nice change of pace.

And yes, she was referring to the handsome detective who had joined their little task force, if only temporarily.

While JJ had gotten to work on the video, attempting to clean up the image in an effort to identify the tattoo Baz had noticed, the men had continued to discuss the case, outlining what they could on the whiteboard. And every time Baz spoke up, JJ's ears perked. There was something intensely erotic about his voice. It wasn't so much deep as it was raspy, every word spoken like he was talking to a lover.

Of course, it didn't hurt that she had some new eye candy to check out. While she had always thought Brantley Walker was the absolute most attractive man she'd ever laid eyes on, Sebastian Buchanan had now taken that coveted spot. Dark blond hair, pretty blue eyes, and lips that looked as though they were made to kiss… Yes, it was safe to say she'd had a couple of fantasies about the guy and she'd only known him for a couple of hours.

It wasn't like she was ogling him though. She had more respect for him than that. However, every so often, she would look up to catch what he was saying. Most of the time she would find his gaze straying back to hers, meeting briefly before he turned his attention to Brantley and Reese. During those moments, there would be a strange churning in her stomach. Anticipation, maybe? Whatever it was, it was both intriguing and annoying.

She was fairly certain there was a hint of interest on his part, but it wasn't like she knew Baz. He could very well look at everyone he worked with like that. And it wasn't like she was going to pursue the guy. As far as she was concerned, she was off men for the foreseeable future. Her life was far simpler when she didn't involve herself in relationships.

"Hey, JJ?"

She jerked her attention away from her computer monitor to find Baz standing in front of her desk, peering down at her with a brilliant smile on his handsome face.

"I'm sorry?" she said, realizing she'd clearly been lost in her thoughts.

"I was wonderin' if maybe you'd like to grab a bite with me. I haven't eaten yet today."

JJ looked over to get Brantley's reaction only to find that the man wasn't there. Nor was Reese.

"I … uh…"

"No worries if you don't," Baz said easily. "Just thought I'd make the offer. Give me a chance to get more information on the case."

His mouth said this was about work, but his eyes were saying something else entirely. And surprisingly, JJ was fond of the combination.

"Sure," she blurted. "Yeah. Late lunch, early dinner's good. Either way. We can go to the diner, if you don't mind."

"Lady's choice."

JJ got to her feet, unplugged her laptop before tucking it into her backpack. She snagged her keys from her top drawer, then led the way to the door.

"This is an interesting setup you've got here."

"Brantley's doin'," she admitted. "He bought the house when he retired from the Navy. Set up shop here. When the governor requested he lead the task force, he converted it to an office."

"So, what? He have hay and horses in here before?"

She grinned. "No. A couple of computers though." She motioned toward the stairs leading to the loft. "As you can see, it's still under construction."

Ever the gentleman, Baz opened the door, holding it for her while she stepped outside. She watched it close, then ensured the lock engaged before gesturing for him to shut the big barn door, concealing the other doors.

"I know it's not my business," he said as they walked toward their cars, "but are Brantley and Reese ... together?"

"Yeah." She peered up at him when she said it, gauging his reaction.

He glanced down, grinned. "No, I'm not homophobic, JJ. To each his own and all that. Just tryin' to get a lay of the land."

"Just makin' sure."

He laughed and she realized she liked the sound of that, too.

"And you?" he asked, pausing beside her car.

JJ stopped and stared up at him, directly into those teal-blue eyes. "What?"

"Is there a husband or boyfriend I should be worried about?"

So she hadn't been imagining that spark between them.

It was her turn to smile. "No. I'm quite single."

And she intended to stay that way.

Of course, if she really meant it, she would've said it out loud.

Chapter Fourteen

TELLING THE GOVERNOR YOU HAD NO NEWS on his missing daughter was not something Brantley ever thought he'd be doing. It also wasn't something he would've ever wanted to do. Unfortunately, that was the gist of their investigation and exactly what he relayed when he made the call later that night, despite the hour. There was no way he would've been able to hold off until morning. Gerard and Trina needed the updates, needed to hold on to hope that they would find their daughter quickly.

Brantley was holding on to that hope as well, although it wasn't looking great. Aside from a grainy image of what appeared to be a tattoo, they were no closer to finding whoever had taken Corinne Greenwood from her apartment.

Now, as the clock ticked around to one in the morning, Brantley knew they had to call it a night. As it was, Brantley and Reese had gone back to speak to Lauren Tyler's mother in an effort to find out what Corinne and Lauren had in common from that day. Who had they hung out with, who did they spend most of their time with, that sort of thing. She hadn't been all that helpful in terms of remembering names, but she had provided them access to all of Lauren's yearbooks from back then. They had brought them back to the barn, started going through them.

"Where'd you run off to this afternoon?" he asked JJ as he got to his feet, stretched his back.

"Baz took me to eat," she said, although she didn't look up at him.

"Really?"

Her eyes flipped up to his. "It wasn't like that. A business dinner, that's all."

"Business." He smirked. "Right."

JJ glared his way, making him laugh.

"What do you think of him?" he inquired.

"Nice guy. Smart."

"Handsome," Brantley inserted.

JJ grinned. "Sure. Some might think so."

Some? Brantley had watched her interaction with the man. She was more than a little smitten if he had to guess.

"I think it's time to call it a night."

She'd been going nonstop since she returned and now she looked as exhausted as he felt.

"You need to head home," he ordered. "Get some sleep and we'll start again in a few hours."

Her eyes swung up to the second floor. "It'd be easier if you'd put a pull-out couch up there."

Brantley looked up at the hayloft. "So what? You can camp out there at night?"

"The thought did cross my mind." JJ's gaze scanned the space around them as she frowned. "Where's Reese?"

"I sent him inside. He was hungry."

"I take it the two of you made up?" She eased back in her chair, stretching her arms over her head.

"Yeah."

"That's good, B. I'm happy for you. I saw him at Moonshiners Saturday night. He looked miserable."

Brantley strolled over, perched on the corner of her desk. "Why aren't you goin' home?"

A half-hearted shrug was the only response.

"JJ?"

"What?"

"Somethin' goin' on?"

"Besides us tryin' to find Dante's missing sister? No."

"Talk to me."

"Nothin' to talk about," she mumbled as she got to her feet.

"This have to do with Dante?" He couldn't imagine it was easy for her to have to deal with him on this case considering the fallout they'd had recently.

"He's been callin' me," she told him. "I asked him to leave me alone, but now he's usin' the case as an excuse."

"Tell him to call me if he has questions."

"I tried. This is Dante we're talkin' about." She sighed heavily. "He'll use any advantage he has."

"I thought you broke it off."

"I did. And he was in agreement. But Dante's not the sort to like to admit defeat."

Brantley narrowed his gaze on her face. "Meaning?"

"Meaning he used that woman as a way to get a rise out of me. He was hopin' to piss me off, to hurt me. When he realized it didn't…"

"He'll continue until he can."

"Unfortunately." She stood. "I just don't want to find him waitin' at my house when I get there."

Although he held in the frustrated growl, Brantley's molars clamped together. That sounded like Dante. High and mighty Dante Greenwood stalking his ex-girlfriend in an attempt to get her to admit she had feelings for him only so he could turn around and dump her. Some people never changed.

"It's fine," she said quickly.

"Maybe we should put up some cameras," he suggested. "That way you can monitor your house when you're not there."

Her eyes cut to his. "I'm not opposed to that idea." She grinned. "On the outside only."

Brantley winked at her as he stood. "Outside only. Now scoot. Go home and get some sleep."

"Yep. Headin' that way now," she said, getting to her feet. "I can grab a couple hours' shut-eye. That way I can be back bright and early."

"You want me to drive you home?"

She wrinkled her nose, offered up a pffft. "I'm quite capable of drivin' myself home, thank you very much."

"Then text me when you get there so I know you made it safely."

"Fine. Slave driver."

Brantley smiled, glad she'd lost that morose look. He hated to think of JJ getting beaten down emotionally by the likes of Dante. Maybe the guy hadn't hit her all those years ago, but that didn't make him a stand-up guy. Emotional abuse was as significant as physical. He only hoped she knew that. Unfortunately, it didn't really matter that she'd broken things off with him, either. Some guys didn't know when to quit.

After walking JJ to her car, Brantley went into the house, found Reese in the kitchen. He had showered and wore only a pair of athletic shorts as he worked at the island preparing something that smelled fantastic. He was quite fond of seeing Reese in this state of undress. Relaxed, all that naturally tanned skin on display. The man truly was a masterpiece, made even more so by his height and those long limbs and sleek musculature.

"Hey," Brantley greeted, coming up behind Reese and sliding his arms around his trim waist, feeling his abs contract when he pressed a kiss to his neck. "Makin' dinner?"

"I am," he said easily, leaning into him. "Salisbury steak, mashed potatoes, and peas. You've got about five minutes before it's ready."

"Plenty of time for a shower." He kissed Reese's neck once more, then released him.

His time in the military had made him fast and efficient when it came to hygiene. He was back in the kitchen in the allotted five minutes, finding that Reese had finished preparing their meal, had it dished up on plates at the island with iced tea to go with it.

They dug in, neither of them saying much as hunger was the driving factor. Not until he'd had seconds did the rumbling in his stomach finally stop.

"What's for dessert?" he asked, downing the last of his tea before carrying both plate and glass around to rinse.

"Me," Reese said, deadpan.

Brantley's gaze slammed into the man, a slow smirk forming. "Just a warnin', I might want seconds of that, too."

Reese smiled, that blush creeping into his cheeks. Why Brantley found that hot, he didn't know. There was so damn much about Reese Tavoularis that turned him on.

When Reese passed over his plate, Brantley snatched it up, set it in the sink as he turned off the water. Grabbing a dish towel, he dried his hands and walked around the island as Reese was getting to his feet.

"Where do you think you're goin'?" he asked, his voice thickened by lust.

"Where do you want me?" Reese countered, unable to move when Brantley backed him up against the island.

Brantley jerked his chin toward the island top. "Up there."

"Here?" Reese smirked, tapping the granite countertop. "Where we eat our meals?"

"Yep. This qualifies as a meal, does it not?"

Because of his height, Reese didn't have to do much to hoist himself up so he was sitting on the granite countertop.

Brantley had been thinking about this all damn day. Getting Reese alone, finding some spare time to make up for what they'd lost this past week. He probably should've been taking things slow now that they were getting back on track, but he couldn't help himself. He was done with slow. They'd gone that route already.

Brantley stepped between Reese's long legs, slid a hand behind his neck, and pulled him in for a kiss. "Touch me, Reese."

While he did, Brantley owned the kiss, dominating Reese's mouth with his own. Their tongues dueled, soft groans escaping as firm hands began to wander.

The man's touch was exquisite. More confident as time passed, but gentle all the same. From the very first time Reese had touched him, Brantley'd been addicted. He could get a high simply from having the man's hands on him.

"Love when you touch me," he muttered, sliding his lips down Reese's jaw as he tugged on the loose-fitting shorts Reese wore.

Those hands disappeared when Reese lifted himself up so Brantley could free him of his clothing, but returned when Brantley had jerked them down his legs, letting them fall to the floor.

"I'll take that dessert now," he mumbled, stepping back and urging Reese to lean back by planting his hand on his chest.

He watched Reese recline onto his elbows, enjoying the way his long, lean body coiled and flexed as he moved. With the thick pads of his chest, the deep grooves of his abdomen, the man was a walking wet dream.

Brantley manhandled him then, turning Reese so his legs were on the countertop, too, that beautiful body stretched longways on the granite.

He started with his mouth, kissing his way down as he gripped Reese's rigid cock, stroking lightly, teasing because he knew Reese enjoyed it. There was no rush, and he took his time, pausing to nibble on Reese's nipples, listening to the dark rumbles that escaped, watching the flex of his abdomen as he rolled his hips in an effort to get Brantley's full attention where he wanted it.

"Brantley…"

"You like when I play with your nipples." It wasn't a question. They both knew it was true. The man was super sensitive, another thing Brantley found ridiculously hot.

"Ahh, God," Reese groaned loudly. "Suck me, Brantley. Let me feel your mouth on me."

Because he asked so nicely, Brantley gave Reese what he wanted. But he wasn't aiming to make him come. Not right away.

No, the pleasure for both of them was in the pace. Brantley took his time, licking, sucking, reacquainting himself with every delicious inch of his rock-hard shaft, the wide head, his heavy sac. He worked Reese for the longest time, light licks followed by forceful suction. Up, down, around. By the time Reese was thrusting his hips, Brantley was ready for him. A strong, demanding hand palmed his head, holding him in place while Reese fucked his mouth, taking his pleasure from him.

When Reese came, it was with a throaty moan and Brantley's name falling from his lips.

Best damn dessert he'd ever had.

REESE WOKE BEFORE THE SUN WAS UP, content to find Brantley still sleeping beside him. He knew the man had difficulty sleeping, but it seemed he did better when Reese was around. And if that wasn't a boost to his ego, he wasn't sure what was.

Rather than get up and get the day underway, Reese spooned behind Brantley, unable to ignore the way his cock hardened even more as he molded himself to all that smooth, warm flesh.

"Mmm," Brantley mumbled, reaching back and sliding his hand down Reese's thigh. "Mornin'."

"Not a good mornin'?" Reese whispered, kissing Brantley's shoulder.

"Not yet, but it's certainly goin' that direction."

Chuckling, he continued his exploration with his tongue and lips, spurred by the soft rumbles coming from the sexy man tucked up against him. He paused only when Brantley leaned away, reaching for the bottle of lubricant on the nightstand. Because he didn't offer a condom, Reese took it to mean he wanted to be teased, so he urged Brantley onto his stomach.

"Spread your legs," he mumbled, brushing his lips over Brantley's shoulder.

His legs widened, allowing Reese to slide his fingers down the crack of his ass. He used only his fingers to fondle Brantley's hole, working in deep, earning more grunts and groans.

"Do you like when I do this?" he asked, not sure what was prompting him to be quite so verbal.

"Fuck, yes," Brantley groaned, his body rocking in an attempt to get him to go faster.

Things progressed from there. Hotter, so fucking hot as Reese impaled Brantley with three fingers, the man's hips rocking, his cock trapped beneath him as he ground his hips into the mattress. Reese continued to kiss his neck and shoulders, letting Brantley's guttural groans work him into a frenzy. Next thing Reese knew, he was mounting Brantley, gliding the head of his dick against the tight entrance to his ass.

"Brantley," he groaned, rubbing his forehead against Brantley's shoulder, resisting the urge to impale him. "I need to be inside you."

Brantley shifted as though giving him permission.

Reese angled his cock, pushed his hips forward, breaching Brantley's hole.

"Fuck..." He was so fucking hot. The feel of his body clamping down on him...

It was too much but not nearly enough.

"Fuck, yes," Brantley groaned, pushing back against him. "Fuck me, Reese."

It felt ... so fucking good. Better than good. Hell, better than anything he'd ever felt before. He sank in deeper. Slow. Easy. Working himself to the hilt before retreating. He tried to maintain the pace, wanting to savor the intensity that coursed through him from the blistering heat. The control he had on himself snapped as he drove into Brantley, fucking him harder, faster. Up on his knees now, Reese gripped Brantley's hips, jerking him back as he watched his cock penetrate him.

It was then he realized why it felt obscenely better than the last time.

No condom.

"Oh, fuck," he bit out, halting his movements, buried all the way inside Brantley. "No condom. Oh, fuck. I'm sorry. So fucking—"

Brantley's hand slapped down on his thigh. "Fuck me, Reese. I trust you and you can goddamn well trust me. Fuck. Me."

Because there was absolutely no question as to whether he trusted Brantley, Reese did as Brantley demanded. He fucked him. Hard. He lost complete control, loving the overwhelming heat that consumed him as he drove them both to heights Reese had only ever found with this man.

"I'm gonna come," he warned seconds before he slammed into Brantley one final time, his cock erupting.

Brantley groaned, his back muscles tensing right before a shudder racked them both.

Reese collapsed on top of him, letting his spent cock slide out.

"Fuck. I'm not sure anything's ever felt that good," Reese muttered. "No. I take that back. I know nothin's ever felt that good."

Brantley rolled to his side, forcing Reese to move off him. Strong arms banded around him, holding him tight.

"Won't disagree," Brantley said, still breathing hard. "Never done that before."

"What? Without a condom?"

Brantley nodded.

And fuck if that didn't swell Reese's head. Yeah, there was no doubt he loved this man, had fallen headfirst, but to know he'd been Brantley's first for something … well, that made him feel like he could conquer the world.

An hour later, Reese joined Brantley at the barn only to find JJ had already arrived. She was sitting at her desk, a cup of coffee steaming at her side, eyes glued to the monitor. She didn't look up, didn't greet him as she usually did.

Casting a quick look at Brantley, he cocked an eyebrow.

"This is how I found her," he said, not bothering to muffle his voice.

JJ didn't seem to realize they were even there.

"I guess she's not that interested in sausage biscuits, huh?"

That got her attention. Not only did she look up, JJ stood, glaring over as though she thought he might be joking.

Holding up the plate of biscuits and sausage, he nodded toward the kitchen. "I'll just put 'em in there."

Brantley's laugh followed him as did JJ's footsteps.

"You're here early," Reese said as JJ snagged a napkin and a sausage biscuit.

"Work," she said around a mouthful.

"Did you sleep at all?"

JJ shrugged. "Hour. Maybe two. Had an energy drink, couple cups of coffee."

Reese had to work to translate the words because she continued to bite and chew as though she hadn't eaten in a month.

While she reached for another, Reese poured himself some coffee, added the requisite sugar and milk, then carried it and the pot toward his desk. He set his own cup down, refilled Brantley's, and returned the pot to the warmer.

"Dare I ask if there's anything new?" He glanced from Brantley to JJ then back.

"She's workin' on the tattoo."

"I was thinkin' about that." Reese perched on the edge of his desk, sipped his coffee. "We can't see what the design is, but is there anyone we've talked to or anyone we've noted as knowing her who has a tattoo in that spot? Maybe we can use that as a lead."

JJ stopped with the biscuit near her lips, then dumped it onto the napkin. "Reese, you're a fuckin' genius."

Yeah. JJ definitely needed to lay off the caffeine.

While JJ's fingers flew over her keyboard, Reese ventured over to the whiteboard on the wall, studied the timeline they'd laid out, the various names of people who had come into contact with Lauren Tyler before her disappearance. Perhaps they were off base, but Reese was going on the assumption that Corinne's disappearance had to do with Lauren's. He didn't believe in coincidence.

"Did we get anything on the guy the professor mentioned?"

"Jason Montgomery," Brantley supplied.

"Yes. Him."

JJ didn't answer, once again focused on her computer screen.

Brantley shrugged, clearly not having an answer.

Rather than pull JJ from her concentration, Reese headed over to the computer that was connected to the big screen mounted on the wall. He keyed in the name, came up with a good dozen.

"Narrow it down by age," Brantley said, joining him.

Reese typed in the range he suspected Jason would be, roughly three to four years older than Lauren was his max, her age the minimum.

"Leaves us with three." Brantley studied the screen, the three images that appeared. "Where did they live at the time of Lauren's disappearance?"

"Drops us to two," Reese noted, eliminating the one who resided in Alaska at that time, as well as currently. "Last knowns are…" He tapped a few buttons, waited.

Brantley chuckled. "Didn't help."

Nope. Both were in the central Texas area.

"What about social media?" JJ suggested, appearing at Reese's side.

Because he knew she was far faster at retrieving that information, he stepped aside, allowed her to pull it up.

Side by side on one screen were two Facebook accounts, the other Instagram.

Between the three of them, they skimmed through images, until Brantley held up a hand toward one photo. "This one. Pull it up."

JJ did, bringing the image into full view on the screen. It was of a man with his arm around a woman, both mugging for the camera. But Reese immediately saw what Brantley had. There, on his right hand, was a tattoo, in the same spot as the one from the image.

"Show me his profile page."

It appeared on the screen and there it was, hometown: Coyote Ridge.

"Well, that solves that mystery," JJ said, relief in her voice.

"Not quite." Brantley instructed her to bring the image back up. "How tall is this guy?"

"Five ten, according to the information we pulled up," Reese answered.

"And Corinne's what? Five seven? Five eight?"

"About, yeah."

"This guy's not as tall as the one from the video," Brantley stated. "That guy had a couple of inches on her. Closer to six one, maybe six two."

"I'm sure there's plenty of guys who've got hand tattoos," JJ added, her disappointment evident.

Brantley glanced back at them. "How tall is Professor William Dugan?"

JJ began tapping keys, pulling up the man's information. "Six…" Her gaze shot to Brantley. "Two."

"What're you thinkin'?" Reese asked.

"Just that it seems awfully damn convenient that Dugan offers up Jason Montgomery's name and the guy who takes Corinne's got the same hand tattoo."

"You think he staged it? To make it look like Montgomery took her?"

"It's possible." Brantley turned to JJ. "Get in touch with this guy. I want to chat with him. I don't think he's our man, but we need to rule him out."

"We should also run through the previous day's footage," Reese stated. "See if Montgomery or Dugan came into the building at some point. If either of them is our guy, they'd have to case the place to know where all the cameras are."

"Good point," Brantley noted, glancing at JJ. "While you do that, we'll pay Mr. Montgomery a visit."

"But you don't think he's the guy?" JJ countered.

"No, but maybe he can give us some insight as to why Dugan would want to put the heat on him," Reese answered, believing he was on the same page as Brantley.

It was something, he figured. Not much, but better than nothing.

CORI SAT ON THE CONCRETE FLOOR, LEGS crisscrossed, staring at the stairs, waiting for someone to appear. From her vantage point, she'd be able to see the person and she wanted to get a good look at the woman, figuring she was her only hope of getting out of here.

Of course, she was also on the lookout for William—or rather Bill, as he had insisted she call him. That was due to self-preservation, of course. She planned to be ready the next time he came in. She had to be. She needed to get out of here but that wasn't going to happen unless she made the effort.

As it was, the woman had continued to bring her food. A tray every few hours. Peanut butter on wheat bread, and a glass of lukewarm water. Although she wasn't hungry, Cori had forced herself to eat it, to drink because she had to keep her strength up. No way could she fight him off if she was starved and dehydrated.

The sound of footsteps signaled someone was coming.

Cori hopped to her feet, held her breath, waited. There was nowhere for her to hide, no element of surprise to be had thanks to the bars that provided no cover.

She doubted they were coming to bring her food since it had only been an hour since they'd delivered the last sandwich. The footsteps were loud, meaning only one thing. This wasn't the woman paying her a visit. It was him.

Oh, God.

A tremor of terror coiled in her stomach at the thought of what he might want. He hadn't come to visit her since he'd forced her out of her apartment at gunpoint and tossed her into this room, and she'd been hoping he wouldn't.

The clank of the lock disengaging sounded overly loud in the concrete room, but Cori remained where she was, held her breath.

"Don't even think about it," came the warning.

Next thing Cori knew, she was being manhandled backward, tossed in the direction of the cot. Her body missed, slamming hard into the metal side as she sprawled onto the floor. Pain ricocheted through her entire body, drawing a cry from her as she slumped to the floor. Despite her best efforts, tears sprang to her eyes.

"It's time for your bath."

Cori's eyes widened in fear, her pain suddenly numbed by the threat she could see in his eyes. "No. I don't want a bath. I want to go home. Just let me go and I swear I won't tell anyone you took me."

The smile that formed on his face was full of menace. "Too late for that, Corinne. This is your new home now."

This man was deranged. Completely out of his mind. What had happened to him? She remembered him well and the principal she'd known had been friendly and quick to smile. This guy … he creeped her out.

"Why?" she blurted, dragging herself up by using the rails of the cot. "Why did you bring me here?"

"It's the only place for you to go," he said simply, as though that was a legitimate answer.

"Where am I?" she asked, although the location didn't really matter, but it would help when she managed to escape. At least if she had her bearings, she would know which direction to head when she made it outside. Because she would make it outside, by God.

"Doesn't matter. We're miles from anyone who can help you." He pointed toward the cot. "Lie down. I told you, it's time for your bath."

Cori shook her head vehemently. "No. Please."

His eyes narrowed. "Don't make me force you, because I will if I have to."

Her gaze swung to the cot, then back to him. She couldn't bring herself to move, even though she didn't think he made idle threats. He certainly didn't sound like he was joking.

"Last. Warning."

Still, her feet wouldn't move. A squeal escaped when his big hand curled around her bicep. He yanked her forward, tossing her like a rag doll. No sooner had she hit the mattress than he was on her, his entire weight holding her down as he straddled her middle. His hands were rough and angry as he gripped her wrist.

Cori fought because it was her only option. It did little to deter him as he restrained her wrists to the metal bars that were bolted to the wall. Her legs flailed when he got off her, but he easily subdued them, pinning them to the bed as he cuffed her ankles to the footboard.

"Please," she begged. "Please don't hurt me."

"No one's going to hurt you, Corinne. But you will have to learn some manners. Believe it or not, you'll come to enjoy it here. After a while. A few years of training, and you'll be a good little girl for me, Corinne."

He sounded crazy. Like seriously insane.

"I should've thought about this sooner," he continued. "Like sisters. The two of you can take care of each other while I'm away at work. And when I'm home, I'll have two young wives to take care of me." His eyes raked over her, brow furrowed. "Although you're a little older than I'd like. It could work."

Bile rose into her throat at what she thought he was saying, but she couldn't speak.

"But don't worry, Corinne. I won't force you. Won't have to. You'll break. They always break." His smile was feral. "Oh, yes. And that will be a lovely day indeed."

Movement near the door had her eyes cutting over. A woman stood in the doorway, her face in shadow, her waist-length hair board straight, her dress... It looked handmade and something from another time period.

"What're you gonna do to me?" Cori whimpered.

"I told you. It's time for your bath. My sweet Emily's going to help you out."

"No!" Cori cried out as the woman stepped closer. "Please. I don't want—"

The words died in her throat as the woman's face came into view.

Oh, my God.

Chapter Fifteen

UNFORTUNATELY, GETTING AHOLD OF JASON MONTGOMERY WAS more difficult than Brantley had expected. However, not impossible. JJ was able to track him down, but rather than warn the man they were coming for a visit, Brantley decided to surprise him.

Reese whistled softly as they stepped into the building occupied by the Montgomery/Jones team of lawyers. "Nice office."

"Law pays," Brantley noted.

"That it does."

"May I help you?" a cheerful young woman sitting behind a fancy glass desk asked as they approached.

"We're here to see Jason Montgomery," Brantley stated.

"Is Mr. Montgomery expecting you?"

"Doubtful, seein' as he doesn't know us."

Seemingly confused by his sarcasm, the young woman's eyebrows dipped.

"Doesn't change the fact we're here to talk to him," he added when she made no effort to get him.

She hesitantly reached for the phone. "May I tell him who's here to speak with him?"

Really? How polite could one person be?

"Brantley Walker and Reese Tavoularis. We're with the governor's task force." He motioned toward the badge on his hip.

There were no signs of recognition, of course. For one, governor's task force sounded like a lie. Definitely had to work on a name.

Thankfully the young woman picked up the phone, then relayed the information to whoever she spoke with.

"You can go back," she said as she set the phone in the cradle, motioned toward a hallway.

"Thank you," Reese told her before they ventured down the hallway. "Might try layin' on some charm. Goes a long way toward gettin' what you want."

Brantley smirked over at him. "Speakin' from experience, are you?"

Reese rolled his eyes.

All sense of amusement disappeared when Brantley encountered another woman manning a desk. This one was older—both the woman and the desk—with shrewd eyes and a no-nonsense demeanor.

"May I help you?" The stern voice came from equally stern lips.

"Are you Jason Montgomery?" Brantley countered.

"Of course not."

"Then the answer's probably no."

"We need to speak to Mr. Montgomery," Reese said, laying on the charm. "We assure you it won't take much of his time, but it's urgent."

"I'm sorry, but Mr. Montgomery's unavailable right now."

"Fine." Brantley nodded. "Since he can't spare us some time, we'll be takin' him into custody. He can chat with us down at the station."

That seemed to get her attention.

Within a minute, they were stepping into Jason Montgomery's posh, pretentious office with its gleaming mahogany ... everything. Inside a well-dressed man, somewhere in his late twenties. Blond hair, blue eyes, all-American boy. His smile was blinding, as was the twinkle in his eyes. He knew how to play the game, that was for sure.

"Gentlemen," the man greeted, getting to his feet. "How may I help you?"

"We're here to ask you a few questions about Lauren Tyler," Brantley stated, getting right to the point.

Recognition glittered in his eyes. "That's the girl who went missing when I was in high school. In Coyote Ridge?"

"Yes." Brantley moved closer. "Did you know her?"

"Please, have a seat." Jason gestured to the two chairs in front of his desk as he took a seat in his lavish executive chair. "To answer your question, no, I didn't know her. I knew of her because we went to the same school, lived in the same small town."

"According to William Dugan, you had a thing for Lauren back in high school."

Jason choked on a laugh. "First of all, Principal Dugan and I weren't on the best of terms back then. Most of the guys in the school weren't. Secondly, Lauren wasn't really my type."

"I thought you didn't know her," Reese stated.

Brantley already knew where this was going, thanks to the photograph he noticed on a bookshelf behind Jason, but he waited the man out.

"I didn't. But since she's female, that makes her not my type."

"You're gay," Brantley acknowledged.

"I am." He reached forward, turned around a framed photograph. "Adam Jones, my partner in every sense of the word. Happily married for going on three years now."

"And the woman you're pictured with on your social media accounts?"

"Probably my sister, Jen." Jason turned the picture back around. "Just out of curiosity, how did I come up in your investigation?"

"Dugan brought up your name."

"Of course he did." Jason steepled his hands on his desk. "Like I said, there was no love lost between me and Principal Dugan. He was a jackass who spent more time eyeing the cheerleaders than managing the school. At the time, he seemed relatively young to me, I guess. More so than the principal before him. And I think the girls liked that. He was a handsome man, carried himself well. One of those men who was hard to miss and worked hard to earn the girls' affections."

Brantley damn sure didn't like the direction this was going.

Jason's keen eyes bounced back and forth between them. "You think he had something to do with Lauren's disappearance?"

"I don't think anything yet," Brantley told him. "But I'm pullin' the threads I find."

"And you're with the governor's task force, I'm told."

"We are. Missing persons. New development."

"Well, I hope you can find out what happened to her. I know it hit Coyote Ridge hard when she disappeared. That sorta thing doesn't happen in small towns."

"We're from there. Know all about it."

"Wait. Walker was it?" Jason sat up straight.

"Brantley, yeah. My partner, Reese Tavoularis."

"Town was built on your land," Jason said with a smile.

"Not my land," Brantley corrected. "My family's. I'm just livin' on it like everybody else. Can you tell us where you were on Saturday night?"

"Home with my husband."

Convenient.

"I've also got some out-of-town guests. His parents are in from Denver. You're welcome to speak to any of them. Why do you ask?"

"Did you know Corinne Greenwood?"

Jason seemed to consider it. "Name isn't familiar."

"Probably went by Cori. She was Lauren Tyler's best friend back in high school," Reese explained. "She went missing on Saturday night."

"You think it's related?"

"Well, I don't believe in coincidence," Reese answered.

"No, I don't suppose you do."

"Do you remember anything that might help us from back then?"

Jason was quiet for a minute. "No. I really wish I did. All I really remember was how upset everyone was after she went missing. The school was in an uproar for a few days, everyone out helping with the search, canvassing the area. I remember Dugan stayed apprised of what was going on, letting the teachers know. And then eventually it just died off, as though she never existed."

For some people, Brantley knew. Others were still suffering the loss.

Getting to his feet, Brantley extended a hand. "Thanks for your time."

"No problem. If there's anything else I might be able to help with, feel free to reach out." Jason grabbed a business card, passed it over, then shook Reese's hand.

Neither of them spoke until they were back in the truck, and Reese was the one to kick it off.

"Okay, no offense here, but did you notice the gay population in Coyote Ridge is pretty significant?"

Brantley glanced over, barked a laugh. "Seriously?"

"Sorry."

"I don't take any offense to it, I just figured you'd be callin' out the fact that Dugan sounds like he was pervin' on teenagers while pretendin' to lead the school."

"Well, there's that, too."

"We should pay Dugan another visit," Brantley said, turning the truck toward downtown. "Think maybe we can catch him in class?"

"Worth a shot."

Turned out, it wasn't worth a shot. Professor Dugan had called in sick both Monday and today. The administration office had no idea when he would be back.

"Coincidence?" Reese grumbled.

"If I believed in 'em, maybe."

"I've got a really bad feelin' Dugan's our guy." Reese's voice was deadly low. "And not only did he abduct and likely murder Lauren Tyler, but he's probably got Cori, too."

Same thing Brantley was thinking.

"Worse than that," Brantley said softly, "we've tipped the motherfucker off."

FROM THE LOOKS OF IT, BRANTLEY WAS right. They had tipped off William Dugan. A quick swing by his house was confirmation the asshole was now officially MIA. Granted, if the guy had been living there, he'd packed up and scooted out fast. From a couple glances through the windows, there wasn't a single piece of furniture left. Although Reese figured the man hadn't actually been living there at all. Probably used the property for an address.

Now back at HQ, they were all working to locate the missing professor, including Baz, who had made an appearance while they'd been at the law office. After relaying what they'd learned, which was a whole lot of nothing, he'd taken a seat at Reese's desk and borrowed the computer.

"What about his parents?" Brantley mused aloud. "They still alive?"

"No," JJ answered, not looking up from her monitor.

"Both deceased," Baz said. "I looked into them first thing. Died a few years ago, left everything to their only son."

"Including real estate? Maybe there's something still in their names, a place he might be hidin' out," Reese prompted even though he was already digging for the information.

"Not that I can tell," Baz answered at the same time JJ said, "None."

"Brothers? Sisters? Cousins?" Reese rattled off, hoping for anything that might give them another thread to pull.

"Only child," Baz responded. "His father had a brother, but he died of SIDS when he was three weeks old. Mother had no siblings. Aside from his parents, Dugan's got no living relatives that I can tell."

"Did you hack the university?" Brantley prompted. "See what his records show?"

Baz looked up, his eyebrow lifting.

"Immunity and means," JJ supplied, grinning. She glanced at Brantley. "And no, not yet. But I will if you give me the go-ahead."

"Whatever it takes," Brantley said, getting to his feet.

Reese watched as he marched out the door and into the brilliant sunshine. The door slammed closed behind him, dimming the room once more.

"You should go check on him," JJ suggested.

"He needs some space," Reese countered.

Surprisingly, she didn't argue, her head dipping down again, the familiar clack of her keyboard telling him she was hard at work.

Reese leaned back on the couch, stared across the room at the whiteboard. How had one missing person case turned into two? And where the hell was Corinne Greenwood? If Dugan had kidnapped her, where would he go?

He spent the next hour skimming any and all information he could find on Professor Dugan. There was a surprising amount. The guy was rather high-profile at the university, a favorite amongst students. He evidently participated in quite a few university-related events, as well, held lengthy office hours during which he would take appointments online. Based on the form, he was eager and willing to personally help any student who needed it.

Interesting, considering Reese hadn't found the guy to be all that likable despite his best efforts to appear as such.

The ringing of JJ's cell phone broke his concentration. When she answered, he figured it was a good time to go check on Brantley.

He found the man in the house, pacing the kitchen island, lost in thought.

"You okay?" he asked casually as he made his way around to the refrigerator, careful to stay out of Brantley's direct path.

After grabbing a bottle of water, he stepped out of Brantley's way, watched as he continued to walk circles as though he couldn't seem to keep still. It probably wasn't the right time for his mind to go astray, but he was beginning to realize his attraction to this man wasn't something he could simply shut off. His thoughts drifted to two nights ago, when Brantley had quite effectively rocked his entire world. In the best possible way. Especially when he'd used his tongue to—

"Problem?"

Brantley's voice yanked him out of that erotic memory. "What?"

The smirk on the man's face said Reese's thoughts were clearly written all over his face.

Brantley stopped moving. "What're you thinkin' about?"

"Nothin'."

Brantley approached, stopping just shy of plowing him over. "Liar."

Reese grinned, the heat coursing in his veins as much due to that erotic memory as the sexy man standing in front of him.

Somehow he managed to hold his ground when Brantley leaned in. The man never touched him, but he didn't have to. The heat of his body was potent, the rasp of his words in his ear a stimulant all their own. "Your mind's in the gutter, Tavoularis. You're thinkin' about the two of us … naked."

A soft groan escaped him, a not-so-subtle confirmation.

"What am I gonna do about you?" Brantley whispered, leaning in and brushing his lips over Reese's neck.

The bottle of water nearly fell when that wicked mouth trailed over his flesh.

"We're supposed to be workin'," Reese said, though it lacked the conviction he'd intended. "Baz and JJ are out in the barn."

"We're takin' a lunch break."

He chuckled because that was something Brantley would come up with, an interesting way to describe the fact they were about to devour one another.

Reese inhaled sharply when Brantley's hands slipped beneath his shirt, sliding confidently over his skin, moving around to his back as he pulled him in.

"I can't help myself," Brantley continued. "I want you, Reese. Every fucking time I look at you, I want you. From that very first day I saw you. You'd think it would slow down some." Brantley shook his head, then trailed his lips toward Reese's. "It hasn't. Opposite. Touch me."

There was nowhere for him to put the water bottle, so Reese simply let it fall to the floor. It clattered and rolled away, leaving Reese's hands free to reach for Brantley. He pulled him in, their lips sliding together, tongues exploring. The kiss was laced with an intensity that seemed to be building the longer they were around each other.

Reese felt the passion, realized he was beginning to crave it like a drug. This was new, it was thrilling, and he'd yet to get his fill of this man. In fact, he doubted he ever would. He got the feeling years could pass before he would even be moderately sated.

"Touch me," Brantley groaned, leaning into him.

Understanding, Reese reached for Brantley's jeans, unbuttoned, unzipped, then jerked them down his hips. His cock was hard as steel, smooth as velvet as Reese took him in his fist.

Another guttural grunt from Brantley, a few creative curse words.

"Don't stop touchin' me," Brantley moaned. "Never. Stop. Touchin'. Me."

Reese wrapped one arm around Brantley's neck, pulled him in close while he stroked him firmly with his other hand. They stood, right there in Brantley's kitchen, leaning into one another while he worked Brantley toward release. He wanted nothing in return because this … touching him, bringing him to orgasm … it was a reward all on its own.

"You wanna come for me, Navy boy?" he rasped against Brantley's ear.

"Fuck…" Brantley began rocking his hips, fucking Reese's fist. "Reese … love when you touch me."

Warmth consumed him, heat he was beginning to get familiar with. The approval in Brantley's tone, the need he could sense. Sure, this was physical, but there was more to it.

Reese stroked him faster, releasing his hold on Brantley's neck, trying to pull back just a little.

"Don't stop," Brantley pleaded.

"Never."

Reese dropped his other hand, let it join in on the action, stroking him firmly as Brantley's gaze dropped down.

"Close," Brantley warned.

Reese didn't hesitate, he went to his knees, never slowing his hands, gripping firmly as he jerked Brantley's cock, eager to send him over the edge.

When he peered up, he saw the heat flash in those beautiful blue eyes. And when he leaned in, taking Brantley's cock in his mouth, the erotic cry that escaped the man was nearly enough to have him coming in his jeans.

"Oh, fuck. Reese…" Brantley's hips jerked forward, his cock pulsing as he came.

Reese sucked him hard, drank him down, loving the contented sigh that came next.

Before he could stand, Brantley was helping him to his feet, pulling him up with one powerful hand. The kiss that followed was explosive, had Reese wishing they had more time so they could move this to a horizontal surface. Unfortunately, he knew there was work to do, but later … later, they would have time for more.

So very much more.

Chapter Sixteen

BY THE TIME THURSDAY ROLLED AROUND, BRANTLEY was beginning to get discouraged.

Not that he would stop pursuing every possible lead they could uncover, but it appeared William Dugan had disappeared the same way Corinne Greenwood had. There was no doubt in his mind that Dugan had her. The question was, where were they? And what the hell were his plans for her? Was she still alive? Or did he discard her in an effort to cover up the fact he'd kidnapped Lauren Tyler?

It was the only thing that made sense.

The four of them had practically camped out in the barn for the past couple of days, bouncing off ideas, utilizing Baz's contacts with the police department and JJ's hacking abilities in an effort to track him down. Unfortunately, they hadn't gotten anything except for finally a warrant to search William Dugan's last known address.

Now as Brantley pulled up at the two-story red-brick house, he could only stare, hoping they would find something inside that would lead them to Corinne. They knew from their previous visit that the house was empty, but Baz had convinced them it would be worth a thorough search. Considering the number of homes Dugan had owned since Lauren Tyler vanished nine years ago, the detective figured there was a reason he moved around so much.

"What's he hopin' to find?" Reese asked as they sat in the truck.

"At this point, anything," Brantley told him.

"Well…" Reese unbuckled his seat belt. "Let's see what we can do to help him out."

Brantley climbed out of the truck, followed Reese to the front door. It was standing open, and from inside the house, he could hear footsteps on the hardwood echoing throughout the empty space.

"Baz?"

"Back here," came the response.

Brantley entered the house, looking around. Based on the fact there was no dust, it appeared the house had been cleaned recently, if, in fact, it had been vacant for some time. Had Dugan come by and cleaned it himself? Had he hired a service?

Before heading toward the kitchen, Brantley shot a text to JJ, asked her to reach out to all cleaning services in the area and see if any of them were handling Dugan's address. Perhaps they could track him down though payments if he was utilizing one.

"I was able to talk to the neighbors across the street," Baz said when they joined him. Wearing a pair of latex gloves, the detective was opening the cabinet doors, leaving them open as he went. "They said the house has been vacant for three months."

"But he didn't sell it?" Reese asked, although it was clearly rhetorical.

"Maybe he's plannin' to move back," Baz said, shifting to the lower cabinets, then the drawers.

"You go through it already?"

"Haven't been upstairs yet."

"I'll cover it," Reese offered, disappearing toward the stairs at the front of the house.

"You lookin' for somethin' specific?" Brantley asked when Baz opened the refrigerator.

"Hopin' maybe he left something behind that might tell us where he moved to."

From the looks of it, the house had been gone over with a fine-tooth comb. Brantley didn't figure they would find so much as a strand of hair.

"I've got JJ lookin' into the possibility he's usin' a cleaning service."

"Speakin' of JJ..." Baz opened the pantry door, stuck his head in. "Is she comin' off a bad relationship?"

Brantley stared. "Kinda random, don't you think?"

The detective closed the door, glanced over, smiled. "Sorry."

"Don't be. And as much as I'd like to play matchmaker between you two, it's not my place. I will say, the last person she was datin' was the governor's son."

"Ah." Baz nodded. "Which means she's off-limits."

"The governor's son's a douche," Brantley told him. "It's been an on-again-off-again thing with them for years. I'm pretty sure Dante's not lookin' to settle down with one woman."

"Gotcha."

"Why? You thinkin' about askin' her out?"

Baz's grin widened. "Just gettin' the lay of the land."

Brantley moved toward the adjoining dining room, changing the subject. "I thought APD detectives worked with partners."

"We do. Usually."

"You're the exception?"

"Let's just say I have to tread lightly right now."

Curious, Brantley turned back toward him.

Another grin from Baz. "They call me hotheaded. My last partner transferred out so he didn't have to work with me."

"Hotheaded?" Brantley wouldn't have described the man that way. Then again, he hadn't spent a lot of time in the detective's company.

"Upstairs is clear," Reese called out, his boots echoing on the stair treads.

The three of them moved through the rooms on the main floor, opening closets, going through bathroom drawers and cabinets. He knew it was a waste of time. There was nothing here to find. If William Dugan was attempting to cover his tracks, he was doing a damn fine job of it.

"Hey, y'all…" Reese shouted. "You might wanna come look at this."

Brantley stepped out into the hall, following the sound of Reese's voice. He found him in what appeared to be the master bedroom.

"Find somethin'?"

Reese had his hand on the closet door, opening it wider as he nodded.

Brantley glanced inside, noticed a wood panel at the back of the closet. "Storage?"

"It's possible," Baz said. "If I'm right, the staircase is on the other side of that wall."

Which meant there could be empty space behind the panel. Whoever built the house likely decided to utilize it for storage.

Pulling the multi-tool he kept on his belt, Brantley stepped into the closet. He used it to pry the panel open, moving the heavy piece of wood out of the way.

"Well, that doesn't look like storage to me," Reese said. "This place have a basement?"

If it did, it would be extremely rare. Most houses in this part of the state didn't have basements.

Baz stepped forward, clicking on a flashlight and leading the way by ducking into the stairwell.

Brantley and Reese followed behind him. There wasn't much space to maneuver. Brantley had to angle his upper body just to make it down.

"Holy. Fuck."

Brantley stepped out behind Baz, right into a room that looked anything but normal.

"This looks like…"

"A cell," Brantley supplied. And based on the irons connected to the floor and the wall, William Dugan had been keeping a guest down here.

Reese exhaled heavily, moving around the room. "Did he keep … people down here?"

"At least one," Baz stated, squatting down and shining his flashlight on the floor. "I've got blond hair over here. Looks to be human."

He was instantly on his feet, making a call, probably to bring the crime scene unit in.

Brantley remained where he was, staring around the space.

If William Dugan had kept people down here, where were they now?

REESE WAS PROPPED UP IN BRANTLEY'S BED, skimming through his emails on his iPad.

Brantley had said he needed to finish up a couple of things, but asked that Reese stay the night again. He'd been here every night since Saturday, when he came to check on Brantley. The only time he'd gone home was to get a change of clothes. At some point he knew he would need to go back to his apartment, sleep alone. He didn't necessarily want to, but he also didn't want to move too fast in this.

Okay, that wasn't exactly true.

For one, Reese didn't think they were moving too fast. In fact, the speed at which they were moving was just right. They were getting comfortable and that was all he could hope for. He'd never been the sort to really think about time as a measurement for a relationship. Their slow pace was more geared toward him getting comfortable on an intimate level. Needless to say, he was past that point now.

"What's on your mind?"

The deep rumble of Brantley's voice pulled him from his thoughts, had a smile forming on his face.

He shifted on the bed. "Not a whole helluva lot. You?"

Brantley strolled around to his side, fell into it, propping himself up on pillows. "Tired. Was hopin' you were still awake."

"Yeah?"

"Thought maybe we could watch something mindless on TV."

That was a good idea, something to take their minds off everything else. Reese had turned the television on, but he had no idea what he was watching. He'd made it as far as the power button before he'd shifted his attention elsewhere.

And now it was shifting again, only this time, he was letting his gaze skim over Brantley from head to toe. He looked so damn sexy sitting there, one knee propped up, reclining back, wearing a pair of shorts. So casual, so … relaxed. It was a good look on the man.

As though he'd done it a million times before, Reese passed over the remote, set his iPad on the nightstand, and flipped off the lamp. He settled back against the headboard. When Brantley leaned into him, Reese put an arm over his shoulder.

They remained like that, watching the news in bed, neither of them speaking. It wasn't an encounter Reese normally would've paid attention to but he couldn't help himself.

This.

This was what felt right to him.

Being here with Brantley.

And when they fell asleep an hour later, it was with Reese spooning behind the man, holding on to him.

They were both up before the sun, their routine one they'd run through every day this week. After joining Brantley for his morning run, Reese went to the kitchen, started breakfast while Brantley hopped in the shower. When they were finished with their respective tasks, Reese took his turn in the bathroom, dressed for the day, and met Brantley over at the barn.

JJ arrived a little after seven. She had a smile on her face and a mug of coffee in her hands. She looked as though she'd gotten some sleep and Reese was hopeful she had. Despite his attempts not to, Reese had overheard a couple of her conversations with Dante and it seemed the man was attempting to use this tragic situation to his benefit, trying to weasel his way back into her good graces. From what he could tell, it wasn't working.

"You're smilin'," Brantley noted, looking up from his computer. "Why?"

JJ giggled. "Am I not allowed to smile?"

"You are, sure." He picked up his coffee, leaned back, studying her. "But you have to explain why since it's such a rare phenomenon."

"It is not," she countered, still chuckling. "And I don't know why I'm smilin'. I just am."

And because they were talking about smiling, Reese found himself doing the same as he stared at his computer, skimming through his inbox.

"Did Baz happen to send the DNA results on what they found yesterday?" he asked Brantley.

"Not yet."

"I haven't seen 'em either," JJ noted. "But I know he has a rush on them. We're hopin' it'll give us a lead to where Corinne is."

"He was askin' about you yesterday," Brantley said.

Reese looked up, noticing JJ's expression. She seemed incredibly pleased by this revelation.

"Me?"

"Yep. I told him you're datin' a douchebag."

"I'm not datin' anybody," she argued, her tone hardening. "Dante and I are done."

Although Reese knew it wasn't any of his business, he was happy to hear her confirm. Dante didn't deserve a woman like JJ. She was far too good for him. Hell, she was far too good, period.

"Well, if you need help makin' him understand just how done you are, just let me know," Brantley told her.

"That won't be necessary. I think he's gonna back off."

A chime sounded, and a second later, Reese's cell phone vibrated. He picked it up, noticed it was an alert for the cameras. He glanced over at Brantley then JJ.

"Why's my phone buzzin'?" he asked them both.

"I did it," JJ admitted. "Set it up so we all get notified if someone shows up here. Figured Brantley's not the only one who needs to know anymore."

"It's Baz," he told them as he peered at the screen, which reflected the camera mounted to the side of the house, overlooking the driveway.

"He said he might stop by this mornin'," JJ said.

Reese glanced at Brantley, grinned when the other man looked back at him. It looked to him like JJ had taken a liking to the detective.

When the buzzer on the door sounded, Reese got up because he was closest. He let Baz in, would've offered the man coffee, but based on the two paper cups he was carrying, he was already stocked up.

"What's this?" JJ asked when Baz approached her desk, holding out one of the cups.

"Caramel macchiato with an extra shot."

Her eyes widened, as did her smile. "Thank you."

"You're more than welcome." Baz took a sip of his own coffee, turned around to face them. "Sorry I didn't get y'all somethin'."

"Sure you are," Brantley joked, then lifted his own mug. "We're set though. Thanks."

Baz nodded, smiled.

"Any news from the crime scene guys?" Reese asked, hoping to get the conversation rolling.

"Not yet. I should hear from them this mornin'." Baz glanced from him to JJ then to Brantley. "Anything on your end?"

"Unfortunately, no," Reese said when no one else answered.

"That's not entirely true," JJ announced, her voice growing louder, her attention on her computer screen. "Holy shit. I think I found somethin'."

Reese and Baz moved around to stand behind her, Brantley joining.

"It's a piece of property owned by a Bill D. Martin. And yes, before you say anything, I know that's not his name. But he is William, which people sometimes refer to as Bill. And D would be for Dugan. Martin's his father's name." JJ tapped a few keys and a map appeared on the large monitor on the wall. All eyes turned toward it as JJ got to her feet, moved over to the other keyboard.

"Before I left last night, I started a property search."

"On Dugan?" Baz asked.

"No. In general. I took in the details of the houses we know William Dugan's owned in the past. I honestly didn't expect much because my main parameter was houses with basements. And we all know how rare those are in this area. I added in any that had storm cellars. There were a few, so I pulled up the owners. This one's about half an hour north of here."

The map on the screen zoomed in, changed to street view.

"Let me put in a call to—"

"No," Brantley interrupted. "Let's go there now."

Baz frowned. "Now? It'll take us a good hour to get there with traffic."

"Your point?" Brantley was already moving to his desk, tapping something on his computer.

Because he was not about to let Brantley go on his own, nor did he want to get left behind, Reese followed.

"JJ, stay here and stay available," Brantley called out on his way to the door.

"I will."

"You know he's right," Reese told Brantley when they were in the truck. "With rush-hour traffic, it'll take an hour to get there."

"You got anything better to do?"

Well, when he put it that way…

CORI WAS COLD. SHE WAS SHIVERING DESPITE the fact she had the scratchy wool blanket draped over her.

It was due more to fear than temperature, she knew.

Lauren.

She still couldn't believe Lauren was here, living in this house with Principal Dugan. Granted, she called herself Emily, as did he. And when Cori had accused him of kidnapping Lauren all those years ago, he had argued—actually argued—that she was wrong, that the woman who clearly looked like Lauren wasn't who Cori claimed her to be.

Of course, he was right to a degree. Lauren was no longer that sweet, kind, innocent girl Cori had grown up with. No. She'd been gone too long for that, held prisoner by this lunatic. Her mind was now warped and she honestly believed her name was Emily Dugan. Professor Bill Dugan's wife.

Another chill raced down Cori's spine.

The woman who was wandering around this house was definitely Lauren. The moment she saw her face, Cori had recognized her, although she had changed drastically in the nine years since she'd gone missing. Her hair was longer, nearly to her waist, but still the same interesting shade of brown it had been. Her face had filled out, no longer radiating with adolescence. But it was her eyes that made her look like an entirely different person. There was absolutely no life in them. As though a part of her had died.

Cori had been hoping Lauren would come back so she could talk to her, but Principal Dugan—Bill—wasn't letting her. No, he had taken over bringing her food, sitting with her while she ate. The man liked to talk, mostly about how happy he was that she was here, how he knew one day she would come to think of this place as home the same way Lauren—Emily—did.

The guy was a complete lunatic. Absolutely batshit crazy.

But Cori had learned that telling him as much wasn't conducive to survival. The first time she'd told him had been when he had Lauren bathe her while she was strapped down to the bed. After he had stripped her of her clothes, cutting them off because of the restraints, he had stood over her, watching intently. His beady eyes had followed Lauren's hands as they dragged a lukewarm washcloth over Cori's naked body.

The thought had her shivering again.

She had to get out of here. Based on her calculations, she'd been here at least four days, maybe five. Or was it six? At one point, she was pretty sure Bill had drugged her, making her lose track of time. He'd put something in her food. When she woke, it was to find him lying on the bed with her, his naked body up against her side. She had gotten violently ill at that point. Partially thanks to whatever drugs he'd plied her with, partially because he disgusted her.

But he hadn't touched her.

Not yet, anyway.

Cori had a feeling it was coming, though.

And she knew she had to get out of here before that happened.

She wasn't going alone, she knew that much. All these years, she had blamed herself for Lauren's disappearance. If only she hadn't been sick that day. If only she'd been there to walk home with Lauren. Now that she knew who had taken her, she wasn't completely convinced she'd been responsible back then. But she was responsible for ensuring Lauren got out of here now.

The question was, how?

Chapter Seventeen

BECAUSE THEY HADN'T MADE A FORMAL PLAN and that was clearly something the APD was familiar with, Baz called him on their way to the house where they suspected William Dugan was holding Corinne.

"How's this gonna play out, boss man?" Baz inquired. "What's your plan?"

"My plan?" Brantley glanced in his rearview mirror, looking at the car following him, the sun glinting off the windshield kept him from seeing Baz's face. "You're the detective."

"And you're runnin' point on this," Baz countered, his voice coming through the truck's speakers. "Not to mention, you ran right over me when I suggested we wait."

"No reason to wait," he argued. If there was a remote possibility that Corinne was at this location, Brantley was going to find her. The longer they waited, the better chance Dugan had to relocate her.

"Again," Baz said, his voice tight, "what's your plan?"

"Let's scope it out first," he told the detective. "Then we'll formulate one."

"Great. You're one of those guys. Fly by the seat of your pants, hope for a soft landing."

Reese chuckled, drawing Brantley's attention.

"He's right."

Brantley turned his attention back to the road. "Just keep up, Buchanan. Or I'm gonna leave your ass behind."

He disconnected the call as they turned onto the highway that would lead them out to the sticks.

"You think she's still alive?"

"I do."

"Because he's kept women before?"

"Yeah." That basement cell in Dugan's house was proof that the man kept women. As for how long, he had no idea. But he had to hope that Dugan had spent too much time on the run in the past few days to have disposed of Corinne. He would much rather think she was chained up in some basement than...

No, he wouldn't think about it. The idea was horrific even if it was better than thinking she was in a shallow grave.

They were going to find Corinne Greenwood and they were going to bring her home.

"You armed?" Brantley asked Reese.

"Of course."

"Good."

"You have a plan, don't you?"

Brantley glanced over. "If Dugan so much as tries to hurt her, shoot him. That's my plan."

"You are the type who likes to get right to the point."

There was amusement in Reese's tone and Brantley appreciated it even if he couldn't laugh. Right now, the situation was bearing down on him and the only thing he could do was focus on getting Corinne home. He hoped like hell they could find some closure for Lauren Tyler, because yes, he did believe these two were connected, but that was secondary.

Brantley hit the button to dial JJ.

When she answered, he bypassed pleasantries. "Tell me you've got some information on the house. Floor plan, at least."

"Both the interior and the property," she confirmed. "Single-story ranch. Twelve hundred square feet. From the most updated map, it looks like there's a storage building on the property along with a separate two-car garage, both relatively close to the house. Kitchen's on the right, along with dining. Center of the house looks to be the living room. Left side has two bedrooms and one bathroom."

"And the basement?"

"There's no records of square footage or anything like that, only that it has one. Or at least it did when the last owners sold it because they mentioned it in the listing."

"If Corinne's there, she's in the basement," Brantley stated. "Do we know if Dugan's there?"

"No idea," JJ said. "We have no eyes nearby."

"Since he's hidin' out, callin' in sick, it's probably safe to assume he is," Reese added.

Brantley sure as hell hoped so, because he had every intention of resolving this today.

Forty-five minutes later, Brantley was leading the way through an outcropping of trees. Rather than pull up to the house, they had avoided his street altogether and parked on a road running parallel so as not to alert Dugan to their presence. Now they were trekking through dense underbrush, making their way toward the house where Dugan was hopefully holed up.

"You bypassin' a lot of red tape here?" Reese asked Baz.

"The whole fucking roll," Baz answered. "I didn't even bother callin' my sergeant. Figured since the governor gave y'all the green light, I'm just along for the ride."

"Until it's time to make the arrest," Brantley noted. "That's your job. Not mine."

"Copy that."

"You military?" Reese inquired.

"No. My older brother was. Marine. Died in Afghanistan."

"Sorry to hear that," Reese said softly.

Brantley kept his attention on the house although he was listening to the conversation.

"Hold up," he bit out before they risked stepping out from their cover.

Both men went quiet, coming to stand on either side of him.

"That's Dugan's car," Reese said. "I remember it from the coffee shop."

Guy had good attention to detail.

"You know he could be in there with a whole harem of women, right?" Baz said. "We have no idea what we'll encounter when we go through that door."

The detective was right. They had no idea. Admittedly, Brantley was used to recon and intel. In the Teams, they'd had it in spades. Not that it was always accurate, but they usually had something to go on. Here, they were going in blind.

"Baz," Brantley stated, "you take the north side. Reese, the south. Do what you can to get a look inside. Text me if you get a visual."

Man, they could really use some comms right about now.

"Front and back," Reese stated. "Where're you goin'?"

Brantley pointed. "See that window right there? Low to the ground? I'm bettin' that's the basement. I need to see if I can get a look. Don't do anything until I signal."

They split up, Reese going to the right, Baz to the left. They would have cover but only for as long as they remained in the trees.

Brantley, on the other hand, was concealed partially by the garage and the shed JJ had mentioned.

Because there was no way to tell whether Dugan was standing there watching out the window, Brantley had to assume the man was busy with other things. Namely the woman he was likely keeping chained up below ground.

He took off at a dead run, heading for the shed. He cleared the one hundred yards, paused behind the rickety wooden structure. He was quiet, listening for noises inside the little shed just to be safe. It was possible he was keeping her out here, but based on the condition of the thing, Brantley doubted it.

Convinced no one was inside, Brantley peeked around in an attempt to get a look at the windows on the house. From this vantage point, he could see they were covered. That was good news for them. The shades were down, which meant Dugan wasn't watching and waiting. Of course, it also meant they couldn't get a look inside.

Didn't mean Dugan wasn't monitoring from a camera, but from what Brantley could tell, there weren't any. The guy was likely convinced no one would find him out this way. A warped sense of safety to go with that warped mind of his.

Brantley peeked around the side of the shed once more, then took off for the house. He made quick work scaling the four-foot chain-link fence, landing on his feet. As he continued to run, he pulled his gun from its holster, held it at the ready. When he reached the house, he paused, keeping his back to the old wood siding.

Up close, the house looked to be in far worse shape than he'd originally thought. There was a ton of rot on the boards, what had once been painted white now a dingy gray. There'd been no upkeep on this place for a while. Including the yard. The weeds were high, but he worked his way toward the window.

Dropping to his knees, he leaned around, tried to determine if there was a covering on the inside. There wasn't. And the shade from the house would hopefully keep his shadow from being projected in when he leaned over.

He glanced left, then right, ensuring no one was coming his way. When he determined the coast was clear, Brantley leaned down for a peek.

His heart kicked hard when he saw Corinne Greenwood sitting on a cot, a dark blanket clutched to her chest. He pulled back, processed what he'd seen. Her back was bare, which he took to mean Dugan had taken her clothes. He hoped like hell that was all the bastard had taken.

Taking a deep breath, he leaned down once more, scanning the entire space.

No Dugan.

That meant the man was somewhere in the house.

Standing tall, Brantley headed around to the south side of the house where Reese was. He attempted to peek into windows on the way, came up empty at every turn. They were locked down tight, shades drawn, windows painted shut.

Wouldn't be going in that way.

His phone buzzed in his pocket.

All clear on this side, was Baz's message.

Stepping around to the back of the house, he nodded to Reese, who was standing on the other corner of the house. He made a mental note to get them some sort of comms. Would've worked a whole hell of a lot better if he had a way to communicate with them. As it was, Baz was basically going in blind at the front of the house.

Taking a second to text JJ, he let her know he had eyes on Corinne and that she needed to make that call to the woman's parents. Once he was done, he tucked his phone back into his pocket.

Holding up three fingers, he nodded at Reese again.

Reese replied with a thumbs-up before leaning back, most likely relaying the information to Baz from a distance.

There was probably a better way to do this, but Brantley wasn't worried about that right now. Corinne was down in the basement, and provided Dugan didn't make a run for it, he wouldn't be able to use her as a hostage.

He moved to the back door, gave it a quick assessment. Door looked new, but the knob did not. No deadbolt either, which would make it easier to kick in. Holding up three fingers, he counted down. On one, he kicked in the door with one well-placed boot near the knob. A second later, he heard the sound of the front door being kicked in.

Baz shouted something; a shot rang out. Brantley kept his cool, sighting with his gun as he moved through the kitchen, looking for the door leading to the basement. He located it, noticed it was closed up tight.

"Get on the ground!" Baz shouted.

Another shot rang out.

Brantley was about to come around the corner to assist when he heard the rack of a shotgun. Turning toward the mouth of the hallway, he came face-to-face with…

Son of a bitch.

WHEN THE GUNSHOTS RANG OUT, REESE TOOK off at a run for the door. No denying his heart was in his throat. The thought of Brantley having taken a bullet was nearly more than he could bear. Yet his feet continued to move, carrying him the distance, up the stairs, into the house.

He was just in time to hear the distinctive sound of a shotgun being cocked, to see Brantley turn, his attention directed down a narrow hallway.

Reese couldn't see who was wielding the weapon, but based on Brantley's expression, it was someone he hadn't expected to see.

"Lauren?" Brantley said softly. "It's okay. We're not here to hurt you."

Lauren? As in Lauren Tyler?

No fucking way.

In the other room, he heard Baz shouting for someone to get on the ground, assumed it was Dugan. Good news was, there were no more shots being fired. Bad news, Brantley was being held at gunpoint by a woman who'd been missing for nearly a decade.

Reese had heard about instances like this. Whoever that girl in there was, it wasn't the same Lauren Tyler who'd gone missing all those years ago. More than likely, she'd been brainwashed and she was going to defend the man she believed was her savior because Dugan was all she had known.

Brantley backed up a couple of steps, coming out of the mouth of the hallway.

"Lauren, my name's Brantley. Brantley Walker. I've been lookin' for you."

Reese saw him make an attempt at a smile.

"Your parents are lookin' for you," he continued. "A lot of people are."

There was no response.

"I'm here to get Corinne," Brantley explained. "You remember your friend, Corinne? Cori? That's what you called her. She was your best friend in high school."

Reese couldn't go through the house without giving himself away, so he backed out through the door that was now hanging by hinges. He took off at a run, making his way around to the front door. Stepping inside, he saw Baz kneeling on Dugan's back, his gun pressed to the back of the man's head.

Baz looked up, motioned for the doorway on Reese's right.

Keeping as quiet as he could, he worked his way to the opposite end of the hallway from Brantley, peeked around the corner.

There was Lauren Tyler, a shotgun aimed at Brantley. She looked as though she knew how to handle the gun, which didn't bode well for any of them.

"Lauren, I'd just like to talk," Brantley repeated calmly.

"My name's not Lauren," she bit out. "It's Emily Dugan."

"Okay, Emily," Brantley said easily. "Like I said, we're not here to hurt you. In fact, if it's all the same to you, I just need to check on Corinne. Can you let me do that?"

"No. She belongs to Bill now."

"Who's Bill?" Brantley asked, clearly attempting to keep her talking.

"My husband," she said sternly. "The man I love. I belong to him. Always will."

Fucking bastard. Nine years of warping and twisting her mind.

"I want to see him," she demanded. "I want to see my husband."

"Okay." Brantley slid his gun into his holster, then lifted his hands up. "We can arrange that."

"Now."

Reese remained where he was, keeping his gun trained on Lauren's back. The absolute last thing he wanted to do was shoot the woman, but he would do what was necessary to keep Brantley safe. It was hard enough knowing she could blow a hole in him at any moment, but he'd spent years training for this. After all, SEALs weren't the only spec ops teams out there.

He only prayed it didn't come down to that.

"Baz. Bring Bill in here," Brantley called out.

There was some shifting, followed by a couple of grunts, then footsteps. Bill appeared at the end of the hall near Brantley, his hands cuffed behind his back.

"Tell her to put down the gun," Brantley instructed.

"I can't do that."

"If you want to see her walk out of here on her own, you'll tell her to put down the gun."

Bill didn't respond.

"You love her, don't you, Bill?" Brantley continued. "That's why she's here. If you didn't, you wouldn't have kept her, right? I can't imagine you'd enjoy seeing her get hurt."

Dugan peered over at Brantley.

"Tell her to put down the gun," Brantley ordered. "Or my partner's gonna have to shoot her."

Reese knew it was only talk. Brantley would not force him to shoot Lauren. Not unless she gave him reason to.

"It's okay," Dugan began, his eyes locked on Lauren. "Remember what I told you, honey?"

"Yes, Daddy," she whispered.

Daddy? What the fuck? She had called him her husband. The guy was so fucking twisted.

"We have a plan, right?" he asked her.

"Yes."

"That's what we need to do, baby girl."

"Dugan," Brantley warned, his gun coming out, aimed directly at Lauren. "Tell her to put down the gun."

They had her trapped between them. There was no way she could do anything.

"Laur—Emily," Brantley correctly. "Put the gun down. We just need to talk."

"I can't do that," she said softly. "Daddy told me what I need to do."

"Emily, no."

Shit.

Reese knew where this was going and he'd be lying if he said his gut didn't churn with anxiety.

Tucking his gun into his holster, he took one step forward as Lauren lowered the shotgun, turning it so the barrel angled up, toward her head.

"Emily, don't do this," Brantley shouted.

Not thinking, Reese cleared the few feet between them, tackling Lauren to the ground, sending the gun clattering to the floor.

In an instant, she was kicking and punching, screaming at the top of her lungs. Lauren Tyler was more animal than human in that moment, which spoke to the hell Dugan had put her through.

Brantley was there, kneeling down, pinning Lauren's hands to the floor as Reese attempted to cuff her with the zip ties he'd brought with him. That didn't stop her from thrashing around, kicking and flailing. She was going to hurt herself if she wasn't careful.

Reese looked up at Brantley, received a nod.

It took a little longer because her adrenaline was flowing, but Reese managed to apply enough pressure to knock her out. He hated to do it, but she deserved mercy. Perhaps the EMTs could give her something to keep her under. At least for the time being.

"Call for backup," Brantley ordered Baz. "And get an ambulance."

"I'll stay with her," Reese told Brantley. "Go get Corinne."

Brantley was on his feet in an instant. The next he had disappeared down to the basement.

Chapter Eighteen

BRANTLEY MADE QUICK WORK OF THE PADLOCK on the basement door before flinging it open and starting down the stairs. He kept his weapon raised, looking for a threat, praying there wasn't one but willing to do what was necessary if there was.

Luckily, the coast was clear. Only one person in the basement and she was on the other side of the metal bars on a cot.

"Who are you?" Corinne called out, her voice trembling.

"Corinne? My name's Brantley Walker. Your parents sent me to get you."

"Oh, God. Please," she cried out, a sob following.

He made it down the stairs, saw the solid door to the room she was kept in. The padlock was a joke and it took him less than thirty seconds with the correct tools to pick it and pull the door open wide.

Brantley didn't make any quick movements as he stepped inside, not wanting to send Corinne into a panic. It was bad enough they'd been holding her down here, naked, with only a blanket.

"Let's get you out of here."

Corinne pulled the blanket aside, revealed her left ankle and the fact that it was shackled to the bed frame.

He could hear the sirens outside, grateful the cavalry had arrived.

Taking out his phone, he called Reese. "Have Baz bring down a blanket. Somethin' from his car. Not from here."

"Will do."

He disconnected the call, looked over at Corinne.

"We've got the police and an ambulance on the way. My partner's upstairs, as is an APD detective helping with the case." He unlocked the cuff around her ankle, then helped Corinne to her feet.

"Is Lauren all right?" She laughed softly, though it was humorless. "You know what I mean."

"Looks like they had a plan if they were ever found. She was supposed to take her own life, but we managed to stop her from doing that."

"Oh, my God." Corinne breathed roughly. "He's crazy."

More than a little, Brantley knew.

"She's safe now. I'm sure it'll be a long recovery for her, but she's okay. Physically, anyway," he assured her.

"I can't believe he kidnapped her. Kept her here all this time."

"Not just here," Baz said when he met them halfway down the stairs. "And not just her."

Corinne stopped short.

"This is Detective Buchanan," Brantley explained as Baz passed over the blanket. "He's workin' the case alongside my task force. Turn around, Baz."

When the detective turned around, Brantley helped Corinne to replace the wool blanket with one she hopefully wouldn't associate with that crazy bastard.

"He's got more girls here?" she asked when she was appropriately covered.

"No," Baz told her, meeting Brantley's eyes.

He saw it then. The truth. There were more girls, but likely, Lauren Tyler was the only one he'd kept alive.

"Come on," Brantley encouraged Corinne. "Let's get you to the ambulance. Have them look you over. Your parents are on the way."

After passing Corinne off to the EMTs, Brantley took a stroll around to the back of the house. He found he wasn't alone though. Reese had already come back here, pacing. Without saying a word, he fell into step with the man and they just walked. No words were necessary.

This was their first official case on the governor's task force, although technically, they'd solved two at one time. Not only had they found Corinne, bringing her home safe and sound, they'd also found Lauren Tyler. That girl had a long, long road ahead of her based on what Brantley had witnessed. She had been willing to take her own life because the bastard who'd kidnapped her had brainwashed her into doing so. He didn't even want to think about what might've happened if Reese hadn't been there to stop her.

He had been there though. That was all that mattered.

A few hours later, after receiving an invite from Baz to join him down at the station to observe Dugan's interrogation, Brantley was standing in a small room. The two-way mirror revealed the brightly lit room where Dugan was sitting at a table, hands cuffed behind his back. There was a sinister smile on the man's face and it took every ounce of his control not to stroll into that room and punch the fucker in the face.

"You've waived your right to counsel," Baz stated as he stepped into the room to join Dugan. "Is that correct?"

"I don't see a reason to pay for a lawyer," Dugan answered easily. "I know my rights."

Baz nodded, then pulled out the chair across from him. "Do you understand what you're being charged with, Mr. Dugan?"

"Whatever it is, it won't stick," the other man stated. "I've done nothing wrong."

"Nothing wrong?" Reese muttered from beside Brantley. "Guy is a complete fucking lunatic."

"Mr. Dugan, we found Lauren Tyler living in your home. She's been missing for nine years."

"The woman living with me is Emily Dugan," the man countered. "My wife."

Brantley noticed the way Baz's shoulders tensed. He could practically feel his anger, the need to get the truth out of this crazy psycho so they could bring closure to Lauren's family.

"She's Lauren Tyler," Baz repeated. "I don't care what you call her, that doesn't change who she is. And she didn't willingly go with you nine years ago, did she?"

Dugan didn't respond.

"Why did you kidnap her?"

Dugan's right eyebrow lifted. "Kidnap her?" He smiled, that evil smirk holding firmly on his face. "I didn't kidnap her, I invited her into my home. I took care of her. I raised her." His eyes narrowed. "I fixed her."

Baz's shoulders relaxed. "Fixed her? What exactly needed to be fixed?"

"Lauren Tyler was a confused young woman when I invited her into my life."

"Confused how?"

Dugan leaned back in his chair. "She fancied herself in love with her best friend. A woman. She was an abomination when I took pity on her."

"That explains what the parents were eluding to," Reese muttered.

Yes, it certainly did.

"I showed her the error of her ways," Dugan continued. "Over time, her misguided ideals were eliminated, replaced by my sweet, devoted Emily."

"And the others?" Baz prompted. "Did you fix them, too?"

Dugan didn't refute that there were others and Brantley wondered if that was Baz's plan. A trap to get him to admit to the other women.

"I attempted to," Dugan said. "Some would last, some wouldn't."

"How many did you fix?" Baz inquired. "And how many didn't ... last?"

"Emily's the only one who truly saw the error of her ways." Dugan's eyes seemed to go blank, as though he was looking into his own past. "The others ... I tried. I tried so hard, but I could only do so much."

"And if you couldn't fix them? What did you do to them?"

"I put them out of their misery," he said easily, still with that far-off look.

"How many?"

"I lost count a long time ago."

Brantley's gut churned at the admission. He wanted to wrap his hands around that bastard's neck and squeeze until his fucking eyeballs popped out of his head.

"And Corinne Greenwood?" Baz asked from inside the room. "Why did you take her?"

"Because she knows too much." His voice turned cold. "I was going to kill her, make sure she didn't talk, but then I figured I could give Emily a playmate. We could be a family."

"Bullshit," Brantley groaned. "He wanted to prove to himself that he'd fixed Lauren. By bringing Corinne in, he could see for himself that she wasn't in love with her. Which made him the hero."

"Guy's a psychopath," Reese stated, his anger evident.

"How'd you bypass the security cameras in her apartment?" Baz asked. "The night you took her?"

"Easy. The little pervert who works the desk. It only cost me a hundred. If I were him, I would've charged more." The asshole grinned, then seemed to come back to himself. "I'd like to see my wife now. I'm sure she misses me."

"I doubt she's going to want to see you," Baz said, his irritation obvious in his tone.

"I'll take that bet," Dugan countered. "In fact, I'll bet my life she'll stand by me through this."

Brantley seriously fucking hoped not.

Two hours later, after briefing the governor on what had gone down and getting an update on Corinne, Brantley, Reese, and Baz walked into the barn to find JJ waiting for them. Immediately, Brantley felt like an asshole because he hadn't taken time to call her, to update her what was going on.

JJ grinned. "We closed our first official case."

"I'm sorry I didn't call you," he said quickly.

"No worries. Baz did."

Brantley glanced over at the detective. "Is that right?"

"What? I figured it's what you would've done if you hadn't been sidelined by the governor. Just doin' my part."

Yes. And the man had done his part rather well. Perhaps he'd be interested in a permanent spot on the task force. Brantley would have to talk to Reese and JJ, get their input.

"We make a pretty good team," JJ said.

"That we do," he agreed.

"So whaddya say we take this team on over to Moonshiners. Grab ourselves a beer?"

"I'm in," Reese said.

Baz chimed in with a "Me, too."

"Y'all go on," Brantley urged. "I'll be along in a bit."

JJ and Baz strolled out together, Reese staying back.

"I'm fine," he told the man. "Just need a few more minutes."

"Somethin' botherin' you?" Reese inquired. "Besides the obvious."

"No. Just thinkin' about that girl. How she turned that shotgun on herself."

"It's always harder with women and children," Reese said softly.

Brantley met his gaze, tried to look deeper. In his previous line of work, Brantley'd come face-to-face with numerous terrorists. Unfortunately, some of them had been women, some children. And yes, it was devastating when it came down to their lives or his. But this ... Emily wasn't a terrorist, but she'd been willing to die for her cause. The question was, how much experience did Reese have with that sort of thing?

"Could've been bad, but it wasn't." Reese stepped up to him, cupped the side of his neck. "Come on, let's head over to Moonshiners. JJ needs this win."

Brantley stared back at him. "She does."

"A few more wins in her pocket and she'll be runnin' the show here," Reese noted. "I think she likes workin' with Baz."

"I think she likes Baz," Brantley corrected.

"And you? What're your thoughts on the guy?"

Brantley shrugged. "I'll answer that after I see him relax a bit."

Reese slid his hand down Brantley's arm, took his hand. "Come on."

"You sure you wanna go out in public?" He hadn't meant to sound quite so insecure about the whole thing.

"I'm sure."

Yeah, he was hesitant about going out with Reese. Even to grab a beer with a group of friends. This was where they seemed to have trouble and he wasn't ready to go through it again. As far as he was concerned, he'd taken enough risks for one day.

Didn't mean he wouldn't go, just that he was hesitant.

REESE OFFERED TO DRIVE TO MOONSHINERS AND was a bit surprised when Brantley hadn't put up a fight. He'd started to think Brantley had a thing about being in the passenger seat. Then again, the man could've been willing because something was up with him. Ever since Reese had agreed to go to the bar, he'd noticed Brantley's reluctance.

Not that Reese wasn't aware of why that was. He was a smart man, and he was more than aware of how his actions had affected Brantley as of late. And while he couldn't promise any PDA, Reese was feeling a bit more confident about this outing. Or rather, he was feeling a bit more confident about his feelings for Brantley.

"Well, if it's not our very own heroes of Coyote Ridge."

Reese glanced up at the woman who had strolled over to the table they'd occupied.

"Didn't expect to see you out and about, Mayor," Brantley said, remaining in his seat but offering a nod in greeting.

Bianca Stewart smiled brightly.

Reese had never really thought about what a mayor looked like, but admittedly, he'd never considered a woman quite like Bianca in that position. She had pretty eyes, a youthful face, and a body right out of a Playboy centerfold. However, he doubted that was what had gotten her elected. While she was definitely attractive, he knew there was more to Bianca than that. Reese remembered her from high school. They'd been in the same grade, shared some of the same friends. There had never been anything between them, but he couldn't deny he'd had a crush on her for a while.

"You know me. I like to be where the action is." Bianca's smile brightened.

Brantley peered around her. "You mean it's girls' night."

Bianca looked back over her shoulder, chuckled. "It is, yes."

Reese followed their gazes, noticed the group of women sitting at the table near the wall. The only one he recognized was Bristol Newton, the woman who owned the day-care center in town and had become a close friend of the Walkers over the years. She was Bianca's best friend, had been since childhood.

"So what brings you over, Mayor?" Kaden Walker spoke up from his seat across from them.

"I thought I'd take this opportunity to remind y'all about our annual fall festival."

Reese took a swallow of his beer, found himself smiling.

"Another festival?" Brantley grinned. "You haven't run outta those yet?"

"You just wait, Walker. I've got more planned for next year."

"I don't doubt that, ma'am."

"This year, we're kicking it off on Friday night. Since Halloween's the following day, we'll have a trick-or-treat in the park, get the kids together."

"Sounds like fun," Keegan told her.

"That's a yes, then?" Bianca looked at all the faces at the table.

Everyone knew better than to tell the mayor they would not be attending one of her festivals. She had them for every occasion and Reese had noticed there seemed to more arranged now than before she'd taken office.

"Of course we'll be there," Keegan told her. "And we'll make sure everyone else is, too."

"I knew I could depend on you."

"For anything," Jaxson Briggs chimed in.

Bianca flashed another smile, sauntered off, which made Jaxson groan.

"You know she's married, right?" Keegan asked.

"Doesn't make me blind," Jaxson retorted.

"Happily married, at that," Kaden added.

"Not like I'm gonna pursue her." Jaxson took a long pull on his beer. "And it's not like that, anyway."

"Then what's it like?" Reese asked, curious.

"She's a witchy woman," Jaxson said, sounding serious. "She bats those eyelashes and it's impossible to say no to her."

That earned some laughs from the group.

"I heard y'all were able to find that girl who disappeared from here, what was it? A decade ago?" Kaden prompted, shifting the conversation.

"We did," Brantley confirmed.

Reese could tell Brantley wasn't interested in talking about it. He'd learned the man was not keen on praise when it came to a job well done. He figured that had something to do with his time in the military. Ops like the one that had gone down today were commonplace in the spec ops community, nothing to be praised. Reese knew from experience.

"And the new guy?" Keegan nodded his chin toward the back.

"Detective Sebastian Buchanan," Reese told him. "Austin Police Department."

"He gonna join the task force?"

Reese couldn't answer that, so he glanced over at Brantley.

"We don't know what direction we're goin' yet," Brantley grumbled, turning to look at Reese. "You up for a game of pool?"

"Yep. I'll get us a couple more beers."

While Brantley secured a table in the back, Reese headed for the bar.

"You look better than the last time I saw you in here," Mack noted as he snagged two bottles from the refrigerator beneath the bar.

"I am better," he admitted, his gaze instantly shifting to Brantley.

As soon as he did it, he knew the move revealed exactly what had altered him these past few weeks. Oddly enough, he didn't feel the need to pretend otherwise. Rather than get defensive, he dealt with the nerves that churned, because yes, they were still there. But Reese had already learned what happened when he allowed them to take control of his life and he damn sure wasn't interested in losing Brantley over it. He would simply learn how to channel the emotions differently.

"Well, it's a good look on you," Mack said. "And those are on the house."

"For?"

"Just because." Mack grinned wide. "Hometown heroes and all."

Now Reese felt the discomfort that Brantley probably had earlier. They hadn't done anything exceptional. They'd merely done their jobs.

Reese nodded his thanks, retrieved both beers, and headed for the back.

JJ and Baz had joined Brantley, the two of them laughing at something.

"You mind if we play, too?" JJ asked, her question directed at him.

"Not at all."

The night was still young when Brantley suggested they head back to his place.

Having spent the past two hours watching Brantley slaughter the rest of them at pool, Reese had been more than happy to agree with him. He had even managed to resist the urge to jump Brantley during the drive home, although it hadn't been easy.

However, all bets were off when they stepped into the house. Reese waited long enough for Brantley to close the door before he had the man up against the wall, his mouth crushed to his.

"I might have to take you out more often," Brantley muttered. "Makes you frisky."

Reese chuckled. He'd never been called frisky before, but it was a good description for what he was feeling right now. He'd never wanted this man more than he did in that moment.

"Thank you," Brantley whispered.

Reese pulled back, met his gaze. "For?"

"Tonight. I know it was hard."

A slow smile pulled at his mouth. "No. Tonight wasn't hard." He leaned in, nipped Brantley's earlobe. "But I am."

"Yeah?"

"Oh, yeah." Reese groaned when Brantley gripped his ass, jerking him forward until their bodies were crushed together.

"Have I mentioned how fuckin' hot you make me?" Brantley mumbled, his lips sliding down Reese's neck.

"Feelin's mutual."

Rather than wait for Brantley to lead the way, Reese gripped his shirt, pulled it over his head, then did the same with Brantley's. And then they were chest to chest.

Oh, fuck yes.

This was where Reese wanted to be. In Brantley's arms, the man's hard body sliding against his own.

"Let's relocate this party," Brantley urged, taking Reese's hand and dragging him down the hall.

They fumbled, alternating between blazing kisses, groping hands, and attempts to alleviate the rest of their clothing. Finally naked, they fell to a heap on the bed, Reese on his back, Brantley's delicious body, all that strength and heat, covering him.

Because he wasn't ready for the foreplay to end, Reese smiled. "I want you in my mouth."

He saw the flash of desire in those blue-gray eyes, the mirroring smile forming on Brantley's mouth.

"Who am I to deny you anything?" Brantley rolled off him, falling to his back on the bed.

Reese followed, but he didn't go right for his cock. Instead, he crawled over Brantley, straddling his hips, planting his hands firmly on the mattress beside his head. Leaning in for a kiss, he slowed things down.

Although he was so hot he was practically combustible, he damn sure wasn't ready for this to be over yet.

So he settled in to take his time.

HAVING GOTTEN HER BUTT WHOOPED AT POOL for the past couple of hours, JJ had decided to call it quits. Of course, she was still in good spirits. No reason not to be. She'd had the opportunity to spend the past few hours with friends, hanging out, laughing. Granted, some of the laughter had been them making fun of her lack of skills at the pool table, but hey, she could take it in stride.

And when Brantley and Reese had opted to call it a night, JJ hadn't been ready to leave. She had to blame it on the man she'd spent the evening with. Sebastian Buchanan. The more time she spent with the handsome detective, the more she liked him.

As a friend, of course.

Nothing more.

"How about I take you to dinner," Baz suggested, as though he'd been tuned in to her thoughts.

JJ peered over at him, unable to hide her smile. "You know I'm not gonna sleep with you, right?"

His answering smile was blinding. She had to admit, the man was insanely attractive. Dark blond hair, teal-blue eyes, the body of a Greek god. He was honestly the polar opposite of the sort of men she usually went for, but the exact replica of the ones she'd always fantasized about. The bad boy with a reckless streak. For that reason alone, he scared her. JJ knew, given half a chance, she could so easily fall for this man. And she wasn't talking only into bed with him.

To her surprise, Baz stepped closer, eliminating the distance between them, ignoring the beers sitting on the high-top they'd commandeered earlier. Somehow he managed not to make her feel crowded despite the fact he was invading her personal space and she was forced to tip her head back to maintain eye contact.

She was aware of his hand lifting, his knuckles sliding over her cheek. A gentle sweep as his eyes stared into hers.

"You should know that won't deter me," he said softly.

"No?"

His eyes glittered with mischief. "No. I'm content with dinner, conversation. I'll follow your lead."

"Why?" she heard herself asking.

Baz didn't move back, didn't drop his hand. "I honestly don't know." The wattage on his smile amplified. "Perhaps you could say I'm smitten."

That made her laugh, but it also sent a frisson of warmth through her. Not necessarily desire, although she felt that in spades.

No, there was something about Sebastian Buchanan. He was different from the men she'd been with in the past. And she truly believed he would not push for sex, that he would be content with dinner and dating for as long as she deemed it necessary.

JJ figured the problem was going to be in managing to hold her ground in that regard.

"What do you say? Dinner? That little diner you like?"

She smiled. "I could eat."

Their eyes remained locked together, their bodies so close she could feel his warmth.

"You want me to kiss you," he whispered softly.

It was then JJ realized her gaze had dropped to his mouth.

His eyes lowered then.

"I think it's the other way around," she replied, her voice low.

"Trust me, JJ, I'd love nothing more than to taste you."

Crap.

Why did this man have to be so polite? So attractive? He wasn't the only one who was smitten, she knew. But the fact of the matter was, JJ had only recently come out of a bad relationship. Or rather, rocky relationship. She wasn't sure she was ready to go down that road again. Nor was she interested in casual sex anymore. And honest to God, that acknowledgement had surprised her more than anything.

"JJ?"

"Hmm?"

"If you lean in any more…" He was warning her.

Oh, fuck it. She had to know if he was a good kisser. That could make or break any sort of relationship, could it not?

Reaching up, she slid her hand behind his neck, pulled him down toward her until their lips met. He was true to his word. He didn't make the first move, allowing her lips to brush softly over his. And when she licked his lower lip, his mouth opened, his tongue gliding against hers, all bets were off.

Baz was a man who knew how to kiss. He allowed her to lead, but only for a few seconds. He took control at that point, but there was nothing overbearing about the way he did it. His hand curled around her head, holding her gently as their heads tilted, the kiss deepening, tongues stroking, lips melding. JJ knew she'd never been kissed like that before. She couldn't imagine what he'd be like in bed.

The kiss lingered for long minutes until the familiar sounds of the bar returned—music, chatter, laughter—causing JJ to reluctantly pull back.

He looked as dazed as she felt, and that was oddly soothing. She definitely didn't want to be the only one who'd been so affected by a kiss.

"Dinner," he urged.

"I'm still not gonna sleep with you," she said, her voice husky from their kiss.

"I'm gonna hold you to that," he said easily, taking her hand and linking their fingers.

"What does that mean?"

"It means there's no rush, JJ. We've got all the time in the world."

Lovely. She'd found the one man she wanted to jump and he was willing to hold out.

Figured.

Chapter Nineteen

Four days later
Tuesday, October 27, 2020

WHEN YOU WERE SUMMONED BY THE GOVERNOR, it wasn't an option to decline.

And while Brantley was more than willing to check in with the man who was currently signing his paychecks, he wasn't keen on meeting with him for the reasons he suspected this was about.

The only concession was that the meeting was taking place in the governor's office, rather than his home. For that Brantley was grateful. A business setting was far easier to deal with.

Now, as he waited for the governor to finish the call he was on according to his secretary, he was thinking about the lunch meeting he would be heading to after this. The one he'd requested so that he could have some time to talk to Baz, get a feel for what the man had in mind for his future at the APD. Brantley still wasn't entirely sure he was going to make Baz an offer to join the task force, but he was definitely leaning in that direction. It helped that Reese and JJ had both agreed he would be a good asset to the team. Brantley was inclined to agree.

"Governor Greenwood will see you now," the secretary stated as she stood and headed toward his office door.

Brantley thanked her kindly as he stepped into the space. Governor Greenwood was standing at the windows, staring at the city laid out before him.

"How's Corinne?" Brantley asked, joining him.

"She's hanging in there. My daughter … she's tough."

"That she is."

"She'll pull through this in time."

Brantley had figured as much. "And Lauren? How's she doing?"

Governor Greenwood turned to look at him. "She's currently under suicide watch. Needless to say, she's distraught."

"Does she know what was done to her?"

"No. She's still in denial. According to her, Bill is her husband and he loves her."

Brantley remembered the way Lauren had referred to him as Daddy. He had to think the man had gotten so many of her wires crossed over the years. It would be a wonder if she came through this at all. But Brantley prayed she did. It was the only acceptable outcome.

"She's got dedicated therapists though. And she's got Corinne. My daughter's insisting she'll be beside Lauren every step of the way."

That was good. Everyone needed someone and with what Lauren was going through, she would need all the friends and family she could get.

The governor moved over to his desk, so Brantley followed, taking a seat across from him.

"I saw the report," the governor noted. "Detective Buchanan had it sent over."

The report the governor was referring to was the one that included a list of women William Dugan had confessed to kidnapping and murdering over the years.

According to the man who was more than willing to share his tale of horror, Lauren Tyler was the second girl he had kidnapped. He had decided to keep her, convinced she could be fixed. The first girl hadn't been so lucky, nor had she needed fixing, according to Dugan. However, the seven who came after Lauren had. Through the years, he had plucked them out of their lives, kept them contained in one basement or another until he determined whether they could be saved from themselves. Evidently he had a set of standards, warped as they might be. According to Dugan, he had continued to buy and sell property to see if anyone would ever figure out what he'd done. He seemed to be under the impression he was unstoppable; therefore, he'd had no fear of his crimes being discovered. Brantley was happy to be one of those who had taken the bastard down.

"It's my understanding they've located the bodies," the governor stated.

"According to Baz, yes. They're in the process of confirming the identities and notifying the families."

"I talked to Lauren's mother. She's happy her daughter's home, as is Lauren's father. They're committed to helping her through this, hoping she will eventually come back to them."

Brantley had no idea what the possibility of that happening was. Lauren Tyler had been emotionally abused, not to mention sexually, for nearly a decade. He doubted it would be easy, but he was happy that she had family to support her. Even if she didn't realize it now, she was lucky to have them in her corner.

"But that's not why I asked you here," Governor Greenwood said. "I actually wanted to talk to you about another case I'd like your team to work on."

"Another missing person?"

"In a sense, yes. There are a number of police departments who've been working on identifying a group who are luring children from their parents via social media."

Brantley didn't need to hear anything more than luring children to know that his team would be fully on board. "We're more than willing to assist."

"Not assisting," Governor Greenwood corrected. "Heading up the task force. I'll put you in touch with the various departments. You can take it from there."

Brantley nodded.

"I will say that I think you'll need more people on your team."

"I'm in the process of making that happen," he admitted.

"Good. I think you're off to a damn good start."

An hour later, Brantley was stepping into Chuy's—the best Tex-Mex restaurant on the planet—where he found Baz already waiting for him, a basket of chips and a bowl of jalapeño ranch dressing in front of him.

"I apologize for startin' without you," Baz said, though there was no remorse in his words.

"Sorry I'm late. Had a meetin' with the governor."

"Well, in that case, you're excused."

The waiter appeared to take their order. Brantley didn't need to peruse the menu as this was his favorite restaurant. After rattling off his selection and allowing Baz to do the same, they both dug into the chips.

"If you don't mind me askin', why'm I here?"

"I'm not one to beat around the bush," Brantley told him.

"Good. Then no need to start now."

Smiling, Brantley sipped his tea. "I did some research on you."

"Yeah?" Baz seemed not at all surprised or bothered by the notion.

"You've got quite the record for closin' cases."

"It's my job."

"It is, yes. You've also got a knack for pissin' off your partners, as well as the brass."

"I'm friendly like that."

"Yet when I worked with you on this last case, I detected no issue with authority."

"Maybe I like you."

"But not the rest of the APD?"

Baz smirked. "It's not the authority I have a problem with. It's the red tape and the bullshit."

Brantley had figured as much. He'd read the man's file, seen the comments made by his bosses over the years.

"I've got a proposition for you."

"You gonna put in a good word with the governor? Ask him to let us do our jobs?"

"Don't need to. I've got a job in mind for you that'll allow you to do just that."

Baz sat up straight, dropped the chip he'd been holding. "A job?"

"I assume you did your own research," Brantley stated. "Into me and my task force."

"Of course I did. Had to know what I was walkin' into on that case."

"And what conclusion did you come to?"

"For starters, you've had quite the military career."

Brantley didn't comment.

"That's if all that redaction says anything." Baz grinned. "And your partner … his record's as secretive as yours. I find that interesting. Two special operators, one Navy, one Air Force, working together."

Special operator? Reese?

Brantley'd had no idea.

"And then there's JJ. She's"—Baz's gaze lowered— "impressive. Let's put it that way."

"To sum it up…" Brantley prompted.

"I'm impressed. Hard not to be, I figure. And I enjoyed working with the three of you. Learned a few things."

"So if I were to offer you a job?"

Baz's expression was almost comical. Clearly he had not expected that, although Brantley wasn't sure why that was. He'd been alluding to it since he sat down.

"Me? A job? With your task force?"

"Yes."

"What's the catch?"

"There is no catch. We're in the early stages, but you got a firsthand glimpse of our mission. We're tacklin' cold cases as well as those that arise. Our objective is to solve as many as we can, do whatever it takes to bring closure to the families." Brantley took a drink, set down his glass. "Sounds like we'll be leadin' some special task forces with various departments across the state. It's why I met with the governor this mornin'."

"And the rules?"

"Conduct yourself appropriately and solve the case. That's what I expect. We'll be teaming up with police departments and other government agencies. We're workin' at the direct order of the governor, but he's not micromanaging. I don't have a lot of rules, provided you can do your job."

"I'll be reporting to you?"

"You'll be reportin' to the team," Brantley corrected. "I'm the team leader because someone's got to bear the responsibility. But, like I said, I'm not gonna micromanage you. I don't have time for that shit."

"And your thoughts on … dating in the workplace?"

Brantley grinned. "If you're askin' whether or not you can pursue JJ, that's y'all's business. Just don't let it interfere with the job."

Baz chuckled. "I'd like to pursue her, don't get me wrong. But I plan to keep my distance."

Brantley could've told him good luck with that. He'd seen the way Baz and JJ were that night at Moonshiners. They were getting closer. Maybe as friends, maybe something else. But he honestly didn't care, provided they didn't let it interfere with work.

"So, what do you say? You in?"

"Salary? Benefits?"

"Your salary'll be consistent with my team, although you'll still have the benefits of the department. Pension and all that." Brantley pulled an envelope out of his pocket. "It's all in there. Look it over later, get back to me with an answer."

Baz took the envelope, set it on the table.

"By the end of the day," Brantley added.

Baz stared at him.

"I might not micromanage, but I never said I wasn't a hard-ass."

That earned him a laugh.

And Brantley highly suspected the rest would earn him a dedicated team member.

"WHAT IS THIS I'M HEARIN' ABOUT A special task force down in Austin that's kickin' ass and takin' names?"

Reese grinned, staring down at his cell phone, listening to Z's rumbling voice coming through the speaker.

"We're doin' what we can."

"Act like it's no big deal all you want, kid. It's a big fuckin' deal."

Reese laughed. "Whatever. How're things with you? How's RT?"

"Good. We're back in Dallas for the time being. Got a couple of clients needin' our services. If we're lucky, we'll sit tight until after the holidays."

Reese knew how much Z enjoyed the holidays. He was big on getting together, hanging out. Reese wouldn't deny he enjoyed them too, mostly because he got to spend time with Z and Jensyn.

"You talk to Mom lately?" Z asked.

"This mornin', in fact," he admitted. "She's doin' good."

"And you? How's the personal life goin'?"

"It's goin'," he said, keeping his tone nonchalant.

"Yeah? You datin' anyone?"

Shit.

He had been hoping Z wouldn't steer the conversation in that direction. Of course, he should've known better.

Reese didn't answer right away and Z evidently picked up on his silence.

"All right, what's goin' on, Reese?"

"It's complicated," he admitted, knowing his brother wouldn't let it go unless he gave him something.

"Complicated? The good kind?"

"You could say that, yeah."

"Well, then I'm happy for you. Y'all been together long?"

"Few months," he admitted.

"Really?" Z dragged the word out, his curiosity clear. "So when'll we meet this lucky lady?"

Reese cleared his throat. He had two options. He could end the conversation, claiming he had something to take care of. Or he could blurt it out now and get it over with. Not like Z wouldn't eventually learn the truth. The last thing Reese intended to do was to lie to his brother.

"I'm not datin' a woman," he said softly. Too softly.

"I'm sorry. What was that?"

"I'm not datin' a woman," he repeated, a little louder this time.

There was no comment on the other end of the line, and for a minute, Reese thought the call had been disconnected.

"Are you tellin' me what I think you're tellin' me?"

Reese closed his eyes, dropped his head back on the couch. "Yes, Z. I'm tellin' you that if I bring anyone around for the holidays, it'll be a man. His name's Brantley Walker."

"Brantley Walker?" Z cleared his throat. "Brantley Walker from Coyote Ridge? Guy I went to high school with?"

Shit.

Reese had forgotten that Brantley and Z were the same age, that they'd known each other growing up.

"Yes."

More silence.

Reese felt his heart pounding in his chest, the sound of his blood rushing in his ears. Christ Almighty. He needed Z to say something. For the past few days, he'd considered outing himself to his brother as a first step. Reese didn't want to keep this a secret, didn't want Brantley thinking he was embarrassed. However, it all seemed good and fine in his head. When it came down to admitting it, that was another thing entirely.

Finally, there was a bellowing laugh. "Holy. Fuck. My little brother landed the bad boy."

He couldn't help it, he laughed, opening his eyes and releasing the breath he'd been holding.

Z's tone turned serious. "How are you doin' with this?"

"With what?"

"Don't play dumb with me, Reese. I know you've never dated a man before. I woulda picked up on it."

"You're right. I haven't. But…" Reese closed his eyes again, pictured Brantley. "There's somethin' about him. I don't know what it is, or when it happened…"

"You're not just datin' this guy," Z stated firmly. "You're in love with him."

"Yeah."

He could hear the smile in Z's voice. "I'm happy for you, kid. Really happy."

"You're not gonna question it?"

"Question what? That you fell in love with a man? Why would I?"

"Like you said, I've never dated a man before."

"So? The heart wants what it wants, does it not?"

That wasn't the first time he'd heard that.

"Do me a favor, Z. Don't tell Mom or Jen, please."

"It's your story to tell, kid. But I might have to make a trip to Coyote Ridge. Check out this guy. Make sure he's good enough for my little brother."

Reese laughed. "I'll buy you a beer when you do."

"About the holidays, Reese. We'd like you to make it up this way this year."

He knew he wouldn't get out of this without Z requesting his presence.

"Thanksgiving or Christmas. Both if you can."

"Let me talk to Brantley and I'll let you know."

He could hear another smile in Z's voice when he said, "Well, now that you completely blew my mind with your good news, I guess I'll get back to what I was doin'. Talk to you later."

Reese disconnected the call, stared up at the apartment ceiling. That hadn't been nearly as difficult as he had imagined it would be. He had been a bit surprised that Z hadn't questioned him about it, though. That was what Reese feared the most. People wanting to know how it was possible to have spent his entire life chasing women only to find himself in love with a man.

He didn't mind the questions so much. It was the answers he feared. There was no explanation.

It just happened.

Reese smiled. Maybe that was what he would tell them if and when they asked.

Chapter Twenty

Friday, October 30, 2020

ON FRIDAY MORNING, BRANTLEY WOKE ALONE IN his bed. No sooner did his eyes open than he reached for Reese only to find the man wasn't there. Only a few nights out of a week and a half that the man spent a night at his own place and Brantley was left wanting the comfort he was afforded by having him there. This was morning three he'd woken up without Reese and he couldn't deny he wasn't fond of it.

Yeah, he said it. He wanted Reese in his bed every night.

Brantley automatically reached for his phone, checked for text messages. There weren't any. Why? Because it was still too damn early.

Disappointed, but not exactly sure why, Brantley forced himself out of bed, pulled on his running shoes. He was out the door, realizing again he missed Reese's presence. The man had been joining him on his morning runs and he missed him.

Damn it.

Although it felt like it took longer than it did, he managed to make the five-mile route, returning to the empty house. Once inside, he grabbed a bottle of water, hit the showers. Twenty minutes later, he walked into the kitchen to confirm that, yes, that was bacon he had smelled when he'd been in the bathroom. He'd thought he was hallucinating at the time.

Good to know he wasn't and all the better because of the man working diligently in his kitchen.

Yep, Brantley loved this man. He missed him when he wasn't around, thought about him even when he was. He knew it was time they took the next step in their relationship and he only hoped Reese would be on board with his plan.

Pausing to admire the man in his kitchen, Brantley watched as Reese moved easily between the stove and the island, prepping one of his delicious meals. He noticed Reese's dark hair was getting longer, a little shaggier on the top, but it was a good look for him. He was sporting his regular attire: a T-shirt (today's was dark blue) that accentuated his finely toned upper body, jeans that encased a rather impressive ass, and boots that gave him that country-boy vibe. Reese truly was a fine specimen.

And yes, Brantley was overcome with the same desire to strip the man naked that he experienced every time he saw him.

Yet he refrained.

"What's this?" he asked, going for nonchalant as he moved closer to the island.

Reese looked up, grinned, and that sexy smirk made his lips itch to kiss him.

Again, he refrained.

"Good mornin'," Reese greeted.

"It's definitely headin' that direction, sure," he replied, moving over so he could greet Reese appropriately.

A quick peck on the mouth was all he could get in before Reese was back to finishing up the meal.

"Can I help?"

"Yes. You can have a seat at the table."

Brantley looked around. "The table?"

"Outside."

Ah. Right. The only table he had was on the patio.

Because it was clear Reese didn't need help, Brantley headed outside. The sky was just beginning to lighten as the sun peeked at the horizon, which explained why the porch lights were on. He came to a stop when he saw there was a white linen tablecloth on the table, as well as a decanter of orange juice, another of iced water. There were glasses, silverware, napkins, even a candle.

Reese had gone all out and Brantley wasn't sure what this was for. Didn't mean he wasn't appreciative, but more accurately, he was curious.

So he sat.

And waited.

When Reese appeared, he was carrying two plates filled to overflowing with all of Brantley's favorites. Eggs, bacon, hash browns, southern-style biscuits, gravy.

Despite his stomach's rather excited rumble, Brantley looked over at Reese.

"What's this?" he asked, repeating the same question he'd asked earlier.

"This is me takin' you out for breakfast," Reese said seriously, his golden gaze looking more vulnerable than Brantley had ever seen. "I know it's not a real date, I know it's not at a restaurant where people'll wait on us and we can chat it up while the courses are delivered. Consider it a do-over."

That was when Brantley understood. Reese was attempting to make up for the clusterfuck of a date that they'd had.

Brantley glanced at the table, took it all in, then looked over at Reese. "This is better than any restaurant, Reese. Like I told you before, I don't need to flaunt this thing we've got to the world. I'm happy. Just the two of us."

Reese smiled, as though relieved to hear that.

"Doesn't mean we won't frequent the diner," Reese told him.

"Of course not." Although Brantley would be the first to say Reese's breakfast was far better than theirs. "So, can I dig in now? Or'd you have somethin' else on the agenda?"

"Yes, you can eat." Reese chuckled. "And I'll just grab the coffee. Be right back."

Brantley didn't dig in, choosing rather to wait for Reese. While the man slipped inside, Brantley poured orange juice into glasses, his gaze skimming the table, realizing the effort that Reese had put into this. Brantley hadn't been lying when he told him this was better than a date. It was. Because Reese wasn't anxious and Brantley wasn't trying to soothe him. This was their comfort zone, where they could relax, be themselves. That was all that mattered when it came to dates, right?

He heard the door being slid closed, followed by Reese's footsteps. Two cups of coffee were placed on the table, but before Reese could sit, Brantley surged to his feet. He grabbed Reese's hand, pulled him in for a kiss. Not the sweet, chaste kind he'd gotten in the kitchen. No, Brantley devoured the man, cupping the back of his neck, holding him firmly.

When he managed to release that delectable mouth, Brantley pressed his forehead to Reese's, smiled. "Good mornin'."

Reese chuckled.

"So…" Brantley pulled back but didn't release Reese. "Do you consider this our first real date?"

Reese glanced at the table, back to Brantley. "It could be construed as such, sure."

"Well, then, you're probably gonna find this a bit forward," Brantley told him.

"What?"

"I mean, we did have sex before our first date," he mused, his eyes locked with Reese's.

Reese smirked. "Yeah. We did."

"Some very good sex, might I add."

He saw the blush on Reese's face.

"Definitely."

Brantley reached up, cupped Reese's neck, turned serious. "Move in with me, Reese."

Those golden eyes bounced over his face as though attempting to find the punch line.

"We don't have to tell the world that we're together," he continued when Reese didn't respond. "But I wanna wake up to you every mornin', go to bed with you every night. We can keep it on the DL. I'm not expectin' you to tell your—"

Reese's hand covered his mouth. "Yes."

Brantley stared, not sure he'd heard him right.

"I'll move in with you, Navy boy."

There was a foreign sensation that filled his chest. Warmth mixed with anticipation, maybe. Brantley had only ever felt it when he was with Reese.

"Under one condition."

"Name it," he blurted.

Reese laughed. "I'm gonna buy us a couch."

Of course he was.

And oddly, Brantley was okay with that.

 STAY TUNED

I hope you enjoyed the second installment of the Off the Books Task Force. There's definitely more to come for Brantley and Reese and the rest of the task force. Each book in this series is a full-length novel involving a new case and the continuation of the relationship for these two men. And I promise not to keep you waiting long for each installment.

If you enjoyed *Without a Trace*, please consider leaving a review.

ACKNOWLEDGMENTS

Of course, I have to thank my wonderfully patient husband who puts up with me every single day. If it wasn't for him and his belief that I could (and can) do this, I wouldn't be writing this today. He has been my backbone, my rock, the very reason I continue to believe in myself. I love you for that, babe.

Chancy Powley – You continue to come through for me in every way. You even tolerate my inability to answer my text messages in a timely manner. I will apologize for that now and for all future instances because we all know, I'm horrible at it. Just keep in mind, you are the absolute best friend I have and I am forever grateful for your friendship.

I also have to thank my street team – Naughty (and nice) Girls – Your unwavering support is something I will never take for granted.

I can't forget my copyeditor, Amy at Blue Otter Editing. Thank goodness I've got you to catch all my punctuation, grammar, and tense errors.

Nicole Nation 2.0 for the constant support and love. You've been there for me from almost the beginning. This group of ladies has kept me going for so long, I'm not sure I'd know what to do without them.

And, of course, YOU, the reader. Your emails, messages, posts, comments, tweets… they mean more to me than you can imagine. I thrive on hearing from you, knowing that my characters and my stories have touched you in some way keeps me going. I've been known to shed a tear or two when reading an email because you simply bring so much joy to my life with your support. I thank you for that.

ABOUT NICOLE EDWARDS

New York Times and *USA Today* bestselling author Nicole Edwards lives in the suburbs of Austin, Texas with her husband and their youngest of three children. The two older ones have flown the coup, while the youngest is in high school. When Nicole is not writing about sexy alpha males and sassy, independent women, she can often be found with a book in hand or attempting to keep the dogs happy. You can find her hanging out on social media and interacting with her readers - even when she's supposed to be writing.

Want to know what's coming next? Or how about see some fun stuff related to Nicole's books? You can find these, as well as tons of other stuff on Nicole's website. You can also find A Day in the Life blog posts, which are short stories about your favorite characters, as well as exclusive contests by joining Nicole Nation on Nicole's website. To join, simply click **Log In | Register** in the menu.

If you're interested in keeping up to date on any new releases and preorders, you can sign up for Nicole's notification newsletter. This only goes out when she's got important information to share.

Want a simple, fast way to get updates on new releases? Sign up for text messaging. If you are in the U.S. simply text NICOLE to 64600 or sign up on her website. She promises not to spam your phone. This is just her way of letting you know what's happening because Nicole knows you're busy, but if you're anything like her, you always have your phone on you.

CONNECT WITH NICOLE

Website: NicoleEdwardsAuthor.com

Facebook: /Author.Nicole.Edwards

Instagram: NicoleEdwardsAuthor

DEAD HEAT RANCH
Boots Optional
Betting on Grace
Overnight Love

DEVIL'S BEND
Chasing Dreams
Vanishing Dreams

MISPLACED HALOS
Protected in Darkness
Salvation in Darkness
Bound in Darkness

OFFICE INTRIGUE
Office Intrigue
Intrigued Out of the Office
Their Rebellious Submissive
Their Famous Dominant
Their Ruthless Sadist
Their Naughty Student
Their Fairy Princess

PIER 70
Reckless
Fearless
Speechless
Harmless
Clueless

SNIPER 1 SECURITY
Wait for Morning
Never Say Never
Tomorrow's Too Late

SOUTHERN BOY MAFIA/DEVIL'S PLAYGROUND
Beautifully Brutal
Without Regret
Beautifully Loyal
Without Restraint